black marks

black marks

a novel by

kirsten dinnall hoyte

AKASHIC BOOKS
NEW YORK

Published by Akashic Books
©2006 Kirsten Dinnall Hoyte

ISBN-13: 978-1-888451-84-9
ISBN-10: 1-888451-84-X
Library of Congress Control Number: 2005903220
All rights reserved
First printing
Printed in Canada

Earlier versions of the following chapters appeared in these publications: "In Nina's House" in *Sojourner,* October 2000 (titled "In Jamaica"); "Why I Drank (Or, the Answers)" in the *Harvard Review,* Spring 2001 (titled "Recovery"); and "Brotherly Love" in *The Hoot and Holler of the Owls: An Anthology of New Black Writers* (Hurston-Wright Publications).

Akashic Books
PO Box 1456
New York, NY 10009
Akashic7@aol.com
www.akashicbooks.com

For Patrice Dinnall and Miriam Bronstein—without these women, this book would never have been written.

And in loving memory of my American grandmother, Patti Ridley Hoyte

Acknowledgments

There are far too many people to thank every individual, but I would like to express my deep appreciation for my wonderful editor Lauren Sanders. I'd also like to especially thank Maxine Rodburg for daring me to write again after a long time away, and my godfather for believing that I could write in the first place.

A big thanks to Karen Thielman, Yael Bat-Shimon, Tayari Jones, Lara Putnam, Steve Axelrod, Ben Stumpf, Susan Bisson, Jessica Roseman, Jayne Stancavage, Lise Brody, Audrey Alforque Thomas and Hanka Ray (for reasons that they each should know). Also, I am very grateful to the Concord Academy community for giving me space, encouragement, and feedback (and putting up with a distracted, too busy, always behind teacher). My colleagues Chris Rowe, Cammy Thomas, and Abby Laber critiqued the manuscript at crucial moments. Lastly, the rewriting of *Black Marks* coincided exactly and rather chaotically with preparing for my doctoral general examination and my son's infancy. I would have never survived any of those events without the support, babysitting, and warm encouragement of his godparents, as well as my family, my professors and my friends from Harvard University, and my [MOMS] list.

contents

For, while the tale of how we suffer, and how we are delighted, and how we may triumph is never new, it always must be heard. There isn't any other tale to tell, it's the only light we've got in all this darkness.

—James Baldwin, *Sonny's Blues*

prologue

everyone knew there was power in names. If an obeah woman got ahold of your true-true name, you were doomed. She'd write it on a slip of paper, and then she'd hold your soul in her fist. Nina claimed that the obeah was nonsense. But I'd heard the cook and gardener whisper that Nina didn't know spit from shit, and obeah magic was strong stuff. So when my mother called, I couldn't help but think that it was caused by the names.

Sonia, the cook, had told me about true-true names when my brothers and I first came to live with my grandmother. I had just turned nine, and Nina started sending me into the kitchen in the afternoons to learn housekeeping. She said those lessons didn't seem to be taking very well.

"Yuh true-true name is the name yuh keep to yuhself. In the dark of night yuh whisper it to gi yuh courage," Sonia told me during one of the first cooking lessons.

"What's your true-true name, Sonia?" I asked. I was sitting on the stool, peeling an overripe mango with my teeth.

"Living in the States has made she fool. Didnah just tell yuh that a private name none must know, nuh?" Sonia was so outraged by my question she slammed the heavy iron skillet on the stove-top. Some curry slopped out of the stew pot. "See what yuh make me do, huh? So yuh chop me onions?"

"Then what's my true-true name?" I began to suck on the mango. Salmon-colored juice trickled down my chin. I hated chopping onions.

"How me supposed to know that? Only oono know." Sonia stopped stirring the stew and stared ominously. "Spare the rod and yuh spoil de child."

"Me nuh know notink!" I wailed, breaking into forbidden patois. Nina did not like us using patois; she said we sounded like the ragamuffin boys who hung out by the harbor. But I'd noticed she spoke patois whenever she got mad or when she was sitting in the kitchen talking to Sonia.

"Worry none," Sonia said, putting her fingers over my lips and glancing at the kitchen door. We didn't want Nina to overhear Sonia's stories. "Yuh know in time. Sometime yuh jus wake up in the day with it on yuh lips. Sometime is animal-name. Sometime is made-up name. Sometime is plain old jane name. But yuh just know is yuh true-true name. Me get fi true-true name when me thirty and fi grandmummy—she die and whisper this African word just to me. She gi she mumma who was the daughta of an African slave her ownself. Now, your grandmummy didnah tell yuh to come to the kitchen to learn suck mango like baby suck teat. Me told about true-true name, yuh can snap me beans."

Sometimes Nina accompanied me for the pleasure of bickering with Sonia in the kitchen. Those afternoons, Nina sat on a tall kitchen stool, balancing herself with the carved wooden walking stick she purchased from a Rastafarian in Runaway Bay. Her short body was surrounded by a thick layer of flesh padding and soft curves—the exact opposite of Sonia, who was as tall and thin as a straight-growing piece of sugar cane. They were the opposite of each other in every opinion as well. The two old women always ignored both the food and me while they fought about recipes and gossiped about the neighbors. Those nights the rice and peas were dry and the meat tough. Nina picked at her dinner while grumbling about the laziness of the help. From my seat near the kitchen door, I could hear Sonia sucking her teeth and muttering about nosy bitches to the garden boy. For the sake of everyone's stomachs, my oldest brother Alex begged Nina to limit her afternoon excursions to the kitchen to once a month or less.

Alex and Chris always made fun of me for spending so much time with Sonia, but they didn't realize that I learned just as much about the world from her as they did from roaming around town with those loud boys from the public secondary school. We all kept our explorations of Jamaica a secret from Nina, as she was unlikely to approve of either the cook's lessons or my brothers' after-school activities. Sonia's topics ranged from obeah to cooking to "special relations," which was what she had with Mr. Sly, but I was not allowed to tell Nina about. As far as geography went, Sonia said the parish of St. Elizabeth, Jamaica, was the center of the world. Kingston and America were nearly as important but filled with a lot of dirty people. Africa was our motherland. The Queen in England used to rule over us until we knocked her flat, and I didn't need to concern myself with the other places. Now obviously I knew that Sonia was wrong about some things. Mother and Daddy still lived in the States, and Nina said that paying attention to church and school was far more important than superstition, but I listened to Sonia just the same. If you asked me, Satan, algebra, and obeah were all equally unlikely.

The bad news came at school after I had been living on the island for almost two years. Earlier that day, Miss Celine announced the winner of the sixth-grade art contest. The assignment was to create representations of good and evil. Practically everyone took it to mean that we should illustrate a Bible story. Grade six had Bible class only once each week, but Mr. Craig, the principal, said that it was the most important hour of the week. Albert Stevens asked, "But what about church, Mr. Craig, sir?" and Mr. Craig sent him to stand in the hall for impertinence. Anyway, I wanted my project to be different. Instead of drawing Cain and Abel or the Serpent like everyone else, I painted an emerald green circle of power in the middle of the paper. Included in the circle was a watery blue pool, a green sky, gold flowers like those in Nina's garden, and the word *home* written in cursive. In the exact center of the circle, a dove perched on an olive branch. Outside the circle, I painted gnashing teeth, glittering eyes, and a series of angry red streaks. In the top left corner, a shadowy figure lurked, watching the circle, waiting intently. Everything inside was still and peaceful with soft colors, unbroken lines, and curves. Outside the images seemed to waver, paint strokes rippled. Shapes that at first glance seemed harmless transformed into howling, furious mouths or sharp talons upon closer examination.

"I am pleased to say the first-place winner is Georgette." Miss Celine gave me a big smile. She was my favorite teacher with her warm brown eyes and dimples. She was not old and sour like the other teachers at Watson; instead of black and gray, she wore soft colors, and on special days she wore a dress the color of the sea. Boys from my brothers' forms often hung around our classroom door hoping she'd let them wash the boards and straighten the desks after school. I was the top student in Miss Celine's class. My marks were always in the nineties, and she exclaimed over how neat my homework was. I never had an absence or got a black mark for misbehavior.

"Class, Georgette has submitted a magnificent example of a

surreal painting," Miss Celine said. I felt hot and embarrassed. I trembled as I went to the front of the class and she handed me the first prize, a beautiful book with a black and red binding, thick and heavy with hundreds of blank white pages. At the beginning of recess, I showed it to Chris, who snorted, but I thought it was real leather and Alex said so too.

Instead of playing, I squatted in the shade of the gymnasium wall admiring my new book. Sarita Cheddie, my best friend, stopped to ask me to be on her netball team, but I shook my head no. The primary-division girls played ball and chased each other shrieking through the yard. As always, the upper-division girls sat on the stone wall by the gate to the school grounds, primly smoothing their blue pleated skirts and crisp white blouses. I hated the jumpers that we had to wear in the primary school. The older girls called them bibs. All the boys, primary in shorts and secondary in long pants, were on the soccer fields except my brothers and their friends. During break, Chris went down to bother the Rastafarians and learn Jah lore, though Mr. Craig said it was forbidden. Alex and his friends hung out in the village with the boys from the local public school—that was also forbidden.

On the front page of the book, I practiced my signature in a smooth, dashing script. Then just for fun, I wrote Nelson Spence's name alongside, then *Mrs. Georgette Spence*. I tried all sorts of combinations. It's not that I really liked him. I was just playing. *Mr. and Mrs. Spence. Mr. Nelson Spence and Georgette Collins Spence, St. Elizabeth, Jamaica.* I drew a picture of the two of us outside a big villa on the cliffs. Suddenly the book was jerked out of my hands. I looked up and realized that I was surrounded by a bunch of older boys from the first and second form. If my brothers had been around, they would have never dared.

"Mrs. Nelson Spence," they hooted, passing the notebook back and forth. Attracted by my shouts, a group of children from all grades gathered. Everyone jeered except Nelson, who looked embarrassed. The older kids towered above him. He was the smallest boy in grade six, and his light skin and chubby cheeks made him look babyish. But he was smart, and he had read all the books in the library, even the ones restricted to the secondary school.

"Georgette Collins will never marry Nelson Spence," an older girl declared severely. "She's American. We will not allow American girls to come over and steal our men."

"Huh! Nelson is scarcely a man! He is still in short pants. He still hides behind his mumma's skirts. He's practically a girl!" Marcus Stewart shouted, and poked Nelson in the arm. Behind his big wire glasses, Nelson's eyes filled with tears. He ran into the classroom building calling for Miss Celine, who came out and got my notebook back. But the front page had been ripped out and the cover was soiled.

During afternoon lessons, I plotted my revenge. I would have Alex beat those boys up. Sarita and I would lure them into a cave by the bay and watch the tide wash them out to sea. I would bribe old Nancy, the obeah woman in the village. Nancy could call a *duppy* to haunt the mocking teens for the rest of their lives. Nelson and I would get married and be the richest people in town so they'd all have to grovel. Absorbed in my fantasies, I was startled to hear my classmates giggling. I looked up to Miss Celine's frown.

"Georgette?" she said.

"Yes, miss." I hurriedly stood up. My classmates were staring at me expectantly. Miss Celine sighed.

"I was remarking to the class that we'll miss you when you move back to America. You will have to send us drawings and paintings of your new school."

"Pardon, miss? I'm not going back to the States."

"Of course you are. During break, Mr. Craig told me that your mother has called asking for a report to send to your new school." While Miss Celine smiled as if I should be pleased, I gaped.

"But miss. I live here now," I said.

"You're visiting here temporarily," she corrected. "You live in America."

"Please, miss," Alice Rowell raised her hand, "may I have Georgie's desk?" But I didn't hear the answer. I grabbed my bag and fled the classroom. As I rushed through the hall, a sixth former tried to stop me.

"Georgette Collins! No running in the corridor. You'll receive a black mark." She reached for my shoulders, but I slipped out of her grasp and headed out the front door and across the yard to the village.

Sarita Cheddie followed. She was the most popular girl in grade six. My first days at the Watson School, everyone else called me a tourist, but Sarita declared that she liked Americans and I could be her friend. Later she whispered to me, "When I moved here from Kingston, the class teased me for being Indian. But I knocked them all down. Then I won the netball tournament for Watson Primary. Now everyone likes me." Sarita was hard and athletic; she was always racing somewhere, her long black plaits flapping behind her. To be honest, I liked her at least as much as soft Nelson Spence.

"Georgie, wait! Miss Celine says to return to class," Sarita said when she caught my arm. I was waving it up and down hoping that a car would stop.

"No, I am going to hitchhike to Kingston. No one will find me there."

"Georgette Collins! Your grandmother will lick you all the way to America if you ride with a stranger to Kingston. And Miss Celine will be angry if I don't bring you back."

"Nina will understand," I said, sounding more sure than I felt.

"Besides, it doesn't matter about getting black marks anymore. Miss Celine says I am leaving."

Always ready for adventure, Sarita (who had many black marks) stuck her arm out as well. "I'll go with you then to make sure you stay out of trouble," she said. Unfortunately, the village road was always nearly empty. No one stopped but Mrs. Redfield, the white lady with the BMW. She only gave us a ride as far as the beach, and she half-laughed and half-scolded when we told her it was the first leg in our journey to the city.

We walked through the scratchy grass, over the sand and rocks, and down to the water's edge. Sarita swung her schoolbag in wide arcs while I wore mine across my shoulders so that the sac thumped my thighs with each step. Kicking rocks and bits of seashell ahead, we moved along the coast trailed by a band of shirtless little boys in ragged shorts and bare feet. They seemed to think we were playing follow-the-leader. When Sarita grabbed my hand and began to run, they followed, giggling and shouting. Finally all of us collapsed on the white sand in a heap of arms and legs. We made growling noises as we tickled each other. Sarita crossed her braids in front of her face and roared out, "Look at me! I'm dangerous and fast like the wind."

My screeches sounded thin next to her hearty laughs and the little boys' yelling.

"Miss Sarita," one of the boys said, "yuh gwine give me dollar. Me give yuh fi treasure."

"Cha! Yuh nuh got notink!" Sarita answered. The seven-year-old grinned, opened one fist, and revealed a tin whistle; in the other hand, he held a sand dollar.

"Aaah!" the boys all murmured, crowding around. Sarita gave him a coin but let him keep his treasure. The boys wandered away. We took off our shoes and socks and spent the next few hours wading and sharing the candy bars from the bottom of my satchel where I had hidden them from Chris and Alex. We walked along the edge point where soft dry sand started to become damp and hard-packed under our feet. I could taste the wind—cool and salty.

Suddenly, Sarita stumbled and sat down hard, grasping her right foot with both hands.

"What's wrong?" I shouted.

"My foot. I've stepped on something sharp."

When I reached her, she was glaring at a bleeding toe. I sat down beside her and examined the wound. "It's not so bad, Sarita."

"Papa says that I run too much," she said glumly. "He says that no real girl would behave this way. Do you think I'm not a real girl? Maybe I'm a boy, or an animal in a girl's skin. Maybe I'm a beastly girl like my father says." I didn't know how to answer. It is true Sarita didn't act like other girls. At least not like Alice, all prim and proper with a flurry of skirts and a sugary voice.

"I hate him sometimes," she added in a matter-of-fact voice.

"I hate Daddy sometimes too," I whispered. "In the States, he's always watching me like he's waiting for me to be bad or like he's surprised I'm still there. And he makes Mama cry."

"Don't go back to America," she whispered, lips close to my ear. "Georgette Collins, you are the only one who lets me be real. Everyone else wants me to be a butterfly or a little meek bird."

"I don't think I have a choice." I kissed her cheek shyly.

"Can we be blood sisters then? Forever?" Sarita asked pointing her toe upwards. I picked up a sharp shell and pricked my finger. The sharp sensation felt good—it meant our friendship was real. The blood was warm and bright. I briefly pressed my finger to her toe, and then we lay down, her back flat on the sand, my head resting on her stomach. We were still lying there silently when Chris found us.

"Sarita Cheddie, go home to your mother," Chris said. "Georgie, Nina is wanting you."

"How did she know where I was?" I asked. Chris shrugged, a Nina-knows-everything gesture. I shivered. Suddenly the magnitude of my disobedience struck me. While Sarita muttered a quick goodbye, Chris pushed me toward the path into town.

"Is she angry?" I asked. Chris refused to say. He moved a few steps ahead of me on the path to make clear his lack of interest in his younger sister. While I dragged my feet, he strolled, carelessly whistling a calypso song and keeping his eyes on the dirt road to avoid cow patties. Each time he heard the motor of an approaching car, without lifting his head he moved to the grass and then back onto the road after the vehicle passed. As we walked through town, we passed groups of women coming from the market. The women carried babies or boxes in their arms, balancing sacks of groceries on their heads. Several called out greetings that I scarcely heard—it took all my concentration not to cry. The mile from the town beach to the house seemed dustier and longer than usual. And my feet dragged on every step on the long drive up to Nina's villa. By the time we arrived, I was sweating, convinced that Nina had a terrible punishment in store.

Nina's house was painted the colors of the Caribbean, cool greens and a dusty pink. At first glance, the house appeared modest, enveloped by a large verandah, wrapping its entire length. However, its reserved exterior masked ten airy rooms that often hosted an endless rotation of visiting friends and family.

Nina greeted me on the verandah. Her small body bristled with energy, but she didn't look angry at all; instead, she stretched out her hand and guided me through the living room, out the wooden doors, and into the back patio and courtyard. The garden was her paradise with flowers ranging from milky white to deep purple. On very still days, I sat there with my head on her knee listening to the sea and breathing in the scent of mint and spices.

"Georgie," Nina said as she strolled along the slate path, "I'm sorry that no one told you about returning to the States. I didn't find out until your mother called today. She's very excited to have you children home again. She has a brand-new house in Cambridge for you all."

I didn't say anything. I thought perhaps I would never talk again.

"Sweetness, I thought you wanted to go home; that is all you talked about when you first arrived here."

"I'll miss you, Nina!"

"You'll be back during the summers. And you'll be near your mother and father again." Nina put a consoling arm around my shoulder and drew me close.

I didn't answer. I had no interest in being with the mother who brought me here and left me for nearly two years. And Daddy no longer even lived at home. Months ago, a telephone call revealed that he'd moved out for good. "Thank God that's over," Mother had said. I would never forgive her.

"I don't want to leave Jamaica. I don't want anything to change. Ever," I finally admitted. "I want us to stay like this always."

"Sweetness, everything changes sooner or later. Look at the water. The waves, they crash in and out, washing some treasures ashore and sweeping others away. It's beautiful, nuh? You like to play there."

I nodded reluctantly. "But what if the waves take away something I really love or bring me something I hate?"

"Oh, it will now, Georgie. That you can be sure of." Nina seemed sad for a moment, and then continued, "But you can still collect what the tide brings." She handed me a book sitting on the wicker bench. It was my art prize. "Your teacher says you forgot this at school."

I took a pen out of my satchel. On the new first page, I wrote my name again. *Georgette Collins, St. Elizabeth Parish, Jamaica, West Indies.* Underneath I wrote, *Georgette Collins, Cambridge, Massachusetts, United States of America.* I turned over the page, and starting with Nina's garden, I began to sketch the parts of the island that I was going to miss. Miss Celine's solemn face breaking into a smile when I got the right answer. Mr. Craig, reassuring and dull, standing in the school hall as he repeated the same old sermons on duty and honor. Nina and Sonia in the kitchen during the weeks before Christmas, baking, wrapping gifts in brightly colored paper, and cooking a huge feast for the Eve. Saturdays weaving in and out of the crowded market stalls. My cousins' and brothers' angry stances as they fought (always to make up again). And Sarita's braids flapping in the wind. I would always draw everything and write down everything. I would never forget.

nina
(part i)

april 2001

i woke one day in my early thirties to discover I had no past. It was early April, and I felt as if I was emerging from a long hibernation or a dream that was fuzzy and difficult to remember. I wondered how long I had been living sound asleep and if anyone around me had noticed. I had a job at a public library branch, a home, which was a one-bedroom apartment, and a bank account with a few hundred dollars. Although I knew I had been living there for more than two years, I recognized very few items in my almost empty apartment.

The bedroom contained a queen-sized bed, nightstand, and dresser, but not much else. Part of my daily routine included keeping the room scrupulously neat and free of any clutter, so the room had a bare or even spartan atmosphere. And there was no furniture and nothing on the walls—no pictures or knickknacks, no signs of a personal life beyond basic survival. The closet was filled with neatly hung, sturdy, practical clothing in sturdy, practical grays, browns, and drab olive tones. The kitchen had an equally stripped-down appearance. The cupboards and refrigerator were nearly empty and the utensil drawer contained just two forks, two knives, two spoons, and a spatula. There were a few pots and pans in a cabinet, but their pristine cleanliness made me reluctant to actually cook in them. I ordered in a lot.

The living room had merely a television and VCR combo and a sofa with broken springs. Like the bedroom, the floor was covered with industrial beige wall-to-wall carpeting. But the tiny study off the living room was crowded, almost claustrophobic because of the four large oak bookcases overflowing with novels I scarcely remembered reading. On the bottom shelf of one bookcase, I found an old shoebox of photographs of myself in foreign places with people whose names escaped me. In this room, the beige carpet was almost entirely hidden by an oriental rug and scattered pillows. The walls were a fresh sunny yellow—a color that struck me as contrived, even desperately cheerful, and the room contained the only picture in the entire apartment, a photograph of a nude black woman staring straight at the camera and laughing, long dreadlocks covering most of her breasts and belly. Though her expression was entirely unfamiliar and I could not remember ever laughing with such abandon, I was uncomfortably certain that woman was a younger me.

I could recite certain facts—I knew where I had gone to school and my siblings' telephone numbers, and I could with little effort list the Library of Congress numbers of most subject areas—but I was unclear on most details. What courses had I taken in college? What were the names of my college roommates? Did I get along with my parents? Who were my close friends? Did I even have any close friends? Trying as hard as I could, I couldn't recall many concrete experiences of my life. There were a few scraps of memory and images such as a cake with candles, a hotel lobby, an anonymous shopping mall, a garden, but these were fragmented and did not seem to be attached to any time or particular place.

The fogginess of the past forced me to cling desperately to the one certainty I had—my routine. I got up every morning at seven, and went to work at eight-thirty. Each day I brought a tuna fish sandwich to work and ate it sitting on the library steps alone. I called my mother and Eric, my stepfather, in Florida on Sunday afternoons when the rates were cheapest. Every Thursday night was movie night, though I couldn't recall more than two or three films that I had seen in recent years.

Meanwhile, I began discreetly to ask my colleagues at work about their memories, without going as far as to admit my lack. My hope was to discover that my confusion was the norm. To my dismay, the people at work could often recall in vivid detail any number of childhood and adult memories from dolls' tea parties, favorite books and films, to past lovers, political affiliations, and dinner parties. Those with their own children had an even greater catalog of events, like the baby's first steps and specific precocious words of their child as a preschooler.

Discovering that the blank slate of my mind was an anomaly, I became uncomfortable around other people. Every day at work, I volunteered to shelve books rather than sit behind the reference desk. I neither wanted to interact with library patrons nor socialize with my colleagues. I especially liked the solitude as I put away books in the annex where I ran into only an occasional student doing research or a sleeping street person. The annex with its floor-to-ceiling bookshelves and its caged cabinets of rare documents was on the over-heated top floor. The dusty room attracted few visitors. I spent long hours there even after my cart was empty and I knew it was past time to return to the main floor. Sometimes attracted by a binding, I would pull an unknown book from the shelves and settle down to consume the afternoon reading. Three weeks went by before my supervisor finally confronted me.

"Georgette, you're a reference librarian but you haven't been working for weeks. You weren't hired to shelve. Is there something wrong?" I wasn't sure whether Esther was concerned or angry. She had called me into one of the back offices for privacy, which might mean she was genuinely sympathetic. On the other hand, the older woman was rather impatiently flipping through a Rolodex as she spoke, and she kept glancing at the telephone's flashing red light.

"I just like to shelve." I stared at the papers on Esther's desk. I saw my name written on a to-do list.

"Well, is there any good reason you can't do the job that you were hired to do?"

"No."

"Okay. Good. I expect you to be at circulation from nine to eleven and the reference desk the rest of the day."

Esther went back to her paperwork while I slowly walked out to the circulation desk. Janet and Marie sat behind it, chatting and pasting barcodes into a pile of un-catalogued books.

"So you're back with us in the land of the living?" Janet looked up and smiled, or maybe it was a smirk. I blinked several times, and Janet went out of focus. As the two other librarians talked, the air in the library became thicker and their faces and voices receded until I could scarcely hear their words.

After I discovered this method of escape the first time, it was easy to use it each day before I got on the bus. I kept my world shadowy and indistinct until the evenings when I was safely back home. Other people ceased to scare me. I couldn't hear their voices when they spoke to me; instead, I learned to lip-read the words devoid of any emotion or need. The student in tears over the paper due the next day became a series of Boolean queries to type into a periodical database. Janet, fearing that her boyfriend was sleeping around, was a soundless blur moving in space. Marie, eating carrot sticks and promising once again to start her real diet on

Monday, was a headline in *Ms. Magazine* about eating disorders.

Mimi was the unofficial leader of the librarians at my branch. She arrived each morning with hair in a bun, clothed in matching coordinates, feet in bobby socks and tennis shoes. At four o'clock, she went into the staff bathroom and emerged with her auburn hair teased, her face carefully made up, and long legs ending in expensive pumps.

"Girls," Mimi would say, as she headed toward the exit in a waft of perfume, "we can't be librarians day and night. Especially not at night!" All the other junior librarians would giggle while Esther would smile slightly and shake her head. I always remained silent.

"Are you gay or something?" Mimi asked abruptly one day. I considered the question, trying the idea on for size. I didn't have an answer but thought that perhaps Mimi knew something about me that I didn't realize myself.

"Why do you ask?"

"Well, you don't seem very interested in any of the guys who come in here. Like the man with the green sweater who was here earlier—he was trying to flirt. But you just looked at him and other guys too with this coolness. It's like you're doing anthropo-logical research or something." As she spoke, Mimi rapidly typed catalogue entries on the computer. I could not tell whether Mimi was embarrassed or just nonchalant.

"Do I look at women differently?"

"No, I guess not." Mimi turned red. "I just thought you might be gay or something."

That night I took the subway to South Station, a stop far away from my neighborhood and my job. I found a magazine seller and bought one copy of *Playboy* and one of *Playgirl*. Later at home, I looked at one and then the other. Even in the privacy of my apart-ment, I felt faintly self-conscious. The models' blatant nakedness seemed to taunt me, not with titillation but with their apparent openness and comfort with themselves. Tara liked roller-blading, swimming, hot men, and mysteries. Steve liked sailing, romantic dinners, sexy women, and beaches. I wondered what I liked, but I felt nothing until I began to read one of the erotic stories in *Playboy*. As the characters eyed each other in a restaurant, there was a momentary warmth in my stomach, almost too subtle to be detected. By the time they were in the stockroom, tearing each other's clothing off, the glow had faded and I was numb. Almost without noticing what I was doing, I went into the study, a room that I generally avoided. I discovered a milk crate of sex magazines near one of the bookcases. I added my recent purchases to the crate and replaced it in the corner of the room. In bed that night, I cried for the first time in weeks.

Sunday afternoon, before making my weekly phone call to Florida, I tried to think of a way to ask my mother about my past. I thought getting them to talk about previous boyfriends or girlfriends might jog my memory. It was somehow shameful to admit that I wasn't sure whether I had always been single. When my mother answered the phone, I had my opener ready.

"Mother, I met someone."

"Oh, what's his name?" My mother didn't hesitate over the question. I smiled.

"Steve," I said. "He's very romantic. We go for long walks on the beach a lot."

"Will you send us a picture?" The voice at the other end of the line sounded hopeful. I agreed, although I had no idea where I would get the picture.

"Actually, I was wondering if you could send me some pictures."

"Pictures of what?"

"I don't know. Me growing up? The family? I just want something to remember everything by." I wasn't sure what I was asking for.

"All right. I'll see what I have." My mother sounded strangely anxious and hung up soon afterwards. Later that afternoon, my eldest brother called and spoke for ten minutes without interruption about my lack of consideration. Would I forever be a thorn in everyone's side, and was I determined to make our mother ill? I had no idea what he was talking about so I listened and apologized.

Nevertheless, a few days later a small brown packet of photographs arrived. Enclosed was a card with a picture of a black child in a pink pinafore on the front. The inside of the card read, *Thinking of Our Little Girl.* Both my mother and Eric had signed. The photographs were of me and my family, from the time I was an infant through mid-adolescence. I recognized the pictures in a vague, uneasy way, like remembering a dream long past. I stared at the most recent. I had my hair braided in long, multicolored extensions, a short black dress, and large clunky boots. I looked sullen, closed in. On the back of the picture was written, *Georgie at 16 (1985).*

The next day at work, a black girl came up to me at the reference desk and launched into a confusing story of a fight with some classmates. The girl looked about thirteen, and she hugged herself tightly as she spoke. Her clothing was bright and fashionable but looked like it came from one of those shops I passed to and from work each day. In the windows hung large white banners with orange neon letters designating all items on sale for $9.99 or less. They never seemed to go off sale. The glittering decals adorning her brightly polished fingernails complemented the clothes. Watching the girl, I felt an almost unbearable panic. I began to blink rapidly.

". . . And Candace said that she'd mess up anyone who came

near her boyfriend. Everyone was screaming and then the teacher told us all to get out. She told us to go to the principal's office. But if I get one more note sent home, I'll be in big trouble," said the girl. I was surprised to notice she was still talking. I blinked again, recovering some of the mist useful for distancing other people.

"So, Georgie, I thought that you might be able to help." Just as the girl began to fade, I heard my name. Somehow, this girl knew me. I looked around hoping that one of the other librarians would come over and help. Everyone seemed busy with some other task. The girl waited expectantly.

"Could you just apologize to Candace?" I offered. The girl stared as if I had suggested that she sprout wings and fly to the moon.

"Forget it!" She turned and was out the front door before I could think of a reply. As I watched the angry back, I was overcome with the first clear memory of myself before that April. I was lying on my stomach on a stone bench somewhere in the city. Red, orange, brown, and black braids fell across my eyes, forming a screen between me and the outside world. The hunger had passed and left me light-headed and airy. Watching the torsos and legs of people passing by, I felt happy. I couldn't see any faces. I felt a shadow over me as someone paused in front of my bench. I looked up to see two people, a white woman and a black man, standing in front of me. The man pointed to a trailer parked nearby. The large white van had blue lettering painted across, *Bridge Over Troubled Waters*. The man was talking, but his words were disjointed.

"Eat . . . need help . . . runaway . . . family . . . Boston . . ." I couldn't make any sense of what he was saying. I smiled and floated away.

Walking home through the park that afternoon, I saw two men playing chess on the stone benches. A crowd had gathered to watch the match. I stood as far to the side as possible in order to remain removed from the bystanders but still see the game. One of the men, the one in dungaree overalls, played there often. I liked his little green-rimmed glasses and the intense concentration with which he played. I liked the way that on the rare occasions he lost, he laughed gracefully and shook his opponent's hand.

There were still many pieces on the board when the man in overalls declared checkmate.

"Damn," the other one said. "You're all that!"

"You lost as soon as you moved that rook. The rest was just playing the game out," said the winner.

"Is that what life is? Is it all predetermined? Don't I have free will?" I didn't think that I had spoken aloud, but the man with the overalls turned and faced me as if he knew what I was thinking.

"There's always free will," he said.

I awoke the next morning to sticky sheets and the smell of cigarette smoke. As the sound of running water penetrated my early-morning fog, I stifled a scream. I stood up quickly and wrapped myself in my robe, cinching the belt tightly. From my nightstand, I snatched up the lamp, ripping its cord out of the bedroom wall. Waiting by the bathroom door, I tried to slow my breathing, but each breath came out as a short gasp, which I muffled with my free hand.

After a few minutes, the door opened to reveal the man from the park. His overalls were gone; instead, he wore only a towel. He was combing his hair out of his eyes as he entered the bedroom. Seeing my right hand wielding the lamp and my left pressed against my lips, the man slowly raised his hands and took a step backwards.

"Who are you? What are you doing here?" I heard myself speaking from a distance; it was almost as if I were watching the whole scene on television. It was too bizarre to be real.

"Calm down. Georgie, what's wrong? What's going on here?" The man's voice cracked as he retreated further into the bathroom. I wanted to laugh. Was it possible that he was afraid of me? The whole scene was absurd: two nearly naked people, a lamp, and neither person knowing what was happening—this was the stuff of TV sitcoms, not real life.

"Get your clothing on and get out!" I moved just far enough to the side to allow the man to pass into the bedroom.

"I . . . Are you all right? What's going on?"

"I said get out! I'll call the police if you aren't out of here in five minutes." To indicate my seriousness, I picked up the cordless phone on my dresser and poised my thumb above the *on* switch.

"I don't get it. I thought we had a good time. I thought that you liked me." The man was almost whining. As I watched him stumble around looking for his shoes, and listened to his unanswered entreaties, I could almost hear the studio audience laughing.

It was not until the man was gone that I felt entirely myself again. My motions and words were no longer being controlled by an invisible puppeteer. I fought the urge to collapse on my bed and cry. Instead, I began my daily routine of brewing coffee, showering, and getting ready for work. Before leaving my apartment, I shoved my sheets and towels into the washing machine with detergent and a cup of bleach. I spun the dial to *extra-soiled*.

That day at the library moved quickly. Patrons blurred together. I was a cold hard automaton, a robotic extension of my computer. I performed multiple database searches with an efficient precision resulting in exact answers to the patrons' often vague queries. I spewed out statistics, facts, citations, and bibliographic references, providing more information than requested.

"Yes, may I help you?" I asked the figure standing silently before me in the late morning.

"Georgie, are you pissed at me? I came back because I thought maybe you'd think about it and change your mind. Tameka says you helped her when she was . . . you know. She says that's why Aunt Fran was all mad at you for giving her the money to do it."

After puzzling over the girl's words, I felt relieved. The girl just wanted money, and she mentioned one of my aunts. She must be a second cousin or the child of some relative whom I hadn't seen in years.

"How much money do you need?" I groped under the circulation counter for my purse. The girl stared at me, fists clenched and scowling.

"I'm not fucking pregnant! I don't want your money. I need your help!"

Once again, the girl's words sparked a memory in me. I was thirteen, sitting on a metal folding chair under fluorescent lighting. I stared at the barren walls listening to the social worker droning on.

When I looked up from my reverie, the girl was gone.

in nina's house

nd it came to pass that the person she once was had disappeared."

Nina always began her stories with the words, *And it came to pass.*

My lover Amanda was curious about my life in Jamaica, but I could never find a cogent way to explain how things were in my grandmother's house. It was there that she told us stories about our lives. These stories shifted in time and place, and sometimes the characters mutated into creatures that we no longer recognized. I think we all had moments when we were listening to her words for the pleasure of their rhythm, but we'd decided the tale was meaningless. I could see the nonbelief in the glances that my mother and aunts and uncles exchanged over Nina's head. As we grew, she began to shrink, until some of my younger cousins were her height.

Sometimes I watched the children chasing each other in circles through the rooms. Their giggles grew to shrieks, and their feet banged into the oak and tile floors so that her house echoed with their joy. This ruckus was nothing new; they were not any ruder or louder or more impudent than we had been. And Nina, as she always had, would call out that they must quiet themselves. The children would try to smother their noise. Often the peace lasted for less than five minutes. Then there were Nina's warnings and threats. And because they were children, chastisement often followed. But when *we* were that small, Nina would cut a switch from her yard. Now, parents were called in to fetch their unruly offspring before they drove her further mad than her eighty years deserved.

"Me tink she mad, pure and simple," the workers would say to one another. I'd heard this talk more times than I could count. When I was ten and squatting in the coolness under the verandah, those whispers would float down from the gate where the garden boy flirted with the young women, baskets and bundles on their heads as they returned from market. Or in the dining room of my Uncle Denton's house where my family would sit around a table laughing at Nina's excesses, which was what they called those wild moods she had. But the servants knew her craziness came from all those years she spent, from thirty to sixty-five, living and working in the States, while my mother and her sisters and brothers were sure this strangeness came after her move back to the island of their childhood. They pursed their lips during her tales, which were meant to direct our lives but often seemed completely removed from our world.

Nina was no fool, however, and she always caught their eyes. "If oono mus look sour like dat, oono catch nuttin but bitterness, yuh know," she'd snap in patois, and my family would be shamed. Most were States born and bred, but they knew patois just the way they knew where they came from. Underneath their stiff ways, they understood that if you listened to Nina long enough or hard enough, the aliens that she described would twist themselves back into recognizable shapes. Suddenly, we'd sit up and say, "Yes, Nina, that is me." She'd just grin and suck her teeth.

We heard our stories in snatched minutes during the slap of playing cards, steaming platters of food, the drunk of rum punch, the traffic of cousins, and the ever-present heat that shaped our days. Early one summer, I was sitting on the floor, my shoulders gripped by her knees while she weaved my hair into tight plaits, which would hopefully last through August. I was enjoying this time alone with my Nina while the rest of the family was still in the States. Nobody else was arriving until at least mid-July.

I hadn't always enjoyed the island. Nina moved back when I was five. Those first several summers, I loved the sun and the beach. When I lived with her, I felt like I belonged. But later, as I grew older, I began to wish that I could attend summer camp like the other girls at my American school. I'd never been to camp but had heard tales of riding and sailing lessons, bonfires and mid-night raids. As a teenager I longed to stay with my boyfriends, believing that each one was my true love and every moment spent apart was a precious moment lost. And I imagined spending the summer waiting tables like my friend Keisha, who wore the cutest black dress with a twirly miniskirt and hung out with college students smoking and drinking after they closed the restaurant each night. Later still, I wanted to bring Amanda to the island to show her the home of my childhood, so she could actually know me. Of course, that was impossible—bringing any woman, but especially a white woman was unacceptable. I was resentful; so those past few summers I insisted, until the very last minute, that I wasn't going. My family could either accept who I was or go without me. But each summer my mother sent me a ticket with a scrawled note dictating that I be at the airport by six a.m. on a certain date. And each summer I relented, leaving my lover behind. At first, Amanda angrily demanded to know if I loved my family better than her. It surprised me that she would ask. Love wasn't even the issue. Having left behind everything else, I could not bear to let go of the island.

"Jamaica was special to me," I tried to explain to her. "For a little while, the couple of years when I lived in Nina's house, everything had seemed just right, magical to me. Then when we moved back to the States, everything was different. I didn't know if it was this country or my parents' divorce or my growing chest, but suddenly I was scared, lonely, and cold. I missed my friend Sarita. Somehow, I just loved her more than any girl at my new American school."

"Oh, no wonder!" Amanda had winked knowingly, trying to kiss me. "Your first girlfriend. A baby dyke at age eleven. You started early." I didn't correct her, but that was not what I had meant at all.

Those early-morning flights from Boston to Kingston were hell. Logan Airport was crowded. We'd wait for hours in the endless line at the baggage counter as each group of travelers frantically shuffled parcels from person to person in an attempt to get below the seventy-pound-per-person maximum. Even my youngest cousins were given two stuffed bags to carry on. Toddlers dragged baskets bigger than themselves. The luggage contained not just our belongings, but clothing, toys, books, toilet paper, and tampons for friends and relatives on the island. It always seemed like every Jamaican in Boston sought my aunts out before we left. *Oh, oono ah go home? Can you bring a lickle sometink fi faada, no? Me pickney? Me aunt? Miss Myrtella, live uppa Brownstown?*

Everyone was tired and irritable as we waited in line. The plane was always delayed. The pale, colorless airline clerks and flight attendants stood behind counters, dressed in blue polyester, smirking with pink-lipsticked mouths. They talked to each other in loud whispers.

"Would you look at those people? They bring everything but the kitchen sink. You'd think they were going on safari."

But there was that wonderful moment when we stepped off the plane in Jamaica. Still exhausted and over-heated, we were in a world where everyone was black. Entering this world was like having a weight lifted off our shoulders; at the Kingston airport, we stood a little straighter, laughed a little more, snapped a little less.

"And it came to pass that the person she once was had disappeared. Georgie had grown up with colors, noise, and warmth. She was a child who played hard and cried hard. And oh how we loved her. We were sorry when she had to leave us to go into the white world, as does every black child in that country over there. Because you know, those white people lead an easier life, but their world is so much harder than ours. Her brothers and her cousins had all gone before her. And perhaps that's where we made our mistake. We thought that she would be like them. They held their hearts protected in a bubble like the skin of a jackfruit. She held hers in open hands for any who asked to gobble it up or slice it into tiny bitlike pieces."

As soon as I heard those words, I struggled to rise. I was not interested in hearing about my heart. I came to this island to escape my heart. Nina's knees tightened. She was stronger than she looked. Sometimes I thought that she merely played at frailty to get her own way and if the pretense of old age didn't work, then she'd cast the mask aside to reveal her true Amazon self.

"Nina," I said. "Let me up. I've promised Catherine that I'll help her with the ackees for tomorrow's breakfast." Nina ignored me. Was there something about old age that allows one to do exactly as one pleases? Last year I wanted to be nineteen forever. But now I'd rather be an ornery old Jamaican woman, sitting in the shade of her verandah commanding her world. Never loosening her grip, Nina picked up the jar of aqua-blue hair dressing from the end table. She gently nudged my left cheek so that my right one rested on her thigh, enveloped in the soft layers of worn cotton and flesh. As she oiled my scalp, she hummed a little under her breath. The gentle pull of the comb, the firm massage of her fingers, and the constant sound of the sea combined to make me feel sleepy and warm. There was a familiar feeling in the air of my childhood, or at least of a time when things were not so hard and I was not so cold. I stopped struggling. Suddenly everything had become very small. There were only three colors. The yellow of Nina's skirt encompassing my head, the green of her garden, and beyond the palm fronds, the barely glimpsed silver-blue glint of sun glancing off water.

When I was completely relaxed and unable to move, Nina chuckled—I could tell by the way her leg vibrated under my head. After she was through laughing, she began again.

"And it came to pass that Georgie has disappeared. We brought her up with love and warmth . . ."

That was how things were in my grandmother's house.

We were both wrong though. It was not always warm, and the family was not always close. As I sat in Nina's grip, I remembered my sixth birthday—loving the feel of the sun and wind on my face as I swung higher and higher on the hard rubber swing. I was sure that I was flying. When I reached the top, I stretched my legs and stared at the cold blue sky. There were no clouds. The teacher had told me that the sun was a star, but I knew that the sun was much too big and warm to be a star. I stared at the sun until the swing carried me back to earth. I pulled my legs in tight as I soared up and back. Now I could see the whole playground.

Beneath me I could see the girl from the fourth grade with the long blond ponytail, a gap in her teeth, and red mittens. She walked over to the swing set and looked at me. I smiled at her. She said something but I was too far up to hear. I laughed, happy that the beautiful girl from the fourth grade was talking to me. When the swing glided down, I dragged my sneakers in the ground to slow it. I jumped off too soon and landed on my knees.

I stood up and smiled at the girl with the blond hair and the red mittens. She smiled back. I could finally hear her saying, "Nigger, Nigger, Nigger." She said this word over and over again. In my head, I sounded out the word. I listened carefully to her voice. It was the voice of my older brother when he had learned a new swear.

I asked her why she was calling me names. In response, she stuck out her tongue, telling me to go away because I was nothing but a dirty nigger. She took off her red mittens so that we could compare the color of her hands. She was right. She laughed again, and I tried to run away from her laughing face.

When I got home, my mother was there. She was angry. She asked me why I was not in school. I told her that I had left early. She slapped me and told me that she did not have time for my nonsense today. She was tired and late for a meeting, and when I asked her if she was a dirty nigger too, she hit me again. She'd had enough disrespect for one day.

"Your head's a mess," she said, pushing me down until I was seated on the hardwood floor. My mother sat on a kitchen chair, gripping my shoulders with her knees. She combed through the knots and snarls. Each pull of the comb sounded like my hair was being ripped out by the roots. Her knuckles dug into my scalp as she began each tight braid. My hand reached up, then was smacked away.

"Mama, you're hurting me."

"If you can't sit still and quiet," she said pulling harder, "we can always cut it all off."

Soon we were in the car. My mother was driving me back to

school. I looked out the window. Children were playing on the sidewalk. Their mothers had bundled them cozy against the wind in hats and striped scarves. They rode red tricycles and bright plastic Big Wheels. Once I had a tricycle, but now I had a two-wheeler. The children on the sidewalk were all beautiful and white like the girl with the blond ponytail. I began to cry again. My mother warned me that she was not in a good mood. I bit my lips.

I slowly walked down the gray hall to my classroom. The girl with the ponytail was coming out of the bathroom. I pretended not to see her.

Yesterday, when I arrived in Jamaica, I had the driver drop me at the main gate at Cha Gully. The gate was unlatched, yet I hesitated, standing with my face pressed against the iron bars, my lips silently forming excuses. The day before, I had changed my ticket and jumped on a plane without telling anyone. How would I explain my month-early arrival, my mother's tight voice when she spoke my name, or my friend who was no longer coming? For the first time, my mother had agreed to Amanda coming with us. And then I went and left her behind. Through the bars, I could barely make out the stucco house; it was almost completely hidden by the palm trees that lined the quarter-mile driveway. Everything was silent—the house, the servant quarters, the entire neighborhood. Where were the sounds of dogs, goats, children, and cars? As a child, I had believed that everything stood still in Nina's world between each summer visit. Perhaps by coming unannounced, I had caught Cha Gully by surprise, and everyone was still in the ten-month slumber. I imagined tiptoeing into Nina's bedroom, kissing her wrinkled walnut forehead, and waiting for the house to come alive. More likely I was asleep. Or perhaps I was actually dead. I thought back to my mother shaking my shoulders last week and shouting, "Do you want to die, Georgette? Is that what you want? That's where you're headed!"

But I was not dead or asleep, and I had forgotten that Nina knew everything. After a few minutes, a shiny black girl carrying a basket appeared on the drive. At first it seemed like she was going to ignore my presence as she stepped outside the gate. Almost as an afterthought, she asked whether I wanted to come to the market with her or go inside and have some tea; the cook had made my favorite, fish stuffed with rice and greens.

Hours later when I finally faced Nina, my back was aching. I couldn't balance baskets on my head like the hired girl; instead, I had to always rest them on my back donkey-style. Nina looked me over. She began with my feet, snorting at my new shoes. She lifted my skirt a few inches to check if I wore a slip. She rolled back my sleeves, glancing at the pattern on my yellow-brown arms, which were pale compared to the polished mahogany of my face, hands, and legs. She didn't speak, just pursed her lips as she concluded by staring into my eyes and tapping each cheek lightly with her palms. Finally, she said, "I want to braid your hair tomorrow. Otherwise you'll be looking like a Rastafarian by the time Verna arrives. Unless you want me to have Catherine put some chemicals in it?"

"No thanks, Nina," I said. "And don't worry about my hair. I don't plan on swimming much."

"Even so."

When I was four or five, before Nina moved back to the island and I began to spend my summers there, my brothers, cousins, and I were intensely curious about Jamaica. It was a place of mystery hidden by the impenetrable cloud of patois, which our parents fell into at times like Christmas, or when they gossiped and did not want us to understand their words. We would spend summer vacation outside in my Uncle Denton's garden helping him dig, or chasing him down to tell stories in the shade of the willow.

"Tell us, tell us," someone would say, "tell us about when you were little and what it was like on Jamaica, and is it true like Nina says that you can go barefoot all year long?"

And Denton would laugh his throaty chuckle. His voice had a deep rasp, which we loved, though it was from smoking too many cigarettes for too many years. He told us stories about the sun and the sparkling blue water and the fish, which you could catch with your hands. And the fields of sweet tough sugar cane growing higher than your daddy's head. Then he'd point to some vegetable and say, "Look at that scrawny nothing—at home the fruits and vegetables grow twice the size they do here. The juice, it runs down your chin, your fingers, and arms as you eat. And that's why the women in Jamaica taste so sweet, their bodies are flavored with mango juice.

"Before my mother, your Nina, moved to the States, we used to live by the coast. Most mornings at dawn, she brought Mercy, Verna, and I to the beach and left us to play on the sand while she walked regal and majestic straight into the water. We played a game where we'd stare at the sea, each waiting to be the first to see her appear. She stayed submerged for so long, Mercy would worry that Mama had stopped breathing under there. But after a while Mama would always come out, dripping but still queenlike, her spear in one hand and a string of fish in the other."

So we imagined Jamaica as a paradise where the sun never set and food fell out of the sky and into your hands anytime you wished. We could never quite reconcile that image with the place we began to visit a year or two later. For it was true that the sun was warm, the water was blue, and the fruit was sweet—but it was also true that up in the hills people lived in shanties no bigger than my brothers' old tree house. And at first, it was hard to understand why in a country where the fruits and vegetables were so big and you could catch fish in your hands, the men and children looked so thin and so hungry. The boniness of the people was a great mystery to us.

"Is it hard, spearfishing? Do you think I could learn?" I asked Nina that day, more than fifteen years later.

"What now, sweetness?" Nina's hands stopped combing. She sounded puzzled.

"You know, remember fishing every morning at dawn when my mother, Mercy, and Denton were real little?"

"Did they tell you that? Cha! Does this body look like it was made for diving?" Nina laughed and began another plait. That was the problem with my family. You could never get a straight answer from anyone, and even when you did, you could not be sure if it was the truth or a fiction.

"I remember Georgie that year or two that she and her brothers lived with me." Nina was relentless in her determination to tell me my story. "They were such little heathens when they arrived. I told Verna to send them to church. But would my child listen? No, she would not. She was too busy fighting with that husband of hers. So when Georgie, Chris, and Alex arrived, they were hungry for love or discipline or both. Georgie was the loudest. I'd tell her to share with her brothers. She'd nod and take whatever was Chris's and share it with herself. If poor Chris wanted to keep any little bit of something for himself, he'd hide it. Else she'd have it in her hands in a second, and if it was food, it would be down her throat lickety-split. Somehow she'd always get Alex to do things for her. He loved that child, though it couldn't have been for her charm."

Nina paused, leaned down, and brushed her lips against my forehead to kiss away the harshness of her words, "Yes, all of us, even Chris, loved that impudent child, though she was as far from charm as north from south."

I wondered if white families had the same sort of fluidity as ours. Nina left her eldest three children on the island with a relative when she first immigrated to the States. For six years she lived alone and worked as a maid to earn enough money to bring her children over. In turn, my mother sent my brothers and me to Jamaica to live with Nina when I was nine and they were twelve and thirteen. My father was gone, and Chris and Alex were running wild, or as wild as possible in a small suburban town. My mother decided that sending them to live in Nowhere, Jamaica would straighten them out. Whether it was the location or Nina or the harshness of our Jamaican school, Chris and Alex were considerably subdued when we returned to the U.S. almost two years later. I was changed as well. Before I left, I could play jump rope and jacks with the white girls in our neighborhood. By the time I came back, I had a funny accent and my skin had turned dark brown, adolescence had struck, my mother had moved into Boston, and junior high at the elite Ellis School for Girls was an endless stream of slumber parties to which I was not invited.

Old habits die hard. Though Nina had plenty of money when she moved back to the island, she was as prudent as ever, and she made us save our shoes for church and school. Saturdays, Alex, Chris, and I went barefoot as our mother, Mercy, and Denton had before us. I still couldn't stand the smell of ripe bananas. It reminded me of walking home through banana plantations with the moist soft feeling of over-ripeness squashed between my toes.

One Saturday, we were hopping up and down in Nina's yard, trying to get a coin out of Chris's hand. We had been on the island for at least six months, as I had already gotten my first report card and was babbling in patois like I had grown up there.

"Yuh say yuh gwine fi buy ice cream with that!" I yelled.

"Me never say nuttin like that. A fi me money." Chris held his hand above my head. My mother had just sent us some money and Alex and I had already spent ours. I had searched Chris's belongings for his, but he was smart enough to keep it on his person.

"Please, Chris. Yuh doan buy me sometink, me can get Alex to mek yuh." I alternately threatened then cajoled. Chris just laughed. I was so much smaller; there was no way I could ever get the money. Every time I jumped up, Chris put his hand behind his back. When I landed, he raised it again. Suddenly Nina appeared.

"What's all this screaming? I can give you something to scream about, you know? Georgie, speak proper English. Do you think your mother sent you here to learn to talk like you've never been to school a day in your life? When she sends for you, she'll be ashamed to call you her child! Both of you, go help Sonia and Enid. Now."

"Yes, Nina," we said. As soon as she turned, Chris shoved me. The last thing he wanted to do was spend his free day in the kitchen or making beds.

"God doesn't like idle hands," Nina said, looking around the yard for more work. "Where's Alex gone to now?" Both Chris and I had seen Alex crawl through the latticework under the verandah, but we just shrugged. There was no use for us all spending the afternoon doing chores. Nina looked at us hard.

"God doesn't like liars," she said suspiciously. We were silent. In the last six months, we had given up trying to please God. Much like Nina, he didn't seem to like much but prayer, study, and silent children. Going to church on Sundays and saying the occasional bedtime prayer was the best we could manage.

I walked as slowly as possible toward the kitchen entrance,

carefully avoiding the cracks in the patio stones in order to protect my mother's back from the hatred that sat like a stone in my heart. And I drooped my shoulders and hung my head to make sure Nina knew how much it pained me to be banished inside to Sonia's chores on such a glorious day. At the door, I glanced back. Nina was watching me, hand on hip. Just as I opened my mouth to protest the unfairness of older brothers, she gave a slow solemn wink. I smiled and went inside.

"I remember when I went to the airport to pick up Georgie's mother, aunt, and uncle," Nina said. "I had been in that country over there for six years without seeing my children! They were so big and grown when they stepped off that airplane. It was winter, and I had brought warm coats for them to wear, hand-me-downs from that dirty bitch I cleaned for. But my children had to be forced into those coats. Instead they ran outside Logan with their arms wide-open and tongues stuck out, foolish they were, giggling hysterical at the white, white snow! During the ride home, we went through that long tunnel, and the taxicab driver, he said to my children that we were driving right under the water. Poor Mercy looked scared. In those days it was a bit much, you know, coming over the ocean in a plane and under the ocean in a taxi all in one day. But Verna was fancy-bold, just like her daughter after her. She bounced up and down and shouted every second or so. 'Aie man, I see a crack and water seeping-sopping in! Mercy, Denton, we've come to America to drown!' And I am wondering if that's what happened as I look at my granddaughter today. Where has Miss loud-and-funny Georgie gone? Why is she so silent, as if her heart has gone?"

I almost laughed. Nina had no idea how silent I could be. Silence was my refuge. I remembered my other grandmother's house as small, dark, and musty smelling. I hated it there. My father lived there after he left. We'd go there every weekend to visit.

I was twelve years old in my other grandmother's house. My father was in the bathroom. I pretended I was much younger by digging my face in the green scratchy sofa. I tried to believe that no one could see me when I hid in that sofa.

I felt someone's presence. I looked up. My other grandmother was standing in front of me. In her hands she held a plate of milk-toast, white and wet. The toast swam in a pool of milk, which covered the pink flowers of my favorite plate. I did not want her toast, this house, my father, or even this country, and I told her so.

Her face crumpled and she began to cry. When I cried it was a loud wailing. But this woman just silently shook. I would like to cry as she does. Her tears were much prettier than mine. I noticed my mother standing in the doorway. She must have been there to take me home. She watched us, frowning. Suddenly she came over and took the plate from the woman. She put it down on the glass coffee table whose surface was decorated with painted green swirls. She leaned forward and shook me. She said, "If you don't have anything nice to say, don't say anything at all."

I didn't speak for weeks after this day. I didn't say anything at all.

The sun was almost down. My hair fell around my face in a hundred tiny braids. Nina was done with her story; she started to play solitaire. She was waiting for some answers, but none were forthcoming. I knew that she loved me, but I did not know what to say. My only thought was that the slap of the playing cards reminded me of the crackle of a paper bag. I could remember walking to my apartment from the drugstore nearby, carrying a small white paper bag. I remembered listening to the rhythm of my walk: the two thuds of my feet hitting the pavement, followed by the crackle of the paper bag against my thigh. I did not know why, but I was filled with intense satisfaction each time I felt the weight in the bag slap against my leg.

Nina got up to light the wicker lamp. Its soft light illuminated the middle of the verandah, leaving the outer edges in darkness. As if she knew what I was thinking, she turned and asked, "Who found you?"

"Amanda," I said, surprised at her bluntness. It was rare in my family for a direct question to be asked. Queries took the form of allegories, and stories were parables.

"Your friend."

I was always forgetting that Nina knew everything. I knew that her statement was asking for more than it seemed, but she would have to wait until tomorrow for answers. Tomorrow I'd call my mother and tell her too. I needed to call Amanda and tell her too. For now, I was content to sit back and watch the moon rise. There were few houses around Cha Gully and no lights on the road. At night it was impossible to see anything but pitch-blackness and stars. But I could hear the chirp of crickets, the thrum of lizards, and the constant crashing of the waves below. From the garden, there was the smell of aloe and fresh mint mixed with the scent of ganja drifting down from the servants' quarters.

Just two days before, I had been fighting with Amanda. The fight began as we loaded up the car. Amanda was carrying bags out of her apartment while I packed the trunk. I leaned over to pick up the cooler. A man sitting on a nearby stoop whistled.

"Hey baby," he said, "need some help with that?"

I knew what to do in those situations. I had known what to do since I was twelve. I continued arranging belongings as if I hadn't heard.

"You aren't very friendly, are you?" he asked, crossing the street. Amanda came out of her building just as he reached me. I stood paralyzed while he began to shove his freckled hand down the V neck of my white cotton T.

Later in the car, Amanda turned to me: "Jesus, Georgie. What is wrong with you? Why didn't you move? Why didn't you run or just tell him to fuck off? It's not that hard. Why? *Why?*" Her voice got louder and louder. Then she paused, waiting for an answer. I knew my silence would infuriate her, but we'd had this argument before; there was nothing new to say. Besides, by that point she wasn't really talking about the man on the street.

"Say something, do something! Please."

I stared at her. I don't usually allow myself to feel intense emotions, but for a moment I truly hated her. I wanted to slap that pale cheek and pull her blond hair. I wouldn't answer. Finally, she pulled over to the side of the road and said, "Then get the hell out!"

My Nina knew everything. She knew how to raise six children, milk a goat, slaughter a pig, and drink any man under the table. Over the years she had been a wife, a servant, and a woman of means. She knew how to love, laugh, cry, and tell stories to negotiate the world in which we lived. Nina knew her family's past, and future. But with all that knowledge, I didn't think she knew how I was that very minute, that day. And I certainly didn't know how to tell her.

Two days before, I had gotten out of my lover's car without saying a word. I took my bag and headed home, cutting through the woods and other people's backyards. Two children were playing with their dog. Those children belonged to the sunburned family that lived in my neighborhood. They were always sunburned. I imagined it was from fabulous vacations in Greece or from skiing in the beautiful Colorado mountains. I always saw the family piling into their station wagon. It was a red station wagon with blue license plates. It looked like a car on TV. Sometimes I suspected that they were the family on channel 5 at eight o'clock, but I may have been wrong.

I opened the door to my studio apartment. Inside, it was dark. I could barely see the futon. Its cover was white with black stripes. At one end of the futon was a hole where the stuffing escaped. The nights I spent alone, I picked at the hole, slowly enlarging it. On the futon was a blanket, frayed at the edges. Nina had given it to me when I was eleven, just before we moved back to the States. The blanket was green with yellow flowers. It was so worn that if a stranger looked at it, she would not have seen its pattern. But that was irrelevant. No one really looked at the blanket but me, and I knew the pattern was there.

amanda

may 2001

Over the next several weeks, a pattern emerged to my days. Rather like the daily routine of April when I had retreated into the annex, this pattern left me feeling numb and detached. However, I had controlled the earlier routine, using it to keep myself safe. The new pattern felt completely out of my hands. In the rare moments when I forced myself to think about it, I was terror-stricken.

Many mornings, I awoke to find a different man in my bed or bathroom. Sometimes I vaguely recognized him from the neighborhood. Other times the face was completely unfamiliar. I pushed them out the door as quickly as possible, emptied the overflowing ashtrays, washed my linen, and went to work.

Lunchtimes, I sat on the steps eating my tuna fish sandwich or took a walk in the park to watch the chess players from a distance. After lunch, most afternoons, the young girl, whose name I'd finally learned was Lydia, appeared. Lydia never spoke to the other librarians, only me. Lydia generally began a complicated story about her parents or a boyfriend or a teacher. I could never quite follow the events, but I heard fear and frustration behind the words spoken in a rapid almost toneless voice. These long monologues were occasionally punctuated by demands for help. But the ideas that I offered—school guidance counselors, the department of social services, friends' parents—were always rejected. The conversations with Lydia inevitably ended in one of two ways: either Lydia turned slowly and left, shoulders slumped and in tears; or she stormed out of the library, almost crashing into other people in her hurry to get away from me.

Snapshot memories of myself as a teenager often followed Lydia's visits. My parents and I screaming at each other. My friends and I sitting in a dark playground, drinking warm beer. My wide eyes staring at the blue sky. The feeling of a weight atop my body and thrust after thrust.

Over the weeks, Lydia began to appear more and more neglected. Her once brightly colored clothes became dingy. The careful manicure was chipped and untended. Dark circles shadowed her eyes. Her cheekbones and collarbone stuck out at sharp angles, and her roots sprouted an inch of nappy hair where the process had grown out. I, on the other hand, was told how good I looked by several colleagues. At first, I barely heard their compliments. Finally, one day as I walked into the library, fifteen minutes before opening, Mimi called out.

"Whatever you're getting, girlfriend, I want some of that!"

"What do you mean?" I felt suddenly self-conscious. For the past few weeks, I had barely noticed the other librarians' presence and thus assumed they did not notice mine.

"Look at you, Georgette: hair, makeup, those clothes. No more Miss Plain Jane for you. You've become a glamour girl."

In the bathroom, I tried to really look at myself. I knew that I had started to dress up a bit more and was trying a new hairstyle, but I was surprised at how radiant I looked. My hair, normally pulled into a tight ponytail, was now permed and fell in curls nearly to my shoulder blades. The silk blouse that I bought on a whim the other day opened in a V neck just shy of risqué. My heavily made-up eyes looked back at me mockingly. I momentarily felt like screaming. Then I smiled and left the bathroom.

I became used to the new weekday routine. Mornings meant unwanted men, dirty linen, used condoms, and terse rejections. Daytimes were for the library, Lydia, and ignoring the gossip of my colleagues. Evenings began with long walks through Boston and ended in welcome oblivion. Errands and housecleaning filled the weekends along with the Sunday afternoon ritual of calling my mother and Eric. The lies about Steve, my fulfilling job, and many friends came without thought. I was happy to try and make them happy.

I should have been worried about both the men and Lydia, who seemed to have no one but me. Actually, one part of my mind, way in the back, was terrified. But the fear acted as a paralyzing agent. I felt frozen and powerless to vary the daily interactions. Once I picked up the phone and called the psychiatric crisis hotline number from the front of the white pages. The voice at the other end asked me a series of questions including whether I felt like I wanted to hurt myself or someone else, if I heard voices, could I tell him the date and the names of the last five presidents. Apparently, I answered all the questions correctly because the voice assured me that I was not in crisis, although it suggested that I might consider psychotherapy. Spending a hundred dollars an hour to pour my heart out to some stranger seemed silly. I did not pursue the matter further.

One day while walking to work, I passed an older man who hailed me. It took me a few moments to recognize my father. I could not remember the last time I had seen him. I rarely thought about Michael Collins, but when I did, I pictured him in his forties, muscular and impeccably dressed. Standing before me that morning, he appeared old, and though his suit was expensive and in good repair, it was rumpled and it hung off a bony frame. He even seemed shorter than I remembered.

"Daddy," I said, "how are you?"

"I'm doing fine. I miss you. How come you never come visit me, little girl? I haven't seen you in months."

I didn't have an answer for him. Instead, I apologized and said that I'd call soon.

"Are you painting? What are you working on now?" Daddy asked. Embarrassed, I mumbled something about not having the time. For months, I had carefully not thought about my artwork. Suddenly my mind filled with a jumble of canvases and collages that I had once created. I wondered how I had gotten from that life to the library.

We chatted for a few more minutes; then my father moved to hug me goodbye. I was overwhelmed by the odor of his after-shave; the scent, a mix of cinnamon and incense, was intensely familiar. As we embraced, I noticed Lydia sitting on the steps of the library; she looked unbearably weary as she propped her head on her bent knee. I had never seen the girl outside before. I was torn between my father and the desire to comfort Lydia, but by the time my father released me, the teenager had disappeared.

The next time I saw her was that afternoon at the reference desk. When I asked what she had been doing in front of the building earlier, Lydia just shrugged.

A few days later, I went to visit my father at his Roxbury apartment. I went with some trepidation but had a pleasant time listening to his memories of my brothers and me as children. "Georgie, it does my heart good to see you," he kept saying, and then he'd tell another funny story of the mischief that Alex, Chris, and I had made. We ran him ragged, he bragged with a charming smile.

Later, Daddy interspersed those recollections with stories of himself as a youngster. As the afternoon passed, he grew even more talkative, describing his teenage exploits and the young women who fell all over themselves to please him. Something about him made all the lovely young ladies weak in their knees, and he was powerless to resist their attention. When he called himself a dog and described doing my mother wrong, his voice had a strange mixture of shame and pride. Each reminiscence was simultaneously an apology and a boast.

In his younger and more foolish days, he had not appreciated what a jewel my mother had been. He pointed out that absence made the heart grow fonder and that he and my mother hadn't realized how much they loved each other until after they broke up. He recalled that soon after the divorce, my mother had gone out and married the light-skinned Eric, who was literally a pale comparison of himself.

"Yeah, poor Verna," he said. "I hear she is still pining away for me after all these years. When a woman falls in love with me, I get under her skin and she can't ever forget me."

I watched him puzzled, trying to reconcile the picture he painted with the man sitting, sipping coffee. Daddy was not quite broken, but he appeared small and more tired than the vibrant booming character of his stories. Every sip of coffee and Kahlua seemed to slow him down more. At first I could not see much of a connection between this slight, hesitant figure and the type of man filled with so much vitality that he drove my mother to distraction all those years ago. *Liar,* I thought to myself, beginning to get angry. Then, out of nowhere, I remembered being very small—not more than five or six. My family was sitting on the back porch of the house in the suburbs. Alex, Chris, and I balanced carelessly on the railing though it was a long drop to the ground. I was fearless then. We were eating huge slices of watermelon and spitting the seeds out into the bright air.

"Next summer we'll have a giant watermelon tree!" Chris shouted.

"Shush!" said Mother. "You're screaming at the top of your lungs."

"Who cares," I giggled.

"The neighbors will hear," was my mother's answer.

"Good," said Daddy. "We'll invite them over to pick watermelons off our giant tree and eat fried chicken with us. We'll play loud music and dance into the night, and all those white folks will be so glad such happy Negroes live in the neighborhood."

Mother frowned and pretended to be mad. Then she threw back her head laughed. My brothers and I looked up at the sound. Her neck, her voice, her smile all seemed impossibly open. Daddy pulled her into his lap, and they kissed. I hopped up and down with excitement, and my brothers punched each other in the arm, clowning for attention until Daddy enveloped us kids into his bear hug as well.

Sitting in my father's apartment, twenty-five years later, I shoved those memories away. I was not sure if there was room in my current life for happy Negroes, or happy families for that matter.

"I've got to go, Dad," I said, shaking my head a little. He seemed to realize that he had pushed too much because he apologized for talking my ear off.

"It is just so rare that I get to see you. I know that you've been mad at your mother and me for divorcing. Sometimes I think it was a mistake too. But there is no use crying over spilt milk, right, Georgie? Let bygones be bygones; your brothers did long ago."

"I've really got to go."

"But wait a second, George. You left some boxes in your old room when you were last here. Why don't you go on back there and take a look?"

As I entered the dark back bedroom, I was flooded with images. Curled up on the bed lay an unhappy child. In the shadows, a furious adolescent kicked the walls. I heard echoes of arguments with my brothers. Sitting on the familiar checked bedspread, I tried to recognize my emotions. Unpracticed at identifying them, I was unsure, but I thought I felt hatred. After a minute or so, I gave up and turned to the boxes. In most of the cartons, I found textbooks and novels. One heavy box was entirely filled with books about African-American history and politics. Another contained several blank journals and pads of yellow-lined paper. Flipping through the pads, I saw pages and pages listing mundane tasks such as combing hair, brushing teeth, paying bills. But in the smallest box, I found loose sketches, scraps of paper, and a small notebook. Digging deeper revealed an assortment of envelopes, some addressed to me and others unopened and marked, *Return to sender.*

"What is that, Georgie?" My father's voice made me jump. I clutched the box to my chest.

"Old letters, I guess. And some artwork and stories I used to write." I could remember a younger me who considered myself creative and eccentric.

"Let me see." Daddy held out his hand for the box. I felt a little reluctant, but I couldn't see any good reason for not showing him its contents.

"Is this one from your Nina?" he asked, showing me a postcard of a Jamaican beach. I looked at the back. There were only two sentences and no signature: *Georgie, we miss you. Come home soon.*

"I don't recognize the handwriting," I said.

"Yeah, I bet it is Nina. Pompous old girl that she was! Who are the other letters from?"

"I'm not sure. I'm going to take this box with me now but leave the other stuff for later, if you don't mind."

"If that means you're coming back again, I don't mind at all."

As I made my way to the door, I promised that I'd visit more often. He grinned and gave me a quick hug. I found myself smiling at how easily I had just made an old man happy, and wondered why it had been so hard before.

strike a pose

O nce upon a time, I found myself living a fairy-tale existence. I wasn't quite sure how I'd arrived at this rich and pleasant life with my rich and sometimes unpleasant lover, but I was pretty content with our routine. During the week, Amanda worked and I painted. Every Thursday, Friday, and Saturday night, we went out to some event or club where we drank and necked and fought. So I was not surprised to find myself feeling petulant one Thursday night in May as my lover and I sat in a cool darkened room listening to a Caribbean woman read her poetry. Amanda and the rest of the audience seemed attentive and composed. Their poised expressions indicated the importance of the up-and-coming poet and the thoughtful comments they were preparing for the reception that was to follow her reading. I was bored with the poet; instead I turned my gaze to the table on my right. It spanned the length of the gallery and was laden with flowers, hors d'oeuvres, and wine. Earlier, Amanda had glanced at the table, appraising the feast. "The wine is completely inappropriate. Port is much too heavy," she had said.

"Besides, they ought to be serving West Indian food. When I dated Sadie, she used to cook curried chicken and other Jamaican dishes all the time. It was wonderful." Her words were no surprise. Amanda liked ethnic food and ethnic women.

As the poet droned on, I began to watch my lover closely. Her blond hair was carefully waved to appear thick and unruly. The muted green of her jacket was almost gray. Under the jacket, I could see a raw silk shirt loosely tucked into a pair of almost white jeans. We had spent forty minutes discussing the desired look: casual and arty, but serious and intelligent. Rather than her usual contact lenses, Amanda wore black-rimmed glasses, which she touched from time to time as if deep in concentration. Soon a little smile appeared on Amanda's lips. The smile let me know that she realized I was watching her and she was fighting back a laugh. For a split second she furrowed her brow and crossed her eyes. Then she winked and just as suddenly smoothed her face back into her contemplative pose. I bit my lip and turned away to avoid giggling. A museum was no place for horseplay, or so the teachers had warned us on countless field trips when I was growing up.

I had been to this museum many times when I attended the Ellis lower school. One spring afternoon, Miss Anders had walked twenty laughing girls two by two through the streets of Boston. Every block, she paused to herd us back into formation. Class Two, the seventh grade, was nearly dancing with the thrill of being outdoors on such a perfect day. At the entrance to the Gardner Museum, Miss Anders counted off heads: nineteen smooth ponytails and my short Afro. With admonishments to stifle our voices and stay with our partners, she ordered us to examine the loveliness of the Renaissance Era.

"No running about. No giggling! Any of you who behave like rude noisy little girls will have to walk with me," Miss Anders threatened. "Such children will be sent to the head's office as soon as we return to Ellis."

When Miss Anders was out of sight, Page, my partner, turned to me. "Hey Georgette," she said, "let's split up so we don't slow each other down. Okay?" She stopped to whisper with the other blond girls, while I went off to wander the galleries by myself. That was the way it had always been at Ellis, and the solitude was relaxing in its familiarity.

Leaving my classmates behind, I walked around the ground floor, ignoring the paintings. I concentrated on the building, feeling its weight, running my hand along the smooth marble columns, and listening to the echo of my footsteps. The rough flagstones that paved the floor were the color of my mother's jade necklace. The polished mahogany of the furniture complemented the floor, as her skin did that necklace.

Though I visited the Gardner Museum often as a child, I never grew bored with it the way I did with the endless school excursions to the other museums in the city. I continued to be awed and delighted by entering the Gardner. Merely crossing under an arched doorway delivered me from the gray sidewalks and buildings of Boston to an extravagant courtyard garden. The never-changing art collection attracted few visitors; often I saw no one else as I wandered the rooms or sat in the courtyard. This quiet emptiness appealed to me. I was sure the exquisite building was not just accepting me but welcoming me; perhaps it was even waiting for me. Perhaps I belonged there.

That afternoon I daydreamed about living in the Gardner. The stuffy paintings could be sold or sent to other museums so that I could take up residence. There was no need to feel guilty for buying such a beautiful building for one's personal use. The Ellis School for Girls had taught me the ethics of affluence. At twelve, I already knew that with money comes obligation and duty. I saw myself every Thursday afternoon graciously ushering an awed public through the elegant reception area to the gardens for the hour or two of open visiting that was necessary to fulfill my responsibilities to the less fortunate.

Although my parents had nowhere near the money of my classmates' families, I had been the charity guest at enough parties over the past year to know exactly what sort of luxuries I craved. I wanted riding lessons, trips to Europe, and Sundays at the country club. I wanted to dance in a floor-length white dress at my debutante ball. And most of all I wanted a home where I wasn't ashamed to bring my classmates. The Gardner Museum was classier than the poshest of their town houses and more majestic than the largest of their suburban homes.

Amanda startled me by taking my hand. As soon as I glanced at her, she let go, never taking her eyes off the reader. I wondered if I had been sleeping or my mouth had been open. I longed for the dull evening to end.

When the audience finally began to clap, I followed, carefully cupping my hands so that they made a loud enthusiastic noise. I was not interested in poetry, but that was scarcely the reader's fault, and habit made me loyal to any black writer, even one whose skin was several shades lighter than mine. I was equally careful to stop clapping when Amanda did. Although I had sometimes taken extraordinary pleasure in irritating other lovers, lately my relationship with Amanda had seemed too precarious to play that sort of game with her.

At the reception, hand on my back, Amanda guided me through the crowd of wealthy matrons and students until she found a thirtyish black woman whose bright clothes were out of place in that crowd of subdued elegance.

"Lena," Amanda greeted her with a kiss, "I want you to meet Georgette, my girlfriend. Georgette, this is Lena Sorrel." I concentrated on not letting the surprise show on my face. Lena Sorrel was a sculptor whom I admired for her ability to mix media. She created boxlike sculptures in which tiny worlds of paintings, photographs, and words appeared. While she had yet to have a solo exhibit, she was doing well for a young artist. She had been noted in several journals recently, and Amanda and I'd seen her work in New York. I was delighted to have the chance to meet her.

"I'm so glad to meet you." Lena shook my hand firmly. "Amanda and I met at the Bearden retrospective last week. She told me you work with collage as well."

I caught Amanda's eye and smiled to silently thank her for the introduction to Lena. I hadn't accompanied Amanda to the Bearden exhibit because we'd been arguing that day. I wanted to make sure she knew that I appreciated the thoughtfulness of her peace-making gesture.

As Lena and I began to talk, Amanda excused herself. A few minutes later, she was back with glasses of wine for the three of us. Lena and I were discussing the advantages of acrylics, when I noticed Amanda silently watching me, smiling politely. Though she owned some originals and frequented exhibits, Amanda was a businesswoman, not an artist. Discussions of technique excluded her. My right hand found Amanda's left, and as soon as Lena paused, I changed the subject. We made small talk for a few minutes until Lena excused herself. It was late, and in the morning she had to drive to Provincetown where she was going to have an exhibit.

"Have a safe trip," Amanda said. "Perhaps we can meet for lunch on Sunday? Georgette and I are going to be in P-town this weekend." Lena nodded and moved away. As soon as her back was turned, I dropped Amanda's hand. Until that moment, I hadn't known we were going out of town for Memorial Day.

* * *

The next day, Amanda and I left her Back Bay apartment. We walked up Newbury Street in silence. We were on our way to Ramon's Salon in the South End to get my hair cut. Amanda and I hadn't spoken since morning. To keep from crying or shouting, I looked into the boutiques, reminding myself that before I met Amanda, I had only window-shopped there. Just the day before, we had gone to the elegant stores and spent eight hundred dollars without a second thought. She had let me pick out whatever clothing and shoes I wanted, only rarely vetoing my choices as unflattering or ill-made. Plus I had all the art supplies and time to paint I desired. Her generosity made my complaints seem like a gross perversion of the women's lib movement.

Some of the men at the laundromat and I had formed a support group. "Househomos-R-Us," we called ourselves. Gerry would gripe about Max staying out late all the time. I complained that Amanda tried to control me. Stan protested his lover's thoughtlessness. But we couldn't take ourselves seriously, at least not on the surface. Our grumble sessions always ended pretty much the same way.

"Do you all use spray or liquid starch?" one of us would distractedly interrupt, as he folded perfect creases into towels.

"Oh, spray, of course. Richard is so particular about his shirts." Then we'd fall into intense discussions about detergents and dishes. Pretty soon, the group would disperse as people ran off to the supermarket or to cook dinner. It all seemed so pathetic.

Ramon was this hairdresser friend of Amanda's from her gym. She said she liked that gym because it was clean, carpeted, and color-coordinated. She insisted on accompanying me so she could talk to Ramon personally. She had despised my last haircut. The angles were all wrong for my face.

Earlier that day, we'd had a fight on the matter. I couldn't stand the idea of her coming with me to a black salon. They were the realm of hot combs and Jheri curls, soul music and gossip. Throughout my childhood, my mother and I had left the suburbs once each month to enter that world where she would undergo the chemical process to relax her tight kinks.

In these salons you'd discover a strange mixture of the city's poor and elite blacks. Sometimes we'd see Karen Pina, the TV anchorwoman whose salary was reputed to be half a million. Right next to her would be sitting Mrs. Emerson, who had grown up with my mother and was still living in that same housing project. I wondered if women like Karen Pina resented having to go all the way to Roxbury to get their hair done. But I suspected they were more like my mother, who seemed to look forward to these visits. The hairdresser was a homecoming of sorts—a breather from the white world in which my family generally existed. Of course, there were always a few whites in the salon, boyfriends and girlfriends of the hairdressers. But these whites had a certain look and an accent that matched the one my mother fell into as she sat under the hair dryer.

Amanda simply didn't belong in a black salon. Her presence seemed like an intrusion to me, as if the Ellis School had taken a culture field trip to the black section of town. So I sneered at her that morning when she announced she was coming. "Just who do you think you are? My lover or my mother?" She was about to turn thirty and sensitive about her age. References to the seven-year gap between us never failed to infuriate her. I spoke hoping she'd get angry enough to stay home, but as soon as the words left my mouth I wanted to take them back. I had opened myself up for a line of attack that she always won and that inevitably ended with me in tears and Amanda glowering.

"For a while now, I haven't been really sure which I am," she replied. "But you can damn well pay for your own haircut if you have a problem with it."

"Stacey said she'd hire me back anytime."

"If you think I'd date a woman who dances in a bar called the G-Spot, think again. This is a small city, and I have a reputation. The appointment is for one-thirty."

She was right. Though we were both Ellis girls, I had no one to embarrass but my parents. She had a whole Brahmin heritage to think about, as well as her wealthy lesbian circle. While they might understand and forgive her taste for exotic young artists, dating a go-go dancer was plain tacky.

It was clear, though, that Ramon resented her interference in his professional judgment. But knowing that she paid the bill, he had to placate her.

"Don't worry, honey," he told her while winking at me, "I'll take care of Georgie. You just sit here and read some magazines."

"Just give her a nice fade," Amanda told him. "Nothing fancy or radical. We're going to Provincetown tonight. Everyone who is anyone will be there, and I want us to look good."

As Ramon led me to his chair, he whispered, "What do you want done?"

"I don't care."

"Girl, I know just the thing for you." Ramon could barely contain his excitement at the blank canvas of my scalp. "We'll give you a Widow's Peak. It will be fabulous. They're all the rage right now. And if Miss Bossy over there has a problem with it, you can blame me."

Ramon began to shave my head in a style that even I found terribly severe at first. But after a few minutes, I realized that I liked the way the style made me look intellectual and relentlessly serious, as if I had no interest or time for frivolity. I decided to buy a pair of thick glasses as well with square, geeky frames to match the haircut. It occurred to me that maybe I should leave Amanda and become a Ph.D. student somewhere. It was true that I had not gone to college—in fact, my senior year of high school, I had barely attended classes—but with this hairstyle, I imagined myself staying up all night in a coffeehouse, passionately discussing politics and poetry with like-minded students. Maybe there was a true Art History professor lurking somewhere inside me beneath Amanda's girlfriend. Maybe the type of woman who actually liked events at the Gardner was in there.

From my salon chair, I could see Amanda in the waiting area. She pored over *Essence* and the other black women's magazines that littered the coffee table. Suddenly, she glanced up and saw Ramon's work. For a moment our eyes met and I looked straight at her. Her mouth set in that hard line I knew so well. It was an expression reserved for when we were alone. Such scowls were too unattractive for public. As she struggled to regain her composure, I looked away as if I hadn't seen. My treachery was cruel and completely uncalled for since I really didn't care how my hair was cut. But I felt no remorse at all. When you're being kept by your lover, small things like haircuts are your only ammunition.

It seemed like every queer person in the Northeast had come to the Cape for Memorial Day weekend. Provincetown was a festival as crowds celebrated the opening of the summer season. Amanda had apparently made our reservations in February, so we had elegant accommodations in a renovated Victorian while most people were packed into fleabag motels or in tents at the local campground. I was torn between loving the bed-and-breakfast where we stayed and hating Amanda for not telling me about the trip beforehand. She said it was meant to be a surprise; I suspected that it never occurred to her that I might have other plans.

The first two days went smoothly. The weather was perfect

and the long days at the beach mellowed the tension that had grown between us that spring. Each afternoon we shopped. In the evening we ate at expensive restaurants where waiters exclaimed over our new outfits, and at night we went dancing at the Bower.

By Sunday night, many of the younger men and women had gone home, and the Bower's DJ was catering to a crowd of older white men by playing disco and Europop.

"Doesn't he know any real music?" Amanda complained. "Then again, this white-bread crowd would probably have a heart attack if he played anything with a funky beat! I wish we were in New York, the crowd is so fierce there."

My irritation returned. I couldn't stop scowling. At first Amanda didn't comment. Then Samuel walked by and asked what was wrong. Amanda pulled me close and whispered, "Fix your face. I don't know what your problem is, but I didn't just spend hundreds of dollars so you can act gloomy."

Biting my lips, I talked to myself firmly. Either get a grip or get a job, but don't make a scene. Going dancing with a beautiful lover isn't a bad price to pay for the sort of life you've always wanted. Don't ruin a wonderful weekend.

And at that moment it occurred to me that my relationship with Amanda was my job. I smoothed out my face and concentrated on thinking of myself as a glorified escort. It was my responsibility to see that she was having a good time. All along I should have been demanding a paycheck rather than depending on Amanda's moods and whims for presents and evenings out. This idea amused me greatly, and I began to have a wonderful night. Pretending to be an escort was like playing dress-up as a child. I wondered why I had never thought of it before.

During the DJ's break, the go-go dancers put on a fashion show. Amanda quickly grew bored with its campy humor, so we moved away from the stage to the back of the club. I sat on a bar stool, leaning against the wall. My arms encircled Amanda's shoulders; she kept one hand on my neck and the other underneath my skirt as we necked furiously. Without opening my eyes, I knew we were being watched by other women in the bar. Their envy delighted me; it meant I was succeeding at my job. I gripped Amanda with my knees. I was suddenly very excited. The night was turning out to be perfect.

The next day at the beach, I woke up to Amanda stroking the backs of my legs.

"Hey, Georgette," she whispered. "Are you awake?"

"Hmm?"

"Look at that woman in the orange walking toward the water. Isn't she sexy?"

I rolled over to face the sea, put on my sunglasses, and slowly glanced around until I focused on a topless black woman with baby dreads tied in a knot at the exact center of her head. She moved confidently like the sand near the water was soft and not the sharp stones I knew it to be. "She's okay, I guess. If you like that emaciated look." My sarcasm was pointless since we both knew that was exactly the look Amanda liked.

"Do you want to go for a walk?" As she spoke, Amanda zipped on her bikini top.

"No." I no longer cared whether my refusal would anger her.

"All right, lazy. I'll see you later. I'm going to the men's beach to find Samuel and the boys." She stood up and put on her shorts. The bare space between the bathing suit and the shorts was perfectly flat. Grabbing her sneakers, she was gone.

I wanted to call after her to bring me back an ice cream or hot dog, but I was not about to leave myself open to her remarks. Instead, I watched her walk down the beach. I loved her straight back and long stride. I had been surprised to find out she never won one of the Posture Prizes given at the Ellis School each year. Once when I complained of the silliness of these awards, Amanda told me that forty years ago when her mother and aunts were Ellis girls, there had also been mandatory classes in deportment and elocution. We were lucky to have gotten away with a few posture lessons each term.

Though Amanda and I had attended the same school, we didn't remember each other. She had been a senior when I was in Class One, the sixth grade, and the lower and upper schools at Ellis were strictly separate. There was no reason for her to notice the girl with the lowest status in the youngest class, and the only time I might have seen her was during assemblies. Twice per week, the entire school would form two lines to march through the corridors and down the stairs to the main hall, which was decorated with one hundred and fifty years of plaques and banners. Two by two, beginning with Class One and ending with Class Six, we would walk down the center aisle singing British hymns, splitting to fill the rows of straight-backed wooden chairs. Then everyone paused, waiting. Finally, Class Seven, the seniors, would arrive. They had the honor of entering the hall in a slow single file. All eyes would be upon them as we sang, "Jerusalem," and they strode to the front of the room. Some looked straight ahead, others deigned to smile at their sisters and favorites among the lower classes. All seemed to float on air. It was not until they arrived and were seated that the last chorus was sung, and the headmistress then gave the signal that the other classes could sit. I tried to remember seeing Amanda, but my memories of the seniors were all blurred together into one large ponytail with a kilt and a field hockey stick.

It was strange. I had spent six years waiting to be adored as I walked to the front of the assembly hall. But when I finally got there, I realized that being elevated to the rank of senior didn't change a thing. I still had the lowest status in the school, and as always, I was alone.

As soon as Amanda disappeared, I rolled down the top of my swimsuit. When the tall dreadlocked woman passed me to go to her towel, she smiled and shrugged with that ironic look that black sunbathers give each other. I didn't hesitate to wink and introduce myself.

The following weekend, Amanda and I drove to Manhattan to go to Foreward. Four hours was a long drive just to go to a boys bar, but the music was better there than at home, and the beautiful black men and women who frequented the place were stylish and hip in a way that made Boston seem provincial.

We arrived in the city around midnight and went directly to the apartment of Amanda's friends, Carlos and Samuel, to change into nightclub attire. An hour later, the four of us made our way downtown. Foreward was almost empty at two, but by five it was packed with dancing bodies. Hundreds of men glistened with sweat and glitter. Scattered among them were a few dykes and even fewer straight couples. At seven, I was worn out and ready to leave. But I knew from previous trips that Amanda and the boys had an endless reserve of energy. They planned to stay until noon when the club finally closed. I didn't want to complain. Amanda would blame my dwindling enthusiasm on laziness. "If you'd just come to the gym with me, or at least exercise more, you'd be able to make it through the night," she had said the last time we were here.

Actually, I wouldn't have minded the long hours so much if she had let me dance by myself, but always having to conform my rhythm to hers was a strain. Sometimes I wondered if our beats were so off because of the difference in our races, or maybe the difference in our heights. In any case, dancing with Amanda often left me exhausted.

Amanda and Samuel had gone to buy juices when two black queens interrupted the dancing. They were going at one another viciously. The men circled warily. First one then the other would get in her opponent's face, then retreat without backing down. The shirtless one wore those transparent mesh overalls that were so popular the previous season. The other was in magnificent drag, with elaborate makeup and an elegant white cocktail dress. I pressed back against the wall. I hated these scenes, even though they broke up the monotony of the night. When Amanda asked why, I told her that witnessing such arguments seemed like a violation of privacy.

When everyone's attention was riveted, the one in the overalls struck with, "You think you so fine. You think you so slick, but you so ugly you've made me sick." She spat out the words rhythmically, punctuating each phrase with a snap of her fingers. "And everyone knows you bought that mess on your head from Kmart," she added, in case anyone was mistaking the brassy but luxurious locks for real hair.

"At least I don't have to walk the streets to get a piece of ass," the other drag queen replied, addressing the watchers as much as her foe. Then, swinging hips first, she slowly, deliberately turned her back on the other.

"Don't you turn your niggerish back toward me, Miss Thang."

"Niggerish? Exactly who are you calling *niggerish*, Miss Polyester Tacky?" The cocktail dress whirled back around. The long press-on nails and rings rushed forward, poised to slap.

"Niggerish, niggerish, niggerish," I heard my Nina mutter as we stood on the downtown sidewalk, trying to hail a cab. She was referring to the two women standing in front of Filene's Basement screaming at each other. She seemed less upset by the profanities they hurled than by the fact they were fighting in public.

"Be quiet," my mother had hissed at her. Words like *nigger* weren't allowed in our house. Just before my mother pushed me into the taxi, I saw one woman pull at the other's shopping bag. There was a tearing sound and clothing fell everywhere.

By now the men were only inches apart. Their arms flailed wildly but somehow, mysteriously, never seemed to land. All the while, their mouths worked furiously, spewing nastiness. I turned to Carlos, who was standing beside me. "Shouldn't they be stopped before someone gets hurt?"

"Please, it's just two queens, Georgette. What's the worst that can happen? A broken nail? A hair out of place?" Carlos's mouth half-smiled at me, but his eyes never stopped scanning the crowd. "Did you notice that gorgeous beast of a man standing next to the Madonna-clone to your right? He's wearing ripped jeans and a shirt tied around his waist."

I slowly turned my head and saw the muscular black man. "Go for it," I said. "I'm going to find Amanda." I tried to keep out of the boys' way while they were cruising. I didn't want to cramp their style.

While I wandered through the crowd searching for Amanda, the DJ turned up the music to drown out the fight. No longer able to hear the slurs, both the spectators and the two queens lost interest. By the time I found Amanda, everyone was dancing again. She greeted me with a kiss, and we started to dance. It was much too loud for conversation.

All night Amanda pointed out the women she found attractive by nodding in a particular direction or leaning forward and shouting a time into my ear.

"At three o'clock," she said. "Isn't she fierce?" To my right there was a sophisticated black dyke in a well-tailored outfit. Amanda had long ago told me that her ideal type was taller and more athletic than I.

"What exactly is 'fierce' anyhow?" I shouted back at her.

"You don't know what fierce means? What kind of black girl are you?"

Jessie, Amanda's ex-lover, had taught her all the black slang. I felt the sick tightness which usually arose in my stomach just before I started to cry. I excused myself and went to the bathroom. I liked the rest rooms in this club more than most. The sale of liquor was prohibited at Foreward, and few bottles escaped the heavy frisking at the door. So the vileness that often characterized club rest rooms was almost completely absent. There was no vomit on the floor. No drunk men, unable to wait in line, urinated in the sink. The scent of perfumes and colognes replaced the usual reek of sweat and shit mixed with industrial-strength disinfectant. The drug dealing and sex were still there, but even they were kept at bay by the bathroom attendant. In an amazing feat of balance, the three-inch-heeled queen kicked in any stall door that remained shut for too long or under which more than two feet appeared.

On my way out, I paused in the ladies' lounge to examine my face. On a red velvet couch sat the two fighting queens, their anger and hysterics already forgotten. Slowly I began to glide a layer of lipstick over already bright lips. My face was fine but I fussed with my makeup in order to eavesdrop on their conversation about cruising.

Apparently as a queen, the trick was not in cruising but in allowing yourself to be cruised. The idea appealed to me: being seduced seemed an almost blameless activity. The one in drag claimed that upon finding the right man, she would give out her phone number or perhaps accompany him home. Miss Mesh-Overalls, however, explained that anonymous but safe sex in an alley was more her speed, as she already had more attentive boyfriends than she knew what to do with. Their advice in mind, I went out to try my luck.

I put on a vacant expression and stood in the corner nearest the rest room to wait. I hoped that one of the women whom Amanda found attractive would approach. Nothing happened. The sweet smell of Angel Dust began to nauseate me. I stared at the rotating silver ball on the ceiling; it refracted the colored lights so that magically strange shadows appeared on the dance floor. A few fags told me my ensemble was fabulous. One asked if the tall blonde in the Chanel outfit was my girlfriend. When I reluctantly admitted she was, he told me we made a beautiful couple. I tried to memorize his face and what little clothing he wore so I could point him out to Amanda. It would please her. We had spent more than an hour in Samuel's bathroom getting ready for the night.

As I waited, I admired the five black men vogueing on the stage at the far end of the dance floor. The dancers were so unified by the music and the desire to impress the crowd, it was hard to believe that vogueing was a competition. With perfect rhythm and control, they challenged each other by dancing increasingly difficult and complex steps. They slid along the stage, twisting around each other like contortionists, limbs intertwining but never touching. Each dancer battled to keep his own identity in the interaction. If one broke routine or touched another dancer, he automatically lost the vogue.

Fascinated by the dancing, I had almost forgotten about cruising when the women began to approach. They were mostly Lipstick. It always seemed funny that the butches were so much shyer. The first two were white so I stared right through them as they looped by me. The next few were black, but faced with success, I was suddenly too shy and embarrassed to continue. Time was running out. Amanda would come looking for me soon. Telling myself that I would never see the cruiser again, and if I did, so what, I smiled at the next black woman who looked interested. Working up the courage to let myself be cruised was hard. The flirting part, however, was a breeze. Within minutes, the woman was pressed next to me. I pushed my hips forward a bit so she could slip an arm around my waist. Our faces were very close. The woman was feeding me some line when I began to examine her. She wasn't that attractive. Amanda would be jealous but not impressed. Mere jealousy didn't seem worth a fight, so I gave my cruiser a small kiss on her neck. I was glad I'd freshened my lips in the bathroom. She'd have a mark to remember me by. I put on my best flaky cheerleader voice: "My girlfriend's probably looking for me. She has a terrible temper. Sorry."

When I returned to Amanda's side, she demanded to know what had taken so long in the bathroom. "I was getting worried," she claimed.

"Just trading makeup secrets with an old queen," I told her. She seemed to accept this explanation.

That afternoon, Amanda and I went back to Carlos and Samuel's apartment to rest before the long drive home. We lounged on the sleigh bed in their loft. She had her arms around me and I started to fall asleep, feeling her chest rise and fall as her laughter mingled with the voices of Samuel and Carlos. It was these moments that I loved, when we weren't fighting, just very close. Then I realized that Amanda preferred talking with the boys about the beauty of the men at Foreward to talking to me about any subject at all. She had a high-pitched eager voice when she talked with them. The voice was saying, *Like me. Accept me. I'll laugh at your jokes and respond the right way.* I knew that voice. It was the voice I had used all throughout school. When they invited us to stay for dinner, of course the answer was yes.

The first time Amanda brought me to the azure apartment of Samuel and Carlos, I was stunned by its beauty and grace. The stained glass windows and muted lighting were the epitome of chic. That spring, we had visited there often; meals didn't begin until ten or eleven and continued through several courses and many bottles of wine until club time, or the first after-hours party began. Carlos cooked while Samuel served to a table of six or seven guests from Boston and New York.

Usually Amanda and I were the only women there, but that evening we met Felice, an Afro-dyke who had known Samuel in Chicago. Perhaps it was Felice's presence or perhaps I was just more sensitive than usual, but internally I began to criticize the vintage-store finds and knickknacks that crowded every surface in the apartment. The trendiness of the art deco objects no longer appealed to me, and the little black Sambos and Aunt Jemimas grated more than usual. Amanda and I often complained to each other about the distastefulness and vulgarity of Carlos's collection. The blatant racism of Jim Crow memorabilia seemed strange in a man who was so refined in the rest of his decor. It was not exactly that we forgave the offense, but Amanda didn't want to alienate their friendship with a confrontation, and I was loath to make a scene. We ate there week after week and never said a word.

The night Felice joined the group, nothing appeared different. But the humiliation of sitting, eating, and trading clever sarcasm in a candle-lit room that was an insult to my very existence, finally struck. I wanted to scream or do something wild, something which would prove I was not the compliant, eager-to-please woman I seemed. But having been silent for so many months, I could no longer remember how to speak. I was merely a little more quiet than usual. I found myself unable to look at the apartment, the boys, or even Amanda. Instead I focused on Felice, whom I both blamed for my frustration and adored for her appearance. I was sure that when we got home, Amanda would talk about how attractive Felice was.

Actually, Felice's face didn't surprise me; it would have been odd to meet an ugly person through the boys. Still, I admired her flawless complexion. I wondered if she actually had perfect skin or if she was also a consumer of Maybelline's Ebony Line. And I was intrigued by her neon outfit, a costume which I might have worn before Amanda, when I was more outrageous than sophisticated. I was positive that my glances were discreet, but near dessert Felice pulled her Lulu bob behind her ears, stuck out her chin, and boldly smiled her bright red lips toward me. I was caught completely off guard. I smiled back. Then I realized the audacity of my behavior. I excused myself to go into the bathroom. As I stood up, I glanced at Amanda. Her face was serene, but her fist was clenched.

A hairless mannequin was posed just inside the bathroom door. Completely nude except for several maroon hand towels draped over an elongated arm, she stared at me as I sat on the toilet gasping. Mouth stretched into an eerie plastic grin, she warned me to watch my step, as if I didn't already know I was treading on dangerous ground, as if I couldn't feel the earth slipping out from underneath me.

As soon as I returned to the table, Amanda pulled me onto her lap, holding me firmly. I knew her gesture was as possessive as it was affectionate, but I was so delighted by the security of her arms. It was not until they tightened that I realized someone had asked me a question.

"Excuse me?" I apologized, hoping that I hadn't missed too much of the conversation.

"We were just talking about love and lust. How did you and Amanda first get together? Nathan here could use some hints on the subject," Samuel said.

Nathan ducked his head and pretended to blush, shyly pushing his long bangs out of his eyes. Everyone laughed. Nathan was just coming out. Barely twenty-one, last night had been his first at

Foreward. You could almost hear the men whispering, "Fresh meat," as they continually circled, each anxious to be Nathan's introduction to the New York nightlife.

"Well, I'm not sure why we first got together," I said, stalling. I wanted to describe a circumstance that would impress people as both sexy and profound. I shuffled through images until I found an appropriate story to tell. "I know. It was more than a year ago, on one of our first dates. Amanda took me out to this totally romantic dinner. Then we spent the night in the Rosewood Inn— that's one of those women's guesthouses out in the country. I remember the room. There was a huge fireplace and one of those big brass beds with a crazy quilt and feather mattress. It reminded me of the dollhouse I used to have—"

"You're getting this out of a Harlequin Romance, right?" Samuel asked, as he opened the evening's fifth bottle of white wine.

"This is for real. If you're not interested in my version, I'll stop and you can ask Amanda for hers."

"No, go on. I'm fascinated." Amanda's slow drawl and stroking hands told me she approved of my recitation, and so I continued.

"Anyhow, I still wasn't sure. I mean, I was dazzled by the whole scene. I felt like I was on the set of a movie or something. But I didn't know about Amanda. I sat down in this armchair with flowered upholstery and waited for her to make the first move. Amanda just talked and talked until the tension was so high I thought I was going to scream. Then all of a sudden, she goes, 'Hold still,' and she reaches forward and takes my silver studs out of my ears. I remember absolutely melting as she kissed me, then undressed me." I stopped at this point.

"Then what? You had great sex?" Carlos said.

"The best," I confirmed.

Of course we had, but that wasn't the point. Amanda and I had already fucked several times by then. I'd had good sex with and been undressed by other lovers. It was the earrings that had gotten me. The pure intimacy of the act had surprised me. Taking them out assumed a familiarity with my body. Nobody had ever breached my privacy that gently, at least not since childhood. I wondered if Amanda had realized her presumption. I was unsure if she knew how close it had made me feel to her and how much I'd later forgiven because of that one act.

"The Rosewood Inn. Didn't you and Jessie use to—" Samuel didn't finish. I imagined Carlos extending his long leg under the marble tabletop, through its cast-iron base, and kicking his lover. While the boys could discuss their affairs and exploits as much as they liked, it was clear that previous relationships were a taboo subject between Amanda and me.

She had had the best sex of her life with Jessie, Amanda informed me after we were together six months. They were still good friends, and whenever Jessie called or came by, I couldn't think. All of my energy was focused on keeping the resentment and jealousy out of my voice. In my battle to be civil, I was only able to mutter small talk and inanities. Amanda had also divulged that my apparent stupidity and limited conversational skills made Jessie wonder why Amanda was with me instead of her. Jessie's judgment and the idea that she wanted Amanda back made me angrier and more tongue-tied. But I couldn't really blame her. I often wondered why we were together myself.

Two days after our dinner with Felice and the boys, Amanda and Jessie had a fight in which Jessie called Amanda a racist. The string of black lovers, the African-American art, the black music and books were all bought by a woman whose own life and culture were so dead that she needed to steal ours. I would never have said such things, but Jessie was more aggressive or perhaps just had less to lose than I. Ordinarily, Amanda would not have told me about the argument since she doesn't like to appear weak. But she was just slamming down the phone as I entered the apartment. She didn't have time to recover her demeanor. Perhaps she told me because I had caught her exposed, or perhaps it was because, as her current black lover, I was in the position to refute Jessie's words.

And as Amanda spoke, I sucked the cold sweetness of vengeance. I listened quietly, patiently. When she stopped, she was trembling slightly. It was this vulnerable side which I loved. She looked at me with such openness, I almost wanted to kiss those soft lips and murmur words of consolation. Very few of my friends realized that under Amanda's glittering exterior was a softness, a yearning need that usually made me forgive all. But rather than speaking the words of exoneration that day, I deliberately spoke in the most caustic tone possible.

"She's right," I said. "You do objectify women. Black women, especially. Amanda, you act like those fags. Looks are everything to you. Women are to be looked at and fucked. I mean, I feel like I'm just another part of your art collection, the latest pretty black piece. You don't even like me. You just want me and think that you can own me because I fit certain labels. I keep on waiting for you to trade me in for a taller model. You shouldn't treat people as if they're only categories. Not only is it wrong, it's shallow, and it's ugly."

Those first few moments after I spoke, as I watched her crumble and start to cry, were exquisite. I had penetrated her shell, and the victory delighted me. My face was cold, my heart steely and hard. I saw Page and the other Ellis girls in front of me. I saw the countless white friends who over the years had hurt me unintentionally by asking me to soothe their guilt and satisfy their curiosity. For a moment, I was no longer stoic nor considerate nor even reasonable. I was strong, and the moment was beautiful.

But as I watched Amanda cry, the joy dissipated as quickly as it had come, and I was horrified at my words. For the truth has many sides and I had chosen to expose only one: the one that made me powerful and her weak. So after that glorious moment in which I hesitated and watched her, I pulled Amanda close to me, wrapped my arms around her, and began to sob as I begged her forgiveness.

Often, Amanda and I went out at night. We danced to pop, house, hip-hop, and reggae. The boys were on all sides of us but we danced very close, each trying to time our movements in sync with the other.

It was not long before I met Amanda that I had worked as a go-go dancer. Physically it was hard work, and I was glad when she started to take care of me instead. Still, there had been the delicious feeling of being suspended high above the crowd. I gyrated, bumped, and grinded to the exact same music then, but it was an entirely different experience. I either danced with the bars of the cage or with my image in the floor-to-ceiling mirrors that lined the opposite wall. Other times I would whirl around, arms extended above my head, faster and faster, making myself dizzy, dancing by myself.

Three nights a week, I arrived at the club in jeans and a T-shirt. In an hour-long ritual, I carefully dressed, usually in velvet or satin, and applied my makeup, body paint, and glitter. Finally I was transformed into a girl who was wanted by women. The euphoria of being desired, even if it was only for my costume, intoxicated me, so I didn't need the drinks the bartenders slipped me behind the manager's back with quick winks and smiles. Up in that box, I could see the women looking. They were shyer than the fags, so they pretended not to, but they looked. And here's the beautiful part: They could only look and adore; they couldn't touch me at all. Even after I descended, there was an aura about me that no one dared penetrate.

On my nights off I'd go to hard-core clubs, the nasty sort, where drunk underaged white boys and girls sneered at each other from black walls and tables. The music was abrasive, the leather-clad, skinhead crowd homophobic, but I didn't care. No one knew me there, and freed from my cage, I could dance in a violent frenzy. Arms slashing, boots kicking, the crowd of individuals on the floor smashed into each other over and over again as if such painful contact could save us from our numbed selves.

So I didn't quite know how to dance with Amanda. Most of the time our rhythms seemed off. Each night we tried to match our motions, but I always started dancing with my image in the mirror or throwing my body wildly as if I were trying to hurt her. Dancing with her was as foreign to me as the smooth, gliding waltzes of old black-and-white films. But occasionally we'd get it right. I'd imagine her taking me in her arms while we floated across the dance floor. If that would only happen, I knew we could be beautiful.

the benefits of travel

maybe I would have never tried impersonating a leather dyke if Amanda and I had been together that New Year's Eve. But I celebrated the holiday alone that year. Amanda was away on business, and most of my friends were visiting parents in other cities. I had always heard stories of people dying over the holidays, their loneliness pushing them to suicide or drunk driving. But I had recently quit working to have time for my art. The endless hours had made me more claustrophobic than creative, and I was delighted with the chance to hang out alone in Amanda's big apartment and go out dancing by myself. I went to Gaby's, one of the girl bars where I'd worked before dancing at G-Spot, before meeting Amanda. She hated the place. I hadn't been there for months.

At the upscale places I went with Amanda, the women were so concerned with their appearance they didn't seem to have fun. Gaby's was a friendlier neighborhood place. As I entered the club, I scanned the room through Amanda's eyes: from the dancers pounding the wooden floor, to the regulars on bar stools chatting and watching videos, to the women playing pinball, darts, and pool. I could hear her snort and define each as too butch, too crude, too fat, or too ugly. None of these women would suit her, but I was attracted to them all.

"Georgie, glad to see you out," Kerry, the manager said, while I hugged the bartenders and bouncer. "We thought you were married to that blond girl with the nose in the air."

"No, I've just been busy," I said.

"What's with you and her?" Kerry asked. "Rumor has it that she keeps you in line."

"Keeps me in style, you mean." I shrugged and winked, gratefully accepting the gin and tonic someone had poured. I felt at home among these women. With Amanda gone, I had found myself again. I would not admit that I missed her when she was not around.

By midnight, I was wasted and had fallen in love with a black woman named C.C. whom I'd spotted near the pinball machines. I was too shy to introduce myself, but Kerry knew that she had grown up in Brixton and worked in a leather bar somewhere in London. Even from across the bar, I could tell that C.C. was everything Amanda was not. She had a gorgeous leather jacket, but her clothes seemed to have been rescued from a dumpster. Her relaxed posture and easy careless laugh were the opposite of Amanda's tight, rigid gestures.

Like most drunken bar crushes, the love was from a distance and ceased when she left the club. I forgot about her in the pain of my hangover and the excitement of Amanda's return from Chicago. I didn't think of C.C. again until summer.

My search for C.C. began as a fight between Amanda and me. I had been sitting in front of the Boston Public Library, waiting for her to pick me up. A man came and sat on the bench beside me.

Although I tried to ignore him, he persisted in talking to me. When Amanda pulled up, he had his arm around my shoulder.

"Is that guy bothering you?" Amanda asked, getting out of the car.

"No, it's okay. Let's just go." I didn't want Amanda to get into a fight on my behalf.

"Look, get away from her or I'll call the police." Amanda pushed past me. Arms crossed, she glared at the man. "You have ten seconds."

"Rich bitch," he muttered, walking away.

Amanda got back in the car without saying a word. I kept my mouth shut hoping to avoid a confrontation. I knew the heat and her job stress were making her cranky. Since the promotion, she had been prone to vent her frustration on me.

At the first stoplight, she pounced. "I hate how you let people treat you like that. It's not just men; last week at the club, I went to the bathroom and I came back to find you in a dark corner with some skanky old dyke. Why don't you tell people to leave you alone?"

I was unable to stop myself from sneering. "You didn't complain when you came up to me at the G-Spot a couple of years ago. Should I have just told you to leave me alone?"

"I'm just sick of always having to protect you. I want a woman who can take care of herself. I swear, you're such a girl sometimes."

"I didn't ask for your protection."

"What if I hadn't been there? What if he had followed you?" She went on and on while I alternated between explanations and anger.

"Can we drop it, please?" I said several times, willing the traffic lights to turn green. I had gotten back from my annual family trip to Jamaica the week before, and Amanda was still livid that she hadn't been invited. I could tell my very presence in the car irritated her, rubbed the wound of being left behind. I prayed to reach the expressway before we overheated and exploded. The cool breeze of speeding down the highway would calm the emotions that threatened to smash the weekend into unsalvageable pieces. As soon as we got to the water, she would calm down. On the beach she would smooth sunscreen on my back, whispering apologies and loving words.

"No, we can't drop it. I feel like I don't have a lover. I have a child. I take care of you in every way. Monetarily, emotionally, physically. I need someone who will take care of *me* for a change."

"Like Toni," I snapped. Tired of resisting her determination to fight, I decided to go on the offense. "I know you're dying to sleep with her. I can see it every time you look at her."

"I'm getting really tired of the jealousy thing, Georgie. It is really not at all attractive," Amanda said.

"Just leave it alone. Neither of us seem capable of saying anything new."

Amanda didn't answer. Meanwhile, the car just sat in the Friday afternoon traffic that was immobilizing Boston's streets. The entire city was headed toward the ocean, trying to escape the relentless August heat and noise. In the silence after our argument, I sat as still as possible, my bare feet propped on the dashboard. The passenger window was stuck shut. The only fresh air came through Amanda's window and felt scorched long before reaching me.

We crawled through downtown, and at each red light the lines at the corners of Amanda's mouth pulled in tighter. I was relieved to see the train tracks of South Station, the final landmark before the expressway entrance. I thought that we had made it through the city, but then Amanda pursed her lips and pulled up in front of the station.

"Get out," Amanda said, double-parking outside South Station.

"What are you talking about?"

"Get out of my car! I don't want to spend the weekend with you. We need some space. Or at least I do." She leaned across me and opened the passenger door.

"You can't throw me out of your car. How am I supposed to get home?"

"Take the subway."

"I haven't got any money on me."

"Well, then walk. You could use the exercise. Look, I really don't care what you do. Just get the fuck out of my car. I'm going to the Cape by myself."

"So you can sleep with Toni?"

"Maybe. If I decide that's what I want."

"Well fine!" I shouted, grabbing my bag from the backseat.

"Fine," she said. I slammed the car door behind me and marched toward the entrance without looking back. A second later, she called out that I'd forgotten my shoes. I kept walking.

"Grow up!" I heard her shout. I lifted my arm above my head and pointed my middle finger straight up toward the sky.

Commuters in gray business suits and briefcases crowded every seat and bench. The men were loosening their ties and the women wore white tennis shoes with bobby socks. They all looked relieved that the weekend had arrived, and they all studiously ignored my bare feet and tears. I sat on my knapsack, leaning my back against the wall. I didn't want to think about Amanda or how she might spend the weekend in someone else's arms. I just wanted to rest and allow my breathing to calm. Then I would try to decide what to do.

I looked around the station. This was the first time I'd been there since its renovations. The grimy atmosphere that existed during my teenage years had been covered with a high-tech gloss and sheen. But the new yuppie appearance was a sham. Only the surfaces had changed. Less than ten minutes after I sat down, men began to approach. Their clothing ranged from immaculate flannels to polyester shirts to jeans, but the offers were all the same. Was there something wrong? Could they help? Did I want to come home with them? No. No. No, I answered over and over again.

"Please. I can help. I have money and a place for you to stay," one man with slick hair and a suede coat persisted. He tugged at my arm. The station was beginning to clear out as the afternoon commuter trains left for Providence and the suburbs. Two police officers stood flirting with the croissant-wagon waitress. I wondered if I should scream, but I didn't want to explain my bare feet and penniless state.

"Look, I've got a train to catch. I don't need a place to stay," I finally said. It was time to leave anyhow.

"All right. All right." He knew that I was lying. "I'll walk you to your train." He escorted me to the platform where I climbed on the first train I saw. While I was sitting down, peering out the window, waiting for him to leave, it occurred to me that I really ought to leave town. It would serve Amanda right if she came home to discover I had disappeared. Some friends had told me that with carefully timed trips to the toilet and dining car, one could get as far as New York or even D.C. before being thrown off the train for lack of a ticket. The conductors hated to fill out the paperwork so there was little chance of arrest. The biggest danger was being caught in some small town in Connecticut or New Jersey, and left there to rot.

On the other hand, I needed to be practical. I hated New York, and at this time of year D.C. was even hotter and more miserable than Boston. Besides, I wanted a bigger statement than the Northeast could make. I imagined calling Amanda from San Francisco or Europe to announce I had left her. Or maybe I wouldn't even bother to call. She could worry herself sick for all I cared. Eager to be on my way, I got off the train, completely forgetting about old greasy head who still waited on the platform.

"Hello," he grinned, "I thought I'd wait just in case. Let me help you. There's nothing to be afraid of. You're such a pretty girl. You don't have a place to go? Come with me. I'll set you up."

The man waited for my reply. For a moment I considered going with him. I would be found cut into pieces in a ditch. How sorry Amanda would be. She'd spend the rest of her life mourning or locked up in an asylum somewhere doing penance for her faithlessness. Unfortunately, she might also dance on my grave and live happily ever after with Toni. I was unwilling to take that chance.

"Fuck you," I tried.

"Anytime, baby, anytime." He burrowed into my neck. I turned and ran down the platform, through the station, and into the subway entrance. I put a slug into the turnstile and stood waiting for the red line train that would take me back downtown. Adrenaline pumped through my system. It was important to keep the momentum up, to get on a bus or a plane somewhere before I could stop to think about the implications of what I was doing. I considered my options. My best bet was to try to borrow the money from one of my friends or ex-lovers. I took the train straight to Cambridge, where I'd lived with my girlfriend, Elaine, before meeting Amanda and discovering the luxury of the Back Bay, fine wines, and trendy restaurants.

Walking through Central Square, I blamed Amanda for the gum, saliva, and trash littering the sidewalk and the hot pavement burning the soles of my feet. I missed that neighborhood. Central Square was more welcoming than the Back Bay. I realized that I needed to be around other blacks to remember my identity. In fact, I needed a black lover. At that moment, I decided to go to London and find C.C., the woman from New Year's

Eve. Never mind that she doesn't know me, I thought, never mind that she had her arms wrapped around another girl. She had said "Hi, honey," in a friendly tone when we passed in the rest room. She was probably still regretting that she hadn't introduced herself.

I found Elaine in her room meditating. Small gold and purple pillows covered the floor. An herb smoldered in her incense dish. On a low table, the altar sat, covered with beads, crystals, and scraps of paper. A new Indian tapestry was spread across the futon and Guatemalan hangings covered three walls. I barely recognized my picture, which still stood among the photographs on the bookshelf. I had painted us naked in bed, with my dreadlocks and her straight brown hair as intertwined as our limbs. The splashy style of the watercolors matched the bright, flowing clothes carelessly tangled around us. Now I had a short Afro and clothing as sharp as the geometric patterns on Amanda's comforter. I looked much older and thinner than the seventeen-year-old in that painting, and my art had changed to mixed-media collage.

Elaine looked up and smiled when I walked in. "Hi, sweetheart, where's your shoes?"

"Hi, do you have any money to lend?" I didn't have time for small talk. The travel agents were about to close.

"I thought you were too busy with Amanda to come visit boring me." She sounded bitter, though our relationship had collapsed more than two years before.

"She threw me out this afternoon and I really need to get away for a while. I don't have a cent."

"Oh, sweetie." Elaine stood and came toward me. "Are you okay? I told you Amanda's a B-I-T-C-H. You can stay here as long as you like." I let her hug me for a minute. I was tempted to allow myself to be comforted. But retreating to Elaine's holistic, whole-grain world would be more pathetic than dramatic. I wanted adventure, danger, and independence. I firmly pushed her away. I needed cash not consolation. Elaine hesitated.

"Please, Elaine." I let a tear fall. I felt desperate. The trip had begun as a vengeful act, but was rapidly becoming a necessity for my sanity. "I just can't take Amanda's temper right now. I have to get out of Boston."

Elaine cupped my chin in her hand and looked at me carefully. "Georgette," she spoke slowly, "does Amanda hurt you?" I didn't answer. There was no need to lie when Elaine had always been quick to draw her own conclusions.

I stared at the floor picturing Toni and Amanda together on the beach, eating dinner, kissing. I imagined Amanda repeating the same words to Toni that she had used to woo me. Tears rolled down my face.

"Georgette?" Elaine repeated. After a few seconds, I looked up and met her eye.

"No," my voice wavered. I began to sob. I whispered, "Please."

"Goddess help me." Elaine kicked the coffee table and crystals scattered across the room. She pulled out her embroidered money pouch. I told myself not to feel guilty. Elaine had put me through hell when we were lovers.

After a quick stop at home for shoes and a shower, I moved on to Keisha's house. She wasn't home but her grandmother was there, ready as always to talk about her no-good daughters and their boyfriends. At one time or another, all three of Mrs. Irving's daughters had left their children with her to raise. "I'm getting too old for this nonsense," she muttered when one of her grandsons and his friends burst into the house laughing and calling out for something to eat. The shirtless teenagers were all shades of glistening brown, and they argued loudly about who had won the last game. Noticing Mrs. Irving's glare, the boys dutifully shushed each other and Keisha's cousin gave his grandmother a kiss on her cheek. Then they tiptoed through the living room, toward the swinging door at the end of the hallway. But once in the kitchen, they sounded a lot like a herd of elephants practicing lay-up shots. Mrs. Irving rolled her eyes.

"Keisha's at work right now. Then I think she's got to go see some professor or school friend. Can I help you with something? You want anything to eat, Georgie?" she asked.

"I just need to get something that I left in her room," I told her. Mrs. Irving waved me toward the back of the house. Keisha's tiny room was meticulous. Visiting her always made me vaguely ashamed of my messy studio apartment. I went straight to Keisha's dresser and opened the bottom left drawer. As expected, her extra uniform was ironed and neatly folded along the crease. Between the shirt and the apron, I found Keisha's savings box. She had begun this "just in case" savings at age seven, the first time that she was dropped at her grandmother's house by a mother who would not return for several months. "Just in case what?" I had asked, seven years old and wide-eyed. My mother had pulled her own disappearing act that summer, but I couldn't imagine how a few dollars and subway tokens would help anything. Keisha just shrugged. By our teenage years, she had somehow managed to squirrel away over a hundred dollars. And now, there was nearly seven hundred.

I took two hundred and in return I left her a drawing of an airplane crashing on Amanda's head. *I promise that I'll pay you back ASAP,* I wrote in large letters under the drawing, then signed, *Love, George.* Like most of my friends, Keisha had been vocal about her dislike of Amanda, so I knew that she would understand this just-in-case emergency.

Two hours, three more friends, and five hundred dollars later, I was on my way to London.

* * *

London might have been a blast if I'd had some money, but on a budget of twelve dollars a day, it was a drag. The youth hostel near Victoria Station cost almost nine dollars, and the Underground rapidly ate my remaining cash. Food became a luxury; I barely had enough money for beer in the bars where I went each night to search for C.C. To make matters worse, I had to leave the clubs by midnight to make the hostel's one o'clock curfew. I worried that I kept just missing C.C.—she hadn't seemed like the type of woman who got to clubs early.

Light-headed from hunger, I suspected I might be going crazy. I longed to talk to Amanda, but each time I picked up the phone, I saw Toni's jeering face. I would call after C.C. and I had our passionate affair. Then Amanda would be jealous and truly repentant. Instead I sent breezy postcards of Buckingham Palace and Princess Di in which I described how much fun I was having.

The hostel had a daytime lockout, and I spent those hours wandering around London in an exhausted daze or sitting on a stoop, dreaming with grim pleasure about starvation and martyrdom. I was strangely satisfied with this wreck of a life. It was nice to have the world reduced to a few simple truths. Amanda was an ogre who used to beat me. Toni was her evil and seductive mistress. I was stranded in London and hungry. And C.C., once found, would be my savior.

I shared room 307 with five young women from Ireland, Australia, and Canada. I knew one hoped to spend the next few years traveling around the world, and two were having summer holidays in Europe before college. Another had said something about a work camp in France. But their stories went in one ear and out the other. I mixed them all up. Their freckles and ponytails looked the same, and I could never keep their names straight. Their carefully planned trips of guidebooks, monuments, and

Eurailpasses were alien to me, and my nightlife left them baffled. One evening they watched from their spotless bunks as I put on a black fringe dress.

"Where do you go?" someone asked.

"I brought a dressy outfit with me," another added. "Perhaps we could come with you one night this week."

I stopped and stared at the friendly faces. While I had envied their candy bars, Vegemite, and camping gear, it had never occurred to me that they might like me or even be jealous of my life. I thought about how pleasant it would be to make friends, join their excursions, eat their tinned goods, but I'd come to London to hit rock bottom, and I wasn't about to let anyone ruin my escape from reality.

"Well, I'm going to a leather bar," I drawled, hooking on my garter belt and rolling up my stockings. Four turned away, but one girl still seemed hopeful.

"A leather bar for lesbians," I elaborated, elongating each syllable. She cringed and picked up her book. After that night, they left me alone.

Despite my nonchalant answers, the leather scene was foreign to me. Amanda believed sex clubs to be dangerous and demeaning. So I was pretty nervous each time that I approached a stranger at a club and asked if she knew C.C. And everyone seemed to know her, but no one actually knew where to find her. One night when I was barhopping from club to club in my usual aimless way, a light-brown woman with dark curly ringlets and almond eyes approached me.

"I hear you're the girl looking for C.C.!?" she shouted over the blaring music. I nodded vigorously, not even bothering to try to be heard.

"Well, I might know where to find her. Who's asking?" The woman leaned forward so that her mouth was directly over my right ear. The skin on that side of my face buzzed and tingled.

"My name is Gigi," I said. It somehow seemed safer to introduce myself by my initials.

"So you're telling me that Gigi is searching for C.C.?" The woman threw back her head and laughed; her eyes and teeth glimmered under the flashing lights from the dance floor. I nodded again. Then we went into the women's room and screwed, ignoring the hoots, whistles, and knocks of the women waiting for the toilet. I thought about words like *safer sex* and *dental dams*, but they belonged to Amanda's cautious rational world. That night I became her official girlfriend. At twenty-three, Deb had already been married once, served two prison terms, posed in a dyke porn magazine, and seemed genuinely unencumbered with things like parents, self-doubt, or even goals. She clearly had some notoriety among a certain group of women, and she walked with a swagger that seemed to fill the room. Overall, I was proud to be seen with her, and a few days later, when she asked me to live with her, I said goodbye to my bunkmates at the hostel and moved to the other side of London. I worried that I was being unfaithful to C.C., but my funds were low and Deb promised that she would help me continue the search.

I never had any idea what Deb and her friends were saying. Their thick cockney accents were incomprehensible, and they seemed to find my American accent hilarious. So we mostly waved our hands wildly, drank, and laughed a lot. The large flat was a sort of halfway house for wayward women who generally stayed a few months, then went on their way. They either left behind extra blankets and mattresses or took with them other women's clothing. It didn't seem to matter. There was always enough to go around if you weren't picky. And the picky ones didn't last. Deb had been there the longest, almost a year.

Those months were a blur from the back of Deb's bike. Nights were drunk and danced away, and days were for sleeping and recovering. Maybe it was the alcohol or maybe malnutrition, but the entire time I felt as light and speedy as a racing car. My fears and insecurities fell away. We were invincible. The world belonged to us. The stealing, the drugs, the casual sex, all had an edge of violence and self-destruction that made emotions sharper and experiences more sweet. I'd finally peeled off the mask of passive pushed-around Georgette; inside the girl, I'd found a strong woman who could manipulate, lie, and cheat without a second thought.

I hadn't brought a camera, but my mind's eye took pictures of London: two women under a strobe light, leaning close together; the slick blackness of the wet nights when we hung on street corners; Deb's walnut fingers rolling endless cigarettes of tobacco and hash, and the flash of her rings as her hand moved toward me. I wanted to save these scenes to paint when I went home. *If* I went home, I reminded myself.

During those months, time passed in a strange jumbled sort of way. At night when I closed my eyes, my heart raced and I tried to organize the images swirling through my mind. My favorite memory was the ferry trip to Deb's cousin's friend's mum's farm— or something like that. We stood on the windy deck laughing into a gray sky while all the other passengers huddled over paper cups of hot tea and chocolate in the ship's cafeteria. By the end the ride, we were drenched with a fine mist and shivering. The drab sea was nothing like the blue Jamaican water that I was used to. And this summer was nothing like my summers at Nina's house. But even though I was cold and the sky was the color of a dull pebble, I still felt a wide-awake aliveness, even a sense of home, which I relished. When Deb and her friends started bellowing, "Jerusalem," I joined in mangling the hymn that I had learned all those years ago at Ellis. Deb wrapped her arms around me and buried her face in my neck. Over her shoulder, I looked out at the nothingness of the fog.

Back at Deb's place, we constantly renovated. The squatters would decide that we needed open spaces and cheerfully knock down some walls; a few weeks later, as everyone began to get on each other's nerves, privacy became the goal and partitions and screens were hurriedly built. The line to the flat had been cut long ago. We used the public telephone on the corner next to a local pub. The sidewalk around the bright red booth and the stone wall surrounding the parking lot became living room furniture. Each evening a group of us lounged there, making calls and plans for the night.

"She's gorgeous. Got bleached-blond hair and the prettiest eyes. Radical femme. I'll see her tonight." Matty told me about her newest girlfriend one night in October, as we waited for the phone. Actually, I caught about every other word. She could have just as easily said, "Got bitching hair and the sexiest thighs. Beautiful femme, she's all right." But I got the basic point. The girl was cute and she was Matty's.

"Hey, get off the phone!" she shouted, pounding on the window. A pub customer had been in there for over twenty minutes. He hung up and came out glaring. After she pushed into the booth, he sat down and bumped me with his shoulder. I pushed it off.

"What's a pretty girl doing with that bulldyke?" he asked, touching my thigh. "She your girlfriend? Why don't you come home with me?" He licked his lips as if seeing his tongue would make me jump up and accompany him home. Matty was immersed in her conversation. Rather than wait for her with that creep around, I decided to go home. I got up and walked away. He followed.

Ignore him. Stay calm. Don't let him know you're afraid, and hurry. I gave myself the list of orders which had safely gotten me through past situations. I began to walk faster. The flat was only a block more. He quickened his pace too. I ran. He ran. He caught up with me as I reached the house. I opened my mouth to scream, and Deb came out.

"Shit," she said. "You all right?" I nodded, gasping, pointing at the man who stood there grinning.

"Oy! Piss off, you." Deb went toward him faster than I had ever seen her move. He ran, and she chased him down the block. When she returned, she asked me again if I was okay and what had happened. As I told her, the man lingered on the street halfway between the flat and the pub. Without another word, Deb went upstairs and I followed. She picked up a piece of wood from the pile of tools and scraps on the kitchen floor.

"Hold this a minute, will you?" She handed me the heavy four-by-four and continued searching the room. Amy and Liz looked up from their card game with interest.

"What's up, Deb?" Amy asked.

"Keys," she murmured. Liz pointed to the hook near the refrigerator.

"Thanks." Deb took the keys, her bike helmet, and jacket. Grabbing the wood, she pounded down the stairs. The rest of us followed.

Outside, Deb was already on her motorcycle. She went straight for the man, who stood there gaping. By the time he turned to run, it was too late. She cornered him against the crumbling brick wall of the next alley. Without getting off her bike, she reached over and swung the wood down. For a few minutes we watched, fascinated, as the blood poured out of his skull. There was a delicious, exhilarated sensation in my body as if I'd just shoplifted or been let out for summer vacation.

"C'mon," Deb said. We helped her park the bike a few blocks

away. Matty showed up carrying a big bag of chips and Jamaican patties that she'd gotten from the dumpster behind the pub. In the garden near the hedges, Deb lit a fire to burn the four-by-four. Sitting on the sidewalk, watching the flames, we ate and described the fight to her. The still warm food tasted wonderful. I ate slowly, savoring the spicy patties. The grease of the chips was a perfect antidote to my hunger. I had a full stomach for the first time in days. I felt clear-headed but exhausted and drained. I was finally coming down from the high that I'd been running on since Amanda had left me in South Station months earlier. The smell of wood and leaves burning was sweet and somewhat sharp.

When the police arrived, the girls and I had just finished the food. The fire had burned down, leaving a few smoldering embers. I was exhausted yet somehow renewed.

"We've had reports of an assault in this neighborhood. Do you know anything about it?" one of the officers demanded.

Deb looked up from the garden where she was burying the remains of the fire. "No sir, I'm just doing a bit of gardening." I expected the policemen to mention that midnight was a strange time for weeding, but they just turned to the rest of us and repeated their question.

"Well, there was a man bothering Gigi here, earlier," Matty offered.

"Yeah, he chased me down the block, then he went that way." I pointed toward the pub.

"American, are you?" the officer asked.

"Sure am."

"Well then," he said, "I suppose we had better go find him."

Minutes after they drove away, Deb and her friends packed their bags and left. No one wanted to risk another prison sentence. I sat alone, deflated, on the remaining mattress, surrounded by pieces of plaster and forgotten belongings. Deb had offered to take me with them, but I was tired of being in a foreign country. When I closed my eyes, I could see the man's frightened face and the wood crashing down. I didn't care about finding C.C. I didn't even care about Toni anymore. I just wanted Amanda. I wanted to go home.

The next morning I called Amanda collect. I was grateful that she answered the phone and not some new lover. I didn't have the energy to get angry and spend another few months in Europe. She sounded relieved to hear my voice. She said that she had missed me and immediately sent the money for a ticket home. I had always known she would. I went to Victoria Station to catch the train to the airport. I hesitated in the huge waiting area, confused about which way to go.

"You look lost. May I help?" a man came over and asked repeatedly, while I looked for an information booth. He refused to take no for an answer. For a moment I shrunk into the twelve-year-old Georgie, vulnerable and scared. A childhood feeling of terror lay at the base of my throat, but almost as quickly the sensation transformed into anger and belligerence. I was anxious to be on the road. It had been a long trip.

"Fine—you want to help me? Give me some money," I snapped.

"Certainly, no problem. Come along with me."

"No way. I'm not going anywhere with you. You just give me the money."

"No, no, no. You don't understand. I can help you, no problem. There is no reason to be afraid."

We went back and forth like that for a while longer. The more we argued, the more determined I became that he should give me his money. He should pay. For years, men had looked me up and down in train stations and bus depots. They had called out obscenities as I walked down the street. They had tried to pick me up in bars and nightclubs, and exposed themselves in parks. Certain men had presumed on my privacy, preyed on my innocence, and betrayed my trust. It was time for me to be paid back for their eyes and their words, and I had chosen this man to be the banker. My fierceness began to frighten him and once he tried to turn away, I grabbed his arm.

"Look, you said you were going to help me. What happened? You promised, now give me the money." I was almost shouting.

Worn down by my determination, or perhaps scared of the scene that we were beginning to make, he pulled out his wallet and handed me twenty pounds. I thanked him politely. Leaving him behind, I went into one of the shops that surrounded the station. There I bought twenty pounds' worth of tacky souvenirs for Amanda. She wouldn't understand the gesture, but the pens, coasters, and coffee cups were tokens of my love. I could already picture her waiting to meet me at the gate.

may 2001

When I got home from visiting my father, I brought the little box into my study and sat on the floor staring at it for a long time. I didn't like that my memories were so fuzzy, nor did I want to be living such an isolated life, but I also wasn't sure that I wanted such a tangible reminder of past connections to other people. Finally, I pulled out the first letter. It was written in a careful script on pink stationery. I quickly scanned to the bottom of the page where I saw the name, *Sarita*.

Dear Georgie,

Mummy has given me this stationery for my birthday. Pink with kittens! What nonsense! I hope you will notice that I've drawn a moustache and sunglasses on each furry face.

We all miss you. Nelson Spence especially. He is such a baby. I am always tempted to knock him down. But Papa says that I must learn to be a young lady now that I am eleven. No more black marks. No more netball. He is always talking in his gloomy voice. He likes to wag his finger at me.

My sisters are such ninnies, they giggle at that. They sound like Alice Rowell who will giggle at anything!

I told Miss Celine what Papa said. She says that it is possible to be a young lady and a netball champion at the same time. I don't know. We'll see. Write back soon. Mummy says perhaps I can visit the States one day.

Your friend,
Sarita Cheddie

Under that letter, I found several yellowing pages filled with my name and Sarita's written side by side. Intermingled with the signatures, the pages held sketches of Jamaican scenes. On the last faded page, there were only two sentences written in large capitals and punctuated with multiple exclamation marks: *I WILL ALWAYS DRAW EVERYTHING AND WRITE DOWN EVERYTHING! I WILL NEVER FORGET!* I was startled to hear the creaky laughter that expelled from my throat—it seemed to come from nowhere, but my body shook with an amused frustration. "Didn't manage to keep that promise, did you, Georgette Collins?" I said under my breath, as I put the pink letter back and pulled out a white linen envelope. Inside the envelope, I found a piece of paper with the handwritten note—*Surprise! Love, Amanda*—and a typeset invitation on cardstock.

Amanda Grace Endicott requests the pleasure of your company at her home for a cocktail reception celebrating new work by Georgette Collins, Friday, October 26th, 1990, 8:00 pm.

Georgette's work is part of the Orion Gallery Emerging Artist Series (Thursday, October 25th thru Sunday, November 4th).

The invitation felt weighty in my hand, important. I put away the box and went to bed.

pink-papered

my family didn't like Amanda. Frankly, except for my father, they weren't about to like any woman I dated, but they especially didn't like Amanda. Alex called her pretentious, and Chris, loath to express dislike of anyone, called her "hard to know." Mother referred to Amanda by the moniker, "that woman." My stepfather was polite but distant.

So, I was shocked when I came home to find them all crowded in my studio with Amanda. First of all, Amanda almost never came to my place. I went to my studio to paint or when I was fighting with her, but she hated the space with its secondhand furniture and smell of turpentine. She certainly looked uncomfortable that day, leaning against a wall while Mother sat in the only chair and Eric was perched on the lumpy futon. Next to their business suits and personal organizers, my apartment appeared even junkier, and my paint-splattered jeans and T-shirt screamed "unemployed." Coming into the room, I fought the urge to turn and run. Although I wanted to shield my eyes and whisper, *Please leave me alone*, I said as casually as possible, "What's going on?"

"This woman," Mother said, barely nodding at Amanda, "called us. She says that she's worried about you. I thought things were better since the summer. What's she talking about?"

"What? Is this some weird sort of intervention thing?" I asked, regretting the piles of dirty laundry and hoping that they hadn't noticed that the refrigerator was empty besides a bottle of white wine, Saltines, and cheese.

To be honest, I could see how an outsider might have drawn the conclusion that I needed help right then, but the timing still seemed odd. For months last spring, I floated around dull and flat. Nothing felt real. The strain of interacting with others left me almost mute from exhaustion. I tried everything to escape my colorless, deadened state. From cheating on Amanda to other self-destructive habits to immersion in my paints and notebooks— nothing had worked until the impulsive trip to London. I returned calmer, happier, and more loving, and life had been almost back to normal. But all of a sudden, my parents and Amanda were ganging up on me?

"You're just so angry all the time, Georgette. I barely recognize you," Amanda said. "I was thinking that you might need to be in a hospital or somewhere."

"I'm so angry all the time?" I repeated incredulously.

"Well, you're always glowering or sullen. You never used to be," she replied. "You've become someone else entirely. Where's my sweet girl?"

"That's neither here nor there, now is it?" I knew my mother's hasty comment was meant to forestall any mention of the intimacy between Amanda and me.

"I'm worried about you, honey," Amanda said, coming over and putting her arms around me. Either Amanda didn't notice my mother's evil looks or didn't care.

"We're all worried about you," Eric finally spoke.

"Yes, I just want to know if I should be worried," Mother said, and glared at Amanda. "Sweetheart," she added as an afterthought, "just explain yourself. Are you okay or are you having those problems again?"

Perhaps she meant the periodic bouts of depression that plagued my adolescence, or perhaps she was referring to the time when she was "pushed to her limit," which is what she called my teenage runaway attempts. With no money, no friends, and a certain ambivalence about actually leaving, I never got far. The third time I was thirteen. A janitor found me curled up asleep under a black metal desk in an unlocked office on the M.I.T. campus. Startled by his rough shaking, I screamed and tried to back away. Somehow my legs became tangled underneath me, and my head smashed back into the wall. After going unconscious, I woke up in an ambulance taking me to the emergency room at Cambridge City Hospital. The nurses bombarded me with questions about who I was and why I had been asleep in the professor's office. I couldn't tell them how I had gotten to M.I.T. because I didn't quite remember, and I wouldn't answer their questions about who I was because I didn't want my parents called. At the time, I thought that if I just refused to give them any information, they would eventually give up and let me go. Instead, another nurse came in and rolled up my sleeve for an IV; she exclaimed over the scars on my arms from cigarette butts and sharp blades. Within the hour, I was put in the hospital's psychiatric emergency room, which is where they quarantined the crazy patients to avoid contamination of the regular ER.

The psych ER was even dingier and more depressing than the medical one. Everyone else was an adult. An older woman in expensive clothing sat in one of the rooms and rocked while muttering under her breath. A drunk, red-faced man was tied to a table with wheels. I felt embarrassed for the man since the table was parked in the middle of the lobby where anyone walking down the hall could see him. He didn't care; he spent hours shouting indecipherable curses at the bored-looking nurse sitting in a glassed-in booth and the grinning security guard stationed just outside the entrance.

After a few hours, a combination of boredom and fear prompted me to spill my guts to the nurse. I told her my name, address, birthday, and everything else that I imagined she might want to know, but she didn't seem interested. I asked if I could call my mom, and she said no. Still, I thought that Mother would come get me as soon as she found out where I was. Imagine my horror, later that same day, to find myself being transferred to Brookwood.

Two uniformed men abruptly entered the ER pushing a wheeled bed. "Is that her?" one of them asked the nurse as he pointed at me. I shrunk away as far into one corner as I could get. Later I learned to recognize the uniforms of EMS personnel and ambulance drivers, but at the time I thought they were some sort of cop. And Daddy had always taught us that black folks should never trust a cop.

"Get on the gurney," one of them said to me, indicating the bed.

"Why?" I remember my voice shaking. The nurse came out from behind the glass.

"Are we going to have trouble here?" she asked. I was still confused—no one had told me about the transfer. I wanted to ask what was happening, but I got on the bed.

When I got home a few weeks later, Alex pieced everything together for me. My brothers were sitting on the floor of my room watching me pack for our annual trip to Jamaica. At sixteen and seventeen, they were still young enough to side with me against our parents. A few years later, the gap between our ages seemed insurmountable. I was still a teenager when they were solidly into adulthood. That night, Alex told me how my parents had gotten a call from a doctor at Cambridge City Hospital. The doctor recommended that they consider sending me to Brookwood, a private hospital.

"Mom and Dad and Eric had a big fight about it," Alex told me. "Dad kept on telling Eric to mind his own business. I've got to hand it to you, Georgie. I never thought Dad would set foot in our house after Eric and Mom got married, but there he was in the living room, eating rice and peas and everything." I wanted to say that I didn't do it to get Daddy to come over. But then I thought, who knows, maybe I did.

"So they decided to just leave me there?" I asked instead.

"Well, at first Dad and Eric didn't want to, but Mom said maybe you would get scared enough to stop acting up. She said that you might as well stay until we left for the island," Alex explained. He twisted the fringe of the braided rag rug and stared at the floor.

Chris looked concerned. "Are you scared enough yet?" he asked. "Maybe they're the ones you should be scared of—Mom and Dad, I mean."

"I'm not scared," I lied.

But the truth is, I was scared at thirteen, and somewhere inside I was scared the day that my parents and Amanda came to my studio. I was terrified of the way my relationship with Amanda was careening out of control. We were both more aggressive than we used to be. Amanda's shoulders were always tense, like there was anger coiled underneath and she was ready to explode any minute. I knew my aggression sometimes looked like passivity to the outside observer, but I was secretly pleased when my non-action fueled our fights. Everything was turned inside out in my strange backwards world; instead of oxygen, unnatural stillness fed fire in this world, and the flames were flickering high, casting shadows dark and eerie and silent. That day in my apartment there was silence as Amanda, Eric, and Mother looked at me expectantly.

"I don't know what you all are talking about," I said with a polite but puzzled blankness.

Mother grimaced. She might have been frustrated, but she also might have been proud. Black women shouldn't show weakness, according to her. Better yet, black women should never admit *anything* is wrong.

"Can I get you all some tea?" I asked. No, no thank you, they murmured. Everyone was momentarily distracted by the type of pleasantries that are exchanged during an ordinary social call. I wondered if they were also unsure of what to do or say. Nobody teaches you how to act when your lover and parents unexpectedly drop by to recommend a hospital stay. As they stared at one another, I knelt by the exposed brick wall on the north side of my studio. My downward momentum caused the knuckles of one hand to graze against the rough brick. I was immediately gratified by the sting of bruised flesh. The sensation gave me courage. The people who notice my scars always want an explanation—as if I know why I do it. I have no explanations. I am helpless to say why the pain makes everything more bearable, I just know that it does.

"Georgette, honey, can't you see that I love you and want to help?" Amanda was saying. I didn't answer. I was thinking back to that first day in Brookwood. I had to take a bunch of tests administered by a social worker. They were the usual assortment that I had been given over the past year and a half by the lower-school counselor at Ellis. With a big frosted-lipstick smile, she kept assuring me that she wanted to help.

"Do I have to use crayons? I'm not five," I complained as I sat in a consulting room. With the tip of my pencil, I shoved the Crayolas back across the folding table. Who knew what kind of psycho-kindergarten cooties covered the box? The woman handed me a case of colored pencils and gave me a look that seemed to say, *You've procrastinated enough. Now draw!*

I tried to draw the perfect family. A big green shuttered house in the suburbs like our Brierly one before my parents divorced, and a mother and father and three happy children with bicycles. They were crowded around a red station wagon outside the garage. Mostly, it was a younger child's quick sketch, primary colors, stick figures, a bright sun with spiky rays, but I paid careful attention to the people's eyes, which I made wide, round, and innocent. This family's biggest worry was deciding between Stove Top Stuffing and potatoes for dinner each night.

"Where are their mouths?" the woman asked when I was done. I stared back at the paper. I had spent so much time on the eyes, I'd forgotten the rest of their faces. Quickly I drew five big toothy smiles. Actually, they looked kind of wolfish in contrast to the bright eyes, but it's hard to erase colored pencils, so the smiles were permanent.

"Where are their hands, Georgette?"

I was getting annoyed with this lady. If she was going to be so critical, why didn't she just draw the stupid pictures herself and I'd sit back and ask the questions?

"Hands are hard—the fingers especially," I explained patiently, as if I were speaking to a preschooler. "I just put them behind their backs or in fists. It's easier that way."

I couldn't even remember this woman's name, but I felt like slapping her. She was wrinkled and sour-looking, like a prune. Wrong color, more like a lemon. Although she was young, she wore what my brothers called *old-lady clothes*, a thick yellow pantsuit and a shiny blouse with a bow. I needed to be out of that room and away from her. "Can I go now?"

"No. We still have forty minutes." She pursed her lips and frowned until she was even more pinched up and sour. "If that isn't your family, will you draw me another picture of your family?"

I clutched the paper forcefully and drew my parents, my brothers, and me in front of a dilapidated hut. I put Alex and Chris in ragged, patched clothing and bare feet. Chris got another wolfish smile, but with several teeth missing. Alex leaned against a crutch like Tiny Tim in *A Christmas Carol*. The Dickensian image spurred me to draw snow falling, weather that made no sense in the Jamaican shantytown that made up the background. The snow was even odder since a giant suitcase sat at my mother's feet and bikinis and sundresses spilled onto the ground. In her hand, she carried the traveling briefcase she used on business trips. Daddy was smoking a cigar and sitting in a big leather armchair as he gazed out the window. A scantily dressed dancer from *Soul Train* sat on his lap. I stood a little removed from everyone else, sporting a Buckwheat Afro and tattered coveralls. I deliberately drew myself flat-chested, though in the last year I had acquired the biggest bust in my eighth-grade class. The whole family was as dark as sin.

Satisfied, I handed the social worker my drawing.

"You're angry at your parents?" she asked.

"No," I said irritably. I wanted to say, *I'm thirteen years old and talking to a lemon-faced lady in Brookwood's adolescent ward. Of course I'm angry at my parents.*

Actually, wedged somewhere between the anger and the fear, there was a part of me that liked being at Brookwood. I felt connected to some of the other kids that I met. I especially liked a gangly girl who always wore bright red lipstick to contrast the almost opaque white base on her face. She generally wore long, rather shapeless smocks that she made dressy by wrapping a faux fur stole around her neck or shoulders. I watched the girl often, but I didn't know her name until the first visiting day. Keisha and her grandmother were my only visitors during the time that I spent at Brookwood. Daddy didn't come until my release day, when he showed up to drive me home in my aunt's station wagon. Mother didn't come at all.

During Keisha's visit, the girl introduced herself. Her name was Harmony. "Get it?" She asked, cracking up as she stuck out her hand. Keisha looked at me for an explanation, but I was too embarrassed to admit that I didn't get it at all.

"Who, or what, was that?" Keisha asked when Harmony left the room. I didn't answer. Keisha was my best friend, and I really wanted to tell her that I thought I might be in love with Harmony, but I didn't know how Keisha would react. I was pretty sure that there was no such thing as a black lesbian. Only white girls could like girls. And I had no intention of saying anything to Keisha that would remind her of the time when she considered me an Oreo and not really black enough. I was relieved when Keisha's grandmother started grumbling about Harmony's clothing and had the whole world gone crazy or what? Only a white parent would let their child out of the house dressed like that girl, with makeup like Bozo the clown, Mrs. Irving pronounced.

"I'm a pyro," Harmony explained a few days later.

"Pyromaniac?"

"*Maniac* is right," she hooted. Then, more seriously, "I like the way lighting the fires makes me feel. Everything gets really intense. Then it burns blue and white and clean. I feel much better after a fire; it really is special."

I had never set a fire before, but I knew exactly what she was talking about. No one believed me about the razors. They only saw the blood and scars, but it was a cleansing act too. It was more than special; it was mine. I showed Harmony the scars that I kept so carefully hidden under long-sleeve shirts, hoping that she would understand. Her merry laughter and response that lots of kids at Brookwood had such scars made me love her even more. Somehow over the next seven years, I went from admiring laughing, cynical girls like Harmony to a relationship with Amanda. Amanda of the silk suits and Italian shoes. Amanda, whose middle name was literally *Grace*. Amanda, who collected black lovers like she collected art.

Amanda, who now stood with my mother and stepfather waiting for an answer to the question that people always seemed to be asking me: "What's wrong with you?"

"Everything is fine. I'm fine," I reassured them.

"She never even comes to my place in the city anymore. She's always hanging out here. Why would anyone hang out here?" Amanda swept her arm around as if condemning my entire existence outside of her. "She could be living in the Back Bay with me."

Mother ignored her, and Eric gave her a half-hearted smile.

"As long as you're okay, I have to get back to work," Mother said. "Darling," she added, shooting a triumphant look over her shoulder as she and Eric exited the apartment. I wasn't sure exactly what she had won. Proving her daughter wasn't crazy? Proving Amanda didn't know me? Or the war of the endearing nicknames?

"What the hell was that?" I demanded as soon as their footsteps had receded on the stairs.

"Georgette, look at you. You're a mess. When was the last time you actually painted or made a collage?"

"I'm working on one now."

"Okay. When was the last time you actually finished a painting or collage?" When I didn't answer, she continued. "I almost never see you. When you do come over, all you do is write in your notebooks or sit in my study reading. We don't even talk."

I wanted to say that we had never talked; instead I said, "Oh, fuck you, Amanda."

"You're a time bomb waiting to explode," she said. "I can see it even if your parents can't. Look at this place. You can barely take care of yourself. What would I find if I opened the fridge? Anything?"

"You're the one who likes me thin. And why should I take care of myself when you're willing to do such a good job, backramissus?" I didn't dare translate, and she didn't ask about *backra,* the Jamaican slang from the old word for *slave master,* the one who made your back raw.

"Watch out, because I won't take care of you much longer," she warned.

"Get out!" I said. I wanted to say, *Help.*

the whore of babylon

after Amanda and I broke up, I was angry at the world in general and my family in particular. Without Amanda, I had no money, no job, and no real social connections. I felt pretty sorry for myself, but I hadn't gotten much sympathy from friends or family about the breakup. Most of my friends disliked Amanda with an intensity that always surprised me. Yes, she was bossy and beautiful, but I liked her that way. Alex just rolled his eyes when I told him about the breakup, and Chris snorted and smothered a laugh before choking out, "How odd! Do you think it'll take this time?" Mother and Eric had finally had enough by the time I turned twenty-one. They said that I had made my own bed and now I had to lie in it. I was not welcome to live with them, and I didn't want to live with Daddy. So I raced back to Jamaica and mooned around Nina's house for a while.

During the weeks that I had been on the island, Nina had tried to talk to me several times, but I kept rejecting her. I didn't need to hear her words of wisdom. I spent as much time as possible in the kitchen with Sonia the cook—I was rather jealous of her since she seemed to have a simple, clear way of looking at the world. She spoke as if her life were unclouded by the ambiguity and confusion that plagued me.

Sometime in the 1980s, Sonia had become a saint in the Pocomanian church. Instead of tarrying with Mr. Sly and dabbling in the obeah, Sonia now practiced her moral perfection as loudly and dramatically as Nina would allow. She dressed in all white, wrapped her head in a turban, and disappeared for long hours with the brethren who came calling at the back gate in a minivan every Sunday at dawn. Though Nina was a fairly religious woman herself and had often complained that the cook was morally lax, Sonia's newfound piety seemed to bother her at least as much as her earlier wickedness.

Every Sunday, Nina would sound newly surprised that her coffee was being made by the serving girl rather than Sonia. "Where is she?" she would demand irritably, and then shake her head and sigh when the girl responded, "Miss Sonia gwane Pocomania."

According to Nina, the writhing, drumming, and speaking in tongues of Sonia's new church was superstition, sin, and self-indulgence all mixed together and masked in biblical rhetoric. I was actually curious about the sect and I'd asked Sonia on several occasions if I could join her. She had always refused.

One day, Sonia asked me to go fetch her aloe vera leaves. While I was in the garden, I heard a harrumph behind me. Shading my eyes with the palm of my hand, I looked up at Nina's stern face. I explained that I was collecting aloe vera for the cook.

"Waa fe? Oono mus leave ma tings be!"

"Nina, don't you know how ignorant you sound? Can't you

speak English?" I asked, trying not to sound too triumphant by this reversal of roles. Even as a child—being nagged by Nina to speak properly—I had noticed her accent was like her stories, always shifting, always chosen carefully to make a point.

"All right, Georgette," Nina said with exaggerated enunciation and a grimace, "I don't want either you or Sonia troubling the plants in my garden. Especially without asking. And why would she need aloe vera anyway? Is she making soap or something?"

"I really couldn't tell you," I replied, staring at her coolly. I pronounced each of my words with equal precision, imagining them enclosed in an ice cube. Then I turned and stalked back to the house. In the kitchen, Sonia crooked her bony finger at me and I came close to hand her the herbs. To my surprise, she grasped my arm and drew me even closer.

"Yah know fe wha mi wanna sinkle Bible?" Sonia's whisper was almost a hiss. I barely understood her words through the thick accent and the patois. Her thumb was pressing into a still-sore welt on the underside of my wrist. The grip was painful but I stopped trying to pull away.

"I have asked the pastor to cleanse this house of your filth. He gwine perform rites to rid the taint." Sonia looked at me triumphantly. I had no idea what was bothering her. "Do you know the whore of Babylon?" she asked, ignoring my wince. I shook my head. "She is the black woman who fornicate with white men . . . Or white women," she added darkly, as I stared. "Through she dat Jamaican trial and tribulation come. She nuh stay chaste nuh clean for black men, an dat harlot brung down the wrath of the Lord unto we, so Paradise become a living Hell."

At that point, I noticed the picture of myself in Amanda's arms on the kitchen table. She leaned against the redwood railing of her condo's deck while I leaned against her. My right hand was intertwined in her left. In the corner of the frame, you could see one of her Adirondack chairs in front of the sliding-glass door that led to the living room. Reddish-brown earthen planters surrounded us, but we were dressed in our trendiest clubbing gear. Amanda and I both looked very seriously at the camera. One of Amanda's friends had asked us to pose for his portfolio; he shot the picture to highlight the contrast between Amanda's pale thin blondness and my brown curves. I'd always liked the picture and kept it dear, because the photo somehow managed to capture both the tension and affection in our relationship. It was impossible to see the picture and not surmise that Amanda and I were lovers. I finally understood why Sonia had been so cold lately—nothing like the cook of my childhood kitchen days.

"Wa mek yuh bringing this rot inna yuh grandmummy's yard? Didna she rear yuh proper?"

"So you are basically calling me a whore and claiming that Nina brought me up badly because of this picture?" I made my voice heavy with sarcasm, though somehow I could not quite bring myself to use the word *lesbian* in Nina's house.

"Only yuh know what in yuh heart. But with the whore of Babylon, it is not enough that she will burn in torment, she take the rest of us down with she." As Sonia spoke, I looked down at my scarred arms. I thought about my last fight with Amanda. Maybe Sonia was right. Maybe she held some knowledge that I was missing and she could show me how to be happy.

"Is there anything that she can do to save herself, to become a better person?"

"Me gwane tell yuh because yuh dear to me. Me pray on it lang, hard, an deep. A lang time mi care fe Georgie, dat poor innocent pickney inna mi kitchen. Den yuh gwane all the way to America to become tainted with the sin of the backra-missus. Now yuh mus repent and lef yuh wicked ways. Oono mus accept the

Lord inna they heart. And yuh mus find a black man to marry and bear him baby."

While Sonia spoke, I imagined what it would be like to belong to a church, to marry, to be sanctified in the eyes of a community. Though they would not say it directly, there was little doubt that my family would rather see me with virtually *any* black man than with Amanda. All the pink triangles and rainbow flags in the world would not change that truth. And despite my bravado of marching in pride parades, I was not so sure that they were wrong. I studied Sonia's face, hoping to see some glimmer of empathy or affection; instead, I saw unyielding blankness. I finally left the kitchen, afraid that I was no longer welcome there. On my way out, I tried to snatch up my photograph, but the tall, lanky cook held it out of my reach.

The next day when I got up for breakfast, Sonia was gone. Nina had fired her despite the cook's decades-long service. Nina would not tell me why, but the servants' gossip claimed Sonia had been driven out for calling me corrupt. The gardener said that Sonia had marched out of the villa brandishing her Bible like a shield. I remembered being nine in my grandmother's yard. I was stamping my feet in frustration while Chris and Alex teased me by singing over and over again, "*Georgie Porgie, Pudding and Pie, kissed Sarita and made her cry. When the boys came out to play, Georgie Porgie ran away!*"

"Georgie's got a boy's name," they crowed, dancing away when I tried to shove them. Suddenly Sonia was standing there, arms crossed, unsmiling.

"Quiet yourselves!" Sonia scolded us. But a few minutes later, I saw her huddled with Nina in the kitchen. And for all the rest of that day, the two bickering women banded together to call my brothers *Christina* and *Alexandra*. And the boys were steaming angry because the servants laughed every time. That day was one of the few times I could remember Nina and Sonia agreeing on any subject.

For years, the two of them had wrangled over cooking, cleaning, and the town gossip. Nina had always complained that Sonia was hard-headed because the cook insisted on having the final say. Apparently this final argument was no different, because I found the photo of Amanda and me torn in half on the kitchen table. The grocery tablet lay open next to the ripped photo. On a yellow lined sheet, Sonia had drawn an indecipherable picture and written in her neat block print, *Let the words of my mouth, and the meditation of my heart, be acceptable in His sight. The Lord is my redeemer. He knows me pure.*

I could not figure out what the drawing was meant to portray until one of the servants showed me the little figure dancing in the flames.

malcolm

may 2001

the next evening after work, I tried reading the small note-book from the box of letters. The journal recorded a teenager's fury and misery. Over and over again, an ado-lescent Georgie had written about wanting to die. I had con-demned my parents' divorce, my father's growing dependence on me, and my mother's growing coldness. With meticulous detail, I had listed purchases of razor blades, cigarettes, and knives, rating each for the amount of damage it was able to cause to my body.

I found a plain white envelope stuffed between two middle pages of the notebook. I did not recognize the name on the return address, *Melody McCabe.* Opening the envelope, I discovered thin paper covered with almost illegible, spider-like handwriting.

Hi Georgie,

I'm writing this letter with my mother's fountain pen. I stole it from her purse yesterday. She's been tearing the house upside down looking for her "favorite fucking pen!" This is the woman who is always telling me to watch my mouth. So

I just smile and look innocent while she's running around like a fucking lunatic.

I'm just writing to tell you that I don't know when I'll see you again. I know we promised to hang out when we both got out of Brookwood, but the parents are sending me to some special school in Nevada or Montana or one of those states with horses and no people. Don't worry about me though. I'll run away as soon as I can. I'm thinking about San Francisco. Have you heard of the Haight? You can come out and visit me there, don't you think?

So, I realized that I never told you about my name. I know you were only pretending to get it. Harmony = Harm On Me. Cause that's what I do, you know, with the fires. I may not burn and cut myself like you do, but I'm harming myself all the same.

Anyway, I was thinking about it the other day and you know what? Maybe that's crap. Maybe I need to stop doing stuff that harms me and start doing healing stuff. Not that I buy all that recovery crap that they sell at Brookwood for $1,000 per day. But the way I see it, I can fuck myself over or I can fuck someone else over or I can forget all the fucking and just have fun. I've tried #1 and I've tried #2. Maybe it is about time to go with #3. (Not that I would throw David Bowie or someone out of my bed or anything! Ha ha!) But no fucking—just making love, if you know what I mean?

Anyway, I'll write more later from some stable or something.

xxox
Melody (previously known as Harmony)

After a while, I stopped reading through the box. *Is this the true me?* I wondered. I recognized a few bits and pieces of my life, but other parts read more like fiction, shaped and deliberately told by a storyteller or a liar. It was not just that I had forgotten certain events, but some directly contradicted my sparse memories. *Do I truly not know or am I just refusing the person I once was? Are these artifacts of my life or are they completely imaginary?*

I thought that perhaps the wisest course would be to throw out the box before it revealed some detail better left forgotten, but I couldn't quite bring myself to destroy what might be tangible proof of my past existence. I settled for sliding the box behind one of my bookshelves.

"Out of sight, out of mind," I muttered, as I got ready for bed. But lying in the darkness that night, I gently ran my fingertips over the ridges and pocks on the arms that had been hidden all summer by long sleeves. In my mind, I could suddenly see the keloid pattern, and I wondered how I managed to not see it before.

The next morning, I surprised myself by shoving my hand between the wall and bookcase to retrieve the box of memories. Ignoring the splinter in my thumb, I buried the case in my bag and hurried out the door. During my lunch break, I sat in the park, the open box perched on my knees.

On top, I found a scrap of yellow paper containing some psalms or Bible verses. Underneath some loose sheets of paper were multiple sealed envelopes held together by a rubber band. Each had my own name in the return address and each was directed to a *Kate Drew*. Someone had circled the name in red pen on each and written, *Return to Sender, Addressee Whereabouts Unknown.* I stuffed the banded envelopes back in the box and rummaged around for more letters.

On my next try, I retrieved a postcard of two women kissing, the caption proclaiming, *I Prefer Girls!* On the back, I read a hastily scribbled note.

Hey Girly-girl,

I'm not positive of your postal address so I am writing care of that diesel bar where you worked. I just wanted to say that I'm sorry that you went back to America. We had some good times.

Also, it is too bad about the cops. But I always said "a crowbar is a dyke's best friend." One good whack and people take you seriously!

Deb

Fascinated yet afraid I clutched the postcard. I sat motionless but churning inside until Lydia's voice penetrated my paralysis. I hastily stuffed the card back into the box and snapped the lid closed.

"Whatcha doing, Georgie?" Lydia asked, leaning against one of the stone griffins flanking the stone steps. She dropped her backpack near my feet.

"I'm trying to figure out who I really am," I said.

"Georgette Collins, duh!" Lydia rolled her eyes. I couldn't tell if her incredulous expression was directed at me in particular or the stupidity of all adults.

"I'm trying to find a person who has disappeared," I tried to explain. I noticed that for the first time Lydia was not asking for help. With her features calm instead of angry and tearful, the curiosity seemed friendly rather than demanding.

"What happened to her?" Lydia asked.

"I'm not sure."

"Oh," said the girl. And then, pointing at my hand, "Doesn't that hurt?"

I looked down. I had been absentmindedly rubbing my right thumb with my index finger. The skin around the splinter was purple and a few drops of blood welled at the corner of the wound.

"No, it doesn't hurt at all."

"You're one crazy lady, George." Now Lydia sounded more like her usual frustrated self. "You're almost as crazy as Fran!"

"Aunt Fran? She's not crazy."

"Are you tripping out or something?" Lydia put her hands on her hips. "She's a nosy bitch. Every day she asks me questions. She don't know nothing about nothing."

"Maybe she cares about you."

"Maybe she should shut her face!" Lydia grabbed her backpack and leapt to her feet as if she were about to take off. Then she hesitated and turned toward me once more.

"I know she'd really like to see you," Lydia said.

"Fran?"

"Yeah, Fran and everyone else. Should I tell them that you're coming? You could come for a Sunday dinner with your father or something." Once again, Lydia stood with hand on jutted-out hip and looked at me inquisitively. I felt panicked at the thought of being surrounded by my father along with aunts, uncles, and cousins whom I hadn't seen in years and would barely recognize. I shook my head mutely. Lydia rolled her eyes again and turned away. The teenager's visits always caused me such intense feelings, an uncomfortable mix of guilt and frustration. As I got ready to return to the library, I decided to visit with my family some Sunday afternoon. *Soon*, I promised myself firmly. *I'll be ready soon.*

double dutch

When Keisha called, I had just finished my nightly ritual of checking off the completed items in my to-do notebook. Study for urban history test: done. Call Malcolm about plans for Saturday night: done. Finish graduate school financial aid form: done. Fold laundry: done. Take daily multi-vitamin: done. Brush teeth: done. I crisply snapped my notebook shut and slid it into the nightstand drawer. As I slid between the bleached-bright sheets, dressed in clean flannel pajamas, I breathed a tired but satisfied sigh and waited for sleep. My life was on track. Perfect, really. The phone rang.

"Hey, George, it's me," Keisha said after I picked up.

"Keisha, what's up?" I tried to sound cheerful, though I wasn't in the mood for a late-night phone call.

At first I couldn't understand Keisha's answer; the words seemed mumbled and indistinct. But after a few moments, I recognized the word *pregnant* and could guess the words I missed.

I asked if Keisha was sure. She replied, "I'm not positive."

When I asked about the father, Keisha burst into tears. I held the receiver with my shoulder and flipped through the appointment book lying on my desk. On the next day's page, I wrote, *Call Keisha in the p.m. PREGNANT*. I underlined the last word three times. After a few minutes of listening to the sobs, I interrupted her.

"Keisha, this call must be costing you a fortune, and I'm really exhausted right now. I can hardly keep my eyes open. Why don't I call you back tomorrow? What time do you get home from work?"

After rushing off the phone, I was unable to sleep. I couldn't stop thinking about Keisha.

We met the summer before I turned eight. My parents had already started to go their separate ways. Daddy was going to West Germany on a business trip, and Mother said that just because he was escaping his home responsibilities, she certainly couldn't be expected to become a single parent for the summer. After weeks of arguing, she finally announced that she would go to Mexico to study Spanish. I could spend the summer in Mattapan with Aunt Fran. Chris and Alex would go to Jamaica to stay with Nina.

The day before I was due to leave, I went to the town library and checked out ten books, the borrowing limit. I chose fantasies about magical adventures and kingdoms: *The Chronicles of Narnia*, several Oz books, and E. Nesbit's *The Enchanted Castle, The Amulet,* and *The Phoenix and the Carpet.* The books, my watercolor set, and the smooth drawing paper, which I loved so well, filled most of the little suitcase sitting on my lavender dressing table. In the remaining space went seven pairs of white briefs and socks, six pairs of shorts, six T-shirts, and a dress. My mother had already promised that Fran would do laundry at least once a week.

Later that night I woke up, my stomach in knots. In a house with four children and another one on the way, Aunt Fran might not have time to get to her laundry. I got up quietly and slid more underwear and an extra T-shirt in the suitcase, then jumped back in bed.

All day long I sat on the stoop outside Aunt Fran's house, reading a book and pretending not to care about jump rope. *Slap*-pause, *slap*-pause, the rope rhythmically hit the sidewalk and the hot sun beat down, and how my head hurt. I had only been at Aunt Fran's a few days, but I already wanted to go home to the suburb of Brierly where I belonged. I longed to be in my own air-conditioned house or in the hammock under the weeping willows in my back-yard. A painting of my house hung on the door of the room that I shared with my cousins, Charla and Peggy.

"I wish I lived in a big house in the country," Charla had said when I first mounted the picture. Embarrassed, I didn't answer. I had painted our rather ordinary colonial as a mansion, and the painted garden was exaggerated into an overly lush and exotic par-adise. Nevertheless, compared to Aunt Fran's cramped decaying brownstone and hot, noisy neighborhood, the Brierly house was roomy and rural.

"Wanta join, Georgie?" I knew that Aunt Fran had told the cousins to ask each morning. But I wanted them to leave me alone. My awkward feet would slow the fast double dutch. The chanting words were too quick and foreign for me. Skipping rope in Brierly was nothing like this Mattapan two-rope craziness. I'd trip and land on my face. The girls sang:

> *Down, down baby*
> *down by the roller coaster*
> *shake it up baby*
> *never gonna let you go*
> *shimmy shimmy cocobop*

shimmy shimmy-wow
shimmy shimmy cocopop
shimmy shimmy-pow
I like coffee & I like tea
I like the colored boy & he likes me
I don't like the white boy
who lives down the street
if he dare come up my way
he'll get his ass beat

A shrill whistle pierced the air. Cousins dropped the ropes and friends stopped jumping. Sneakers pounding the pavement, they chased the ice cream truck ringing down the street. Up and down the block, games of twenty-one, hopscotch, and stickball ended. Children came out of hiding places, over fences, and through parking lots. The truck stopped at the far corner and was immediately surrounded by small sweating bodies, all shades of brown. "I scream, you scream, we all scream for ice cream," they giggled and shoved.

I was left on the stoop with the two little boys whose mother couldn't afford milk, let alone ice cream. Earlier that morning Aunt Fran had offered me fifty cents for ice cream and candy. I had firmly replied, "Mama says I'm not to eat sweets between meals."

As I spoke, my cousins rolled their eyes. Peggy, the eldest, said, "Ma, give me her fifty cent. I'll hold onto it in case she changes her mind."

"Peggy, you ought to be ashamed of your lying self," Aunt Fran laughed, and then said, "All right, honey, maybe tomorrow you'll want something."

I just wanted to sit on the stoop reading my book, counting the days until my parents' return.

"You want some of mine?" someone asked with an odd, slurred accent.

I looked up to see a girl about my age holding an ice cream sandwich.

"I don't take food from strangers, but thank you anyway." I didn't want to appear snobbish. I began to read again, assuming the girl would start playing with the others.

"You sure? 'Sgood." The girl sat down beside me and unwrapped the bar. I nodded, trying to remember exactly why I was not to eat sweets between meals. And could a little girl really find a way to poison an ice cream sandwich? Before I could come to a conclusion, the girl opened her mouth wide.

"Ma says, *Waste not, want not*," she grinned, and the ice cream disappeared in two bites. The girl licked her fingers and crumpled the wrapping into a ball, which she began to toss up and down. "Want to play something, Georgie? I'm not from around here neither, and these tired-ass children bore me nearly to death. Let's us go to Washington Park."

I stopped searching my pockets for a napkin or tissue to give her. Now I stared. "How do you know who I am?"

"Girl, the whole neighborhood knows who you are, Georgette Nose-Always-in-a-Book Collins." The girl had a smirk, which she immediately softened to a smile. "I just asked 'cause you looked by your lonesome, and I am too. I'm Keisha. I'm from D.C. I stay down the street with my grandmother, but just for a while. My mother just had a new baby."

It was almost dark when Keisha and I got back. Aunt Fran looked about to scold me for a minute, but then she only made us promise to tell an adult or Peggy before leaving the block. As I headed for the kitchen and the dinner I had missed, I could hear Peggy's outraged voice.

"Ma, Georgie disappeared for hours! Aren't you going to yell at her?"

"No, I'm just happy that she made a friend."

"But Keisha Irving! She's crazy. She's always boasting about how great things are in D.C. and how she's going back any day now, as soon as her mother sends for her."

"So what?" Aunt Fran asked.

"So she's a bad influence. I heard you say to Mrs. Johnson that you've known Keisha's mother since you were a girl, and that woman couldn't get it together if her life depended on it."

"Be quiet, Peggy. And stop sticking your nose where it doesn't belong."

By the end of the summer, I almost didn't want to go home. I couldn't remember exactly when I had stopped missing my hammock and backyard. Somewhere in between collecting bottlecaps, teasing Peggy, and playing at the hundreds of other games Keisha knew, Brierly and the air-conditioned house had faded. When my father came to pick me up, I made him promise I could come visit Keisha one weekend soon. Keisha shrugged and said that she'd be back in D.C. by then.

The day after Keisha's call, I couldn't concentrate on my classes. I kept thinking about Keisha's pregnancy. Why did she call me? I hadn't seen her for nearly three years. Then I realized that she needed my help. That evening I called her back.

"Hey Keisha," I said. "I've got a long weekend coming up. Why don't I come to D.C.? Maybe I can help out. Besides, I've been wanting to visit you since you left Boston."

"Help out?" Keisha sounded surprised. "I don't think there's much you can do unless you want to move here for the next nine months."

Over the next week, I devised a plan to get her life back on track. Though I knew Keisha was against abortion, I would convince her that terminating the pregnancy was the best solution. If Keisha was adamant, I would advise putting the child up for adoption. I would say that she would be behaving irresponsibly if she tried to raise it herself. Once the problem of this pregnancy was taken care of, Keisha could finally return to M.I.T. to fulfill the potential that I knew she had.

I planned to use Keisha's own mother as an example of the wrong solution to an unplanned pregnancy. Belinda Irving had seven children. Because the eldest was born when she was seventeen, she never had the chance to complete her education or give her children any material advantages. She had been a burden to her friends, relatives, and the state. Keisha would have to admit her childhood would have been much more stable if her mother had had fewer children or the children had known their fathers. Keisha spent half her childhood being shuttled back and forth between her mother's and grandmother's. Her mother kept promising that Keisha could come home, and then breaking that promise. Keisha said she didn't care, but I was sure the instability must have bothered her.

On the first day of third grade, I was amazed to discover Keisha sitting among the EMERGE kids in my homeroom at the Brierly Primary School. EMERGE was a voluntary program that the people of Brierly had set up with the city of Boston. Sixty black students from Mattapan and Roxbury were bused to integrate the almost all-white schools in Brierly. It was generally felt that the Boston children could benefit from a suburban education.

"What are you doing here, Keisha?" I was delighted.

"Going to school, same as you. We came on a bus." She grinned. "Surprised, Georgie?"

"Everyone calls me *Georgette* here," I automatically corrected. "I thought you were going back to D.C. when school started."

Apparently Keisha's mother was still having problems, but any day now, Keisha said, she would send for her daughter.

Meanwhile, Keisha and I chose adjoining desks. We whispered secrets, passed notes, and saved places in line. During recess we picked the same teams and sat on the playground singing popular songs. By Christmas, we were best friends. *Any day now* stretched into next month and then into next summer and then into next year. By fourth grade, I assumed that Keisha was never really going home.

The first day of school, the entire fourth grade was given a long exam. Afterwards everyone was assigned to new rooms for math, English, and science. At first it wasn't too bad. Keisha and I shared math class for the first few weeks of the year—that is, until my mother discovered her daughter had been placed in the Robins math group.

I can still remember sitting on the hardwood bench outside Mrs. Fratus's office, a seat usually occupied by children sent to the principal by frustrated teachers and lunch monitors. I couldn't stop worrying that the kids walking through the hall would see me. They might think I was in trouble, or worse yet, they might hear my mother's insistent voice through the half-open door.

"I would like her to be put in the Bluebirds. I'm sure she can handle the pace. Her father and I will help her."

"Mrs. Collins, I'm afraid our testing has shown that Georgette's ability is more suited for the Robins. I assure you that she'll progress quite satisfactorily with them." I cringed as the principal's words boomed out. Everyone in the whole school knew that being a Bluebird meant that you were a Brain, and Robin stood for Retard. The conversation went on and on. The language remained polite, but their voices grew angry and loud.

"My taxes pay your salary, and she will not be left with the Robins. Am I making myself clear, Mrs. Fratus? Georgette Collins, come in here right now." I entered the room quickly, hoping prompt obedience would appease them.

"Mrs. Fratus says that you don't work hard enough in math. There will be no TV or library privileges until you start taking your schoolwork more seriously. Do you understand?"

"Yes, Mother." I watched Mrs. Fat-Ass angrily purse her lips and prayed no one I knew was listening outside the door.

"All right, then. Thank you so much for your time, Mrs. Fratus. I expect Georgette will be moved on Monday."

My mother pushed me out of the office and down the hall, muttering, "I don't work my fingers to the bone and live in this stuck-up white town so that my child can be some goddamned Robin. We'll hire a math tutor if need be. Are you listening to me, Georgette?"

"Yes, Mama." I was already tuning out the lecture that I knew was coming.

A few weeks later, I glanced around the cafeteria, searching for someplace to sit. The lunchroom was a daily challenge. The dirty pastel walls and fried-food, stale-milk smell made the atmosphere oppressive. Some children sat by themselves; others wandered around the room, flitting from table to table like miniature social butterflies. At last I spotted Keisha in the corner where the bused kids always sat. As I approached, I felt something close to fear. For the first time she had chosen to sit there instead of saving me a place at one of the middle tables. All the chairs were full, so I stood close to Keisha, awkwardly leaning against the stained wall. I didn't want to stay, but I knew that to leave would be to lose. At the middle tables it was mix of cafeteria trays, lunch boxes, and brown paper bags, so you could always squeeze in more kids. At the EMERGE table, everyone ate the school hot lunch; the trays sat edge to edge on the tabletop, leaving no room for extras. Keisha acknowledged my presence with a nod. The other children exchanged glances. A boy I didn't recognize was talking.

"Hi, Georgette. Look, Keisha, it's Georgette. Keisha, why don't you go sit with Georgette? Maybe she'll trade desserts with you. I bet she's got Oreos in there." The boy pointed to my Jackson Five lunch box. Recently my mother had given in to my begging and started packing my lunch. I didn't tell her my reason; she wouldn't have approved—I wanted to fit in with the Brierly children whose mothers could afford to stay home.

"Naw," said Keisha. "I think I'll just stay right here and eat this delicious hot lunch. I wouldn't want to waste the school's free meal." She didn't say another word and neither did I. Instead, I spent the rest of the lunch period silently pretending I was not part of the world around me.

Later that night, I sat in my mother's lap being rocked as if I were a much younger child. I cried the inconsolable tears of someone who has lost her best friend and knows that the world will never be the same.

"It was terrible," I whispered, "just terrible, Mama. They all laughed at me."

"They're just jealous, sweetheart. Of your nice house and big backyard."

My father tried to comfort me: "Think of how you'd feel if you had to get up each day and ride a bus into a strange town where all the children were different from you."

Chris patted me awkwardly on the back. "They'll forget about it in a few days. Don't worry. Alex and I have lots of friends from the city. Keisha will come around."

"Why do we have to live in this no-account town anyhow?" Alex burst out. "The white kids think we're monkeys. The EMERGE kids think we're sellouts. If you ask me, moving to Brierly was a lousy decision."

"I don't recall anyone asking for your opinion," my mother snapped, pushing me off her lap in order to stare down Alex.

"That's my point exactly." Alex picked up his jacket and backpack. "I'm going to spend the night at Ty's."

"You aren't going anywhere, Alexander Collins, except upstairs to do your homework. Michael, talk some sense into your son, please."

"Leave him alone, Verna. If he wants to go into town, why not, it's not a school night. Alex is a teenager now, he deserves our trust." My father rarely raised his voice, but he expected his calm words to be final, never realizing that the calmer and quieter he spoke, the more he enraged my mother. Ignoring my mother's scowl, he picked up his keys to drive Alex to the station. He liked to joke that Alex spent more time flirting with strange girls on the train to Boston than anywhere else. Daddy always grinned and said, *Like father, like son*, when Alex asked for a ride to the commuter rail.

After that day, Keisha and I ignored each other. We didn't speak again until one day the next month at afternoon recess. Deanna and I swung a single rope while Tacy jumped, blond pigtails bouncing. They chanted a song about teddy bears and meadows.

I let the rope fall when I noticed Keisha approaching from the far side of the playground where the bused kids spent recess. She stood waiting and watching. The other girls moved toward her, forming a barrier.

"You're-invited-to-my-birthday-party-next-Saturday-at-two," Keisha said without pausing. With one rapid motion, she shoved a card into my hands and retreated across the pavement.

"I didn't know you hung out with retards, Georgette," Deanna said loudly, aiming her words at Keisha's back.

"Who was that anyhow?" someone new asked.

"Nobody," I said, dropping the invitation to pick up the rope. "Let's play."

Three months later, my parents sent my brothers and me to live with our grandmother in Jamaica. My last day at Brierly Primary, I cried and told Tacy, Deanna, and the others how much I'd miss them; it didn't occur to me to say goodbye to Keisha, and by the time we returned to the States two years later, she had moved back to D.C.

Remembering the Robins and the Bluebirds made me nervous. What if Keisha had grown to hate me again? I had almost forgotten Keisha by Class Four, the ninth grade at Ellis. Then one weekend, I was visiting my father in Roxbury where he had moved after we sold the Brierly house. Mother claimed it was no surprise; he had always loved his family more than us anyhow. As usual, I escaped the apartment as soon as possible. It was dark in Franklin Park, and I had been sitting unmoving on the swings for a long time when I looked up to catch Keisha Irving sitting on a picnic table watching me.

"What's wrong with you?" she asked.

"Nothing." Silence was best.

"Who are you waiting for?"

"Nobody." I was waiting for my father to get fed up enough to send Chris to look for me, but I wasn't about to tell her that.

Keisha studied me for a minute and then said, "Do you want to sleep over at my grandma's?" Saying yes was as easy as slipping on a pair of comfortable old shoes.

We fell back into a friendship with an ease that amazed me. We pretended that we had never heard of Bluebirds and Robins and had parted merely because Keisha had gone home to Washington unexpectedly. After a few months, it was hard to remember who had betrayed whom. Suddenly, weekend visits with my father weren't so bad. And although the school week was hard, even the worst days at the Ellis School for Girls were merely stories to laugh about with Keisha each night on the phone. Page, Caitlin, Clarissa, and the others were just pompous snobs to mimic and giggle over during the frequent nights I spent at Keisha's grandmother's house. We spooned in the dark on top of a scratchy mattress, sometimes silent and other times screaming with laughter. One night Keisha taught me how to do some sort of meditation thing. "Picture yourself floating above everything," she said. "Nothing can touch you. The air is golden, the clouds are purple, and you are light as a feather." I liked the images she used and practiced the meditations often. Soon I could float off within a few minutes of shutting my eyes. Keisha didn't ask why I never invited her over, and I didn't ask what she was doing back in Boston. Our parents and home lives were silent forces that did not bear speaking of.

Keisha no longer took the bus to Brierly. Instead of participating in EMERGE again, she went to one of the local high schools. For years my parents had told me about the problems of the Boston public school system, but Keisha seemed to thrive there while I floundered at Ellis. My parents were well off but nowhere near the old-money rich of the Ellis girls. The $10,000 yearly tuition that my mother demanded from Daddy merely meant attending an exclusive school without the right accessories. While my classmates' mothers hosted charity luncheons and supervised class outings, my mother worked and rarely appeared at Ellis events. The white girls smirked when I spoke in class, and I was equally estranged from the few other black girls who attended Ellis. They seemed to know some secret to navigating the school that eluded me. Their table in the corner of the dining room was as impenetrable to me as the EMERGE table in the Brierly cafeteria.

* * *

Two weeks after Keisha's call, I was getting ready to head to D.C. Moving restlessly around the apartment, I opened my suitcase and purse, checking and rechecking to make sure I hadn't forgotten anything for the trip. I put away the dishes drying by the sink, unplugged the appliances, and double-checked the oven and faucets. Finally, desperate to calm my nerves, I filled a large coffee mug with white wine and forced myself to sit down and watch television. I put on the music-video channel; I always found the collage of color flickering across the screen and the methodic beat soothing. I remembered Keisha trying to keep a straight face while teaching me the latest dance steps. I remembered late-night talks as we did each other's hair. It was real, I told myself, turning up the volume. I stood and practiced long forgotten steps.

While dancing, I thought about being fourteen at one of those get-togethers that began as an afternoon barbecue and ended well after midnight. My mother, her brothers and sisters, and what seemed like half the Jamaicans in Boston were there. As the evening went by, folks came indoors to escape the mosquitoes. Children and babies were put to sleep in the bedrooms or sat half-awake and heavy-eyed in their parents' laps. Most of the women were crowded in the kitchen, where great pots of food continually simmered. The men sat in the basement drinking rum punch, playing cards with friendly but serious intent. The only sounds were the occasional whistles of appreciation for the winner and sympathetic laughter for the losers. In the living room, the young people gathered. Music played loud enough that you could feel the beat, but not so loud that the women in the kitchen came in for the third time to complain they couldn't hear themselves think.

I was with the other teenagers. I danced to the funk with the sexiest boy I had ever laid eyes on. The handsome Eddy Richardson—he must have been at least eighteen—surely could dance, not just the careless one-two of someone who was enjoying the music, but the dancing of someone who commanded admiration. He displayed his sinewy muscles, first moving each individually, then rippling them in long, perfect, unbroken waves. He stepped in all directions, always in time with the music. Of course, he was showing off, but his motions were so smooth and fine, he had every right to do so. No one minded; the boys, girls, and young adults laughed and clapped, swaying back and forth with the beat, occasionally breaking into special steps and gestures. I was the only one who felt uncomfortable. Still, I held my own, moving a bit this way and that, following Eddy but never attempting his wilder gyrations.

The record ended and the teenagers shouted their requests for the next song.

"Kool and the Gang!" shouted one cousin.

"No, Bob Marley," said someone else.

"The Jacksons!"

"Uh-uh, none of that old-time music, play Funkedelic, they're bad." My cousin Lisa grabbed a record and headed for the turntable.

With the music paused, you could hear the women in the next room. My mother spoke, loud and penetrating in the tone saved for when she needed to be heard or the times she felt comfortable, like around other blacks.

"Yeah, I know the girl's got no rhythm. It's not my fault. That's all those white folks she grew up with."

I hoped the room was dark enough to hide my face. Donna Summer blared out. Some kids clapped. Others groaned. *Not that old shit. Better watch your mouth or I'll tell Ma.* Eddy Richardson grinned and held out his hand. I shook my head, no, I didn't want to dance anymore. I sank down into the sofa and silently watched for the rest of the night.

* * *

While I waited for the taxi to the airport, I sat at my kitchen table, trying to concentrate on my homework. Distracted, I looked around the small but cozy and clean apartment. I loved its oak floors and carefully stained woodwork. I had selected the furniture, the rag rugs, and curios, sometimes searching for weeks to find just the right piece. The place was sparkling from the hours I had spent polishing and cleaning the night before. For a moment I pictured the dark, chaotic apartment where I had lived in my early twenties. There had been little furniture but wall-to-wall clothes and piles of papers, books, and magazines littering the floor. Forcefully I expelled the memory. That was a different Georgie. This clean, organized home was mine now. This was a real life with a future, and that's all I wanted for Keisha. A husband, a good job, a calm place to live, a place where fear and uncertainty could not exist.

Malcolm and I had begun to talk about living together, but we weren't sure that we were ready. I knew that he was Mr. Right, but we had so many arguments. Our discussions began as rational talks or political debates but degenerated to slammed doors and stony silences.

The last fight began with Malcolm speaking proudly of his family and neighbors who preferred to live in all-black sections of Chicago though they could afford more affluent communities. He couldn't stand those folks who got a little bit of money and abandoned the race for suburban homes and white middle-class values.

Feeling like my parents and my whole life were being attacked, I responded by saying that wasn't the case. Take myself, for example: Although I had grown up in Brierly and went to white schools, I remained faithful to my heritage. I pointed to my books, records, paintings, my coursework in African-American visual art, and my NAACP membership. In fact, after graduate school I planned to work with low-income youth. Like my parents had always said, black folks have to support each other. I reminded Malcolm that living in a ghetto was not a requirement for being Afrocentric and that I might know African-American culture better than some blacks who grew up in all-black communities.

"Georgette," Malcolm said, "you don't know shit."

"So, what, my parents were supposed to stay in the city and send me to public school there? That would have been a better choice?"

"At least you'd know who you are. You can't *study* our culture. You've got to *live* our culture." Malcolm ran his hands down my shoulders and kissed my neck. Sometimes I wondered if our fights were a kind of foreplay to him. I pushed his hands aside.

"Let me tell you something about the city of Boston. It is filled with racist crackers and no-account niggers." My tongue felt thick and foreign in my mouth. I couldn't remember ever having used the words *cracker* or *nigger* before. I quoted one of my father's uncles—the one who eventually moved to Atlanta because he said that at least you knew what you were getting down there.

"Why are you getting so mad?" Malcolm asked. He seemed genuinely puzzled at my reaction.

"Because you seem to think I'd be better off, more real or something, if I was like my friend Keisha. She grew up in Boston and D.C. She went to city public schools and got all As. And where is she now? Dropped out of M.I.T. because an A from Trinity Tech High doesn't mean shit, Malcolm. Every time she writes or calls, she tells me that she's going back next semester or as soon as she gets her money saved. She's not going anywhere."

I concluded by repeating something I'd heard my mother say. "Keisha will probably end up like her mother—lots of kids and no prospects."

As soon as I had said it, I felt ashamed. I wanted to take my words back. I knocked on wood. Instead of continuing my argument with Malcolm, I thought about calling Keisha for the first time in months, but didn't. A few days later, she called and said that she might be pregnant.

Keisha met me at the airport. We took the Metro from National Airport to Metro-Center Station, then a local bus to her neighborhood. The early-afternoon ride took a long time, the overcrowded bus moved slowly, groaning on the turns. At each stop it picked up children on their way home. The older ones were loud, drinking Cokes, cracking gum and jokes. The younger ones were more solemn, escorted by their mothers and older brothers and sisters. Many were dressed in green-and-brown plaid uniforms—girls in jumpers, boys in slacks and ties.

At times the bus turned down a street that was decimated by poverty. Stores were abandoned, windows were boarded up, and shattered glass covered the sidewalks. In the shadows of doorways, old men sat with vacant faces. A few streets later, the bus would pass freshly painted houses and meticulously kept lawns.

Keisha and I got off at one of the busy intersections. Large signs everywhere proclaimed, *MONEY ORDERS AND CHECKS CASHED HERE* or *LIQUORS* or *GROCERY—FOOD STAMPS AND WIC ACCEPTED*. Keisha's apartment was a few blocks away, and we walked slowly, suddenly shy, having run out of small talk, questions about each other's health, boyfriends, and the weather. The three years since we had seen each other stretched into decades. It was a struggle to recapture the old closeness and warmth. I wanted to talk about school and my plans for the future but felt that to do so would highlight the glaring fact that Keisha seemed to have none.

Our reversal of fortunes seemed vaguely embarrassing. Right

after high school, she had gone to college full of high hopes and big plans, while I had drifted through a series of white girlfriends and dead-end jobs. But here she was, single, possibly pregnant, stuck in the worst part of D.C. And here I was, in a serious relationship with an ambitious MBA student, about to graduate from Harvard, and planning for a career helping people like Keisha.

We walked in silence, interrupted by Keisha's occasional greetings to passing friends and neighbors. She lived with her younger sister, Tracy, and Jamie, Tracy's three-year-old son. The toddler moved around the apartment making a mess and a nuisance of himself. As soon as his curiosity overcame his shyness, he chattered nonstop with me, insisting on showing off all his books and toys.

Finally, his exasperated mother announced bedtime. She picked up the child, kissing his stomach and face. "Never," she said to Keisha and me, "never have children. They drive you crazy."

"I don't plan to," I answered in the same joking tone. Immediately I felt guilty. I doubted the nineteen-year-old had planned to either.

Throughout the visit, I gathered evidence. The cheapness of the furniture and the unpaid water and gas bills were ammunition that I stockpiled for the upcoming fight to convince Keisha that a baby would be a disaster. I grimly looked forward to meeting Belinda Irving and Keisha's younger siblings. The meeting would confirm my understanding of the situation.

The next day I had the opportunity. I attended church with the entire family. There were Mrs. Irving, Keisha, Tracy with Jamie, and the four youngest Irvings, who were washed and brushed with the loving care parents only have time for on Sundays. The last time that I had gone to church regularly was during my childhood years in Jamaica. Walking down the aisle was like walking backwards through years of my life to arrive at age nine. Like Nina's church, the Irvings's church was over-crowded and over-heated and felt like home. The reverend began his sermon quietly and slowly, but soon he was nearly dancing on the pulpit as he shook with emotions and loudly declared his love for God.

The room got hotter as the churchgoers worked themselves into a fervor. The older women praised the Lord and shouted *hallelujah*. They openly prayed for God to give them the strength to make it through another weary day. Somehow, they knew the suffering they endured on earth would be alleviated in the Promised Land. The heat that spread through the room was not the angry dryness of a too-hot day or the wilting humidity of a summer storm; rather, it was the warmth that emerges from people united.

The preacher was calling for souls to stand up and be delivered. All around me, people were rising. The preacher looked right at me, urging me to come forward. I could almost hear God, but instead I heard the voice inside me, which said, *No*. The frenzy climaxed when all were on their feet but me. Keisha reached down to touch my shoulder, and for a moment we smiled at one another. The gospel choir broke into song. And while the brown shiny people sang hymns, which I barely recalled, I was filled with an overwhelming sense of loneliness.

I thought about being in eleventh grade when *The Cosby Show* came on the air. One Thursday night, Keisha and I were watching the happy, wealthy black Huxtables. She turned to me and said, "When we were little, that's what I thought your life was like. I was so jealous!" I told her that she was sort of right back then. But it is not at all like that now, I said.

"Sometimes you seem real nervous around your father," she said carefully.

I replied, "Well, he's not really a Heathcliff Huxtable, now is he?"

* * *

After church and Sunday dinner, Keisha's younger siblings and her nephews were in the front yard playing. They had gratefully put away their Sunday clothes and were determined to catch every last ray of sunshine; they would stay out until their mother called her last warning that they had better get in the house, *now*. Mrs. Irving and Tracy were in the kitchen, talking in slow afternoon voices. The youngest babies sat drowsy in their mothers' laps. Keisha and I cleared the dining room table, finally having a chance to talk alone.

"What should I do?" Keisha asked, low enough to be masked by the TV. Though she had been financially independent for years, I knew she still feared her mother's wrath.

"Shit, Keisha," I said. "I don't know what you should do. How should I know?"

mr. right

i n late October, Malcolm and I went to Northampton to have lunch. Although the town was not too far from my graduate school, I rarely went there. The place was packed with lesbians, and it made me uncomfortable. But there was a Thai restaurant in the center that Malcolm liked, so once in a while I caved in and we went. That afternoon, we had barely sat down when things started to go very wrong.

"Georgie, that woman sitting over there keeps looking at us. Do you know her?" Malcolm pointed at a table out on the patio. Two women, one black and one white, were drinking cocktails. The white woman stared at me. She looked familiar, but I couldn't come up with a name.

"Uh, no, I don't. Are you sure you want to eat here? We could go someplace else." My anxiety was pulling me in two different directions. Part of me thought the solution was to run as fast as possible; another part was desperate for a drink. If we left, we would have to decide on another restaurant, walk there, get seated, and order. It might be another half hour before I got a glass of wine.

"Georgie, why are you so nervous? Let's order." Malcolm looked at me and smiled. I smiled back, gratefully reaching across the table for his hand. Before he could even signal a waiter, one came over with a drink, which he placed in front of me.

"A Tanqueray and tonic, compliments of the table over there," the waiter said, gesturing back to the same patio table.

"Hey, that's your favorite drink. Who are those women?" Malcolm craned his neck, trying to get a better view.

"I'm not sure," I said, although by that point I had recognized Amanda. A few minutes later, she came over. She wore cropped forest-green pants and a fitted chocolate silk jacket. Though her blond hair was now long, it was perfectly styled; clearly, she still visited her salon weekly. Five years had put a few more fine wrinkles near her mouth, and the pair of Perry Ellis glasses implied her vision was no longer 20/20. Otherwise, she looked the same—handsome, rich, and commanding.

"Georgette." She leaned down for me to kiss her. Her perfume was the scent we had chosen together during some New York shopping expedition. I brushed my lips to her cheek, silently willing her to move away. She stood her ground, waiting for an introduction.

"Amanda, this is Malcolm. Malcolm, Amanda." They both looked blank. I had never mentioned Amanda or any of my girlfriends to Malcolm, and she and I had not seen each other since before I started dating him. When she realized that I was not going to add any context to the introduction, Amanda gave a tiny shrug and pulled out a business card.

"Give me a call, Georgette. I miss you." She handed me the card, then indicated the black woman whom she had left on the patio. The woman half-stood and gave a small wave. "By the way, that's Cheryl, my partner." Cheryl was also elegantly dressed and even taller than Amanda.

"Is that woman a dyke?" Malcolm whispered as she moved away. When I nodded, he asked me how we knew each other. I told him that we had been friends a long time ago. Malcolm's forehead knotted and then his expression became distinctly malicious. Before I realized what was happening, he followed Amanda back to her table, and they spoke for a moment. Malcolm was over six feet, but Amanda's posture and self-possession made her appear nearly his equal. Next thing I knew, the waiter was setting two extra places at our booth, and Amanda and Cheryl joined us.

"So tell me how you and Georgie know each other," Malcolm said as soon as they were settled.

"Georgette's never mentioned me?" Amanda's voice was serene, but her eyes glittered stone. I was pretty sure she knew exactly what she was doing. "Georgette and I were lovers for over two years."

I refused to meet Malcolm's eye. I drained my drink and waved down the waiter.

"I think my girlfriend would like another gin and tonic," Malcolm told him.

"Oh, so you two are together." Cheryl laughed. She seemed to be the only satisfied person at the table. "Amanda talks about you all the time. I used to get so jealous. You know. *Georgette was such a great painter. Georgette was so great and creative and smart. Blah, blah, blah.* But I guess I have nothing to worry about."

Amanda muttered something under her breath. From my seat, it sounded like, "Creative, smart, and crazy." I ignored her, gratefully gulping my fresh drink. It was going to be a long lunch.

Later, driving back to the university, Malcolm demanded to know why I had never told him about Amanda.

"Are you angry?" I asked.

"Don't you think I'd have liked to know that my girlfriend was some sort of bulldagger? Do you think I liked finding out from a pretentious white woman? And by the way, I noticed she's a little free with her hands."

I sighed. There was no point in arguing. Amanda had touched me several times while she reminisced about our relationship. To an untutored eye, her brief caresses might have been a friendly, fond relic of the past, but I knew she was marking her territory. Amanda couldn't stand to lose. Though our breakup had been mutual, the idea that I was dating anyone, especially a man, probably irked her.

"Do you think I'm homophobic or something? Is that why you didn't tell me? You know I'm not like that."

I didn't really have a good rationale for my silence on the matter. When we first started dating, I already had to explain so many hard topics. What I had been doing immediately after high school and why I had started college four years later than most people; the scars that marked my arms; my estrangement from my family at the time. Why add another item to the list? And then as the months passed, the girlfriends, gay bars, pride marches, and Provincetown faded; blurry, faint, and incomprehensible, they all belonged to a different person's life. Part of the truce with my mother included an unspoken pact to forget past disappointments. We were all anxious to delete the old Georgie from our thoughts. She never existed.

"Malcolm, I know you aren't homophobic. The topic just never came up. Can we drop it, please?" Now that I thought about it, Malcolm was a lot like Amanda. Always wanting to discuss problems and process our relationship. Neither understood that there were things better left unsaid. I wondered how Malcolm would feel if I said he reminded me of a lesbian.

"Are you going to call her?" he asked.

"No." I was as terse as possible, hoping he would let the topic go.

"And she said that you danced in a nightclub for women. Is that true?" Malcolm kept coming back to Amanda. He seemed horrified, though I had always heard men were titillated by such things.

"Oh, I don't know. I barely remember. I might have done something like that when I was a teenager. It was all a long time ago."

"Why? Why would you do such a thing? It's not like your parents don't have money." Now there was the weird part. Normally, I would never have answered his question. The truth was too close to my heart. I didn't know why I decided to take a risk.

"When I was growing up, all my cousins and brothers could really dance. I mean, they were totally hot out on the floor. And I couldn't. People laughed and said I danced like a white girl. Later, I got better. It was like my body suddenly stopped trying to fight the music and I could hear it instead. And I felt so free. So when this club said that they would actually pay me to dance, it was like some sort of proof that I wasn't some sort of freak or mutation. Black girl with white genes, you know."

"But dancing for a bunch of women is just plain old freaky, Georgie."

"Did you even hear what I just said?"

"Yeah, but if you were so afraid of being labeled a white girl, why date one?"

I shrugged. Pressing my forehead against the car window and staring into the passing woods, I thought about how much I wanted out of the car, away from him. Fall in western Massachusetts is a brilliant mix of gold, red, and brown. I imagined the door opening and falling out at the next stop light. I would roll through the crackling leaves, enveloped in a world of flaming color. Walking through the autumn weather, I always feel at peace, though the very beauty is a sign of death.

"Georgie? Are you upset?" Malcolm's voice intruded on my daydream.

"It's okay. Really."

"You're a great dancer. You don't need some freaky women to prove that. And your rhythm, well, it's certainly unique." Malcolm laughed. I joined in. It didn't seem worth explaining to him how much he had just hurt my feelings. Malcolm said that I felt things too deeply. *Thin-skinned girl*, he called me. "You think too much. Stop over-analyzing things. Just live a little."

Malcolm grew up in the South Side of Chicago. His father was a teacher, his mother a nurse; they probably could have moved to the suburbs, but they chose not to. They sent their children to a mostly African-American and Latino Catholic school in the neighborhood. A school *peopled with color* was the current lingo these days. This difference in our backgrounds came up over and over again. He enjoyed looking at my paintings of urban landscapes. Those he liked, he declared real. *That's so real, you know what I'm saying. It's like that*, he'd say. Others just made him snort and turn aside. Apparently the weekends I spent at my father's and cousins' in Roxbury and Mattapan didn't take. Somehow, I never became real.

Malcolm felt perfectly at home when we visited my father. Sitting on the stoop, he could be as foul-mouthed as the posturing teenagers. At the corner drugstore and hanging out at KFC, he joked with the waitstaff, always flirting with the high school girls. When he stood amidst a crowd of other young men, it always took me a moment to recognize him; his drooping jeans, colorful shirts, and Nikes matched the uniform they all sported, and Malcolm blended into anonymity. Or when we went out for the evening, he wore the requisite tailored black suit, but on his head was a red, gold, and green hat and a narrow band of Kente cloth hung around his neck, Afro-dressy style. I noticed, though, each time he went on a job interview, he was as conservative as if he were following the dress code at my brothers' prep schools. When he finished his MBA, he was bound to be snapped up by some prestigious firm. So, I wondered, was *I* really the one who was the chameleon?

I remembered the first weekend that my brothers and I spent with my father after my parents divorced. Daddy was staying at Grandma Annie's house. Alex, Chris, and I had only been back in the United States for a few months. Daddy was so broken-hearted about Mother and Eric's engagement, he wouldn't get out of bed except to go to work. He liked me to stay upstairs in the bedroom with him so I could rub his back and scratch his head; it was the only thing that made him feel better, he said. Through the grate in the floor, we could hear all my aunts' loud voices rising from Grandma's front parlor.

"Michael needs to get himself up out of that bed and find a place to live," Aunt Fran declared.

"Uh huh, there's no use lying around like the world's coming to an end. Verna was never our kind of people anyway. Those Jamaicans aren't as clean as regular black folks." Grandma Annie had always been clear about her animosity for my mother.

"You know, he's got Georgie locked up in that room with him." My Aunt Audrey was still childless. Everyone liked to say that's why she tried to raise other people's offspring. "The air in there's stale from those cigarettes. It's not healthy. He'll end up burning himself up and the whole house too."

"Georgie," my grandmother called up the stairs. "Go outside and play. Leave your daddy. He'll be fine. The man will get up when he's good and ready."

The women shooed me outdoors where I was left blinking on the sidewalk, unsure of what to do. I was eleven; too old for dolls and not yet ready for boys. Two unfamiliar girls came walking up the street.

"Who are you? Do you stay here now?" one of them asked. She looked about my age, though she was smooth and flat where I had begun to push out in a mortifying manner. Her head was covered with tiny braids and intricate beadwork. The other girl's hair was straightened. It was 1980, and I knew my Afro was a throwback to the '70s, but my mother refused all ideas of processing.

"My name is Georgette Collins. My grandmother lives here," I said without much hope. The girls fell against each other laughing.

The girl with the beads pinched her nose and took on an exaggerated British accent. "Oh, she tawlks moighty fine, does she not?" She over-enunciated every syllable. I tried to change tactics.

"Shut your rass mouth before I box it fe yuh nasty bumbo-clat self," I snapped. The girls just laughed harder.

"Banana-boat nigger," they jeered over their shoulders, continuing their promenade as if I was a momentary amusement, barely worth pausing over. I don't know how much time passed before my cousin Peggy found me crouched in the small side yard next to the chain-link fence. Peggy was almost an adult and beautiful. Aunt Fran let her perm her hair. Or maybe she was so grown she didn't even need to get her mother's permission. I wasn't sure.

"Do you want to come to the store with me? I'll buy you some Twizzlers or something," she said, then realized I was upset. "What's wrong, Georgie?"

"I can't come. Daddy needs me." I was afraid of running into the two laughing girls; besides, my father's sadness weighed on me, ever-present and crushing.

* * *

Weekends with Daddy in Mattapan were preceded by a long, anxious week in Cambridge with Mother. Mother's new condominium was smaller than our Brierly house and we all got in each other's way. Chris and Alex hated sharing a room, although Alex was away at boarding school most of the time. Downstairs there was only a kitchen, dining room, and living room. Mother no longer had a study, and my brothers and I no longer had a family room/den where we could hang out and make noise. Actually, the walls were so thin, noises reverberated throughout the whole duplex. I remember always trying to get away from the sound of my mother crashing pots and pans in the kitchen. She was a noisy cook and dishwasher when she was tired. And Mother said that busting her ass to be taken seriously in the courtroom made her tired all the time. As a black woman, she had to be twice as good to get the court's respect.

Late one Sunday evening, I tried to drown out the clatter by turning the TV on as loud as I dared. I watched old black-and-white movies on channel 28's Shirley Temple Film Festival. Little Miss Sunshine swung her arms back and forth as she marched down an airplane aisle singing "Animal Crackers in My Soup." Warbling and giggling, she was almost coquettish as she winked merry eyes at the passengers. When her adoptive father lifted her, the baby doll dress (which I just knew was sky-blue) rode up and I could see her underwear peeking out. No one seemed to mind, but I looked away, momentarily embarrassed.

"Georgie, move. I want to watch football." Chris stood in the living room doorway scowling. "Mom! Make her move!" he shouted. There was a crash from the kitchen. Chris winced. Mother appeared behind him.

"You kids are working my nerves! I'm trying to cook dinner, and you're shouting and hollering. What's wrong with you?"

"Georgie is watching those dumb old Shirley Temple shows again, and I want to watch football. She hogs the TV."

"Shirley Temple?" Mother said in her exasperated voice. "Between that and all the *Little House on the Prairie* you watch, anyone would think you want to be a little white girl. I didn't raise my child to want to be a curly blond, tap-dancing fool."

When I didn't respond, Mother came and sat next to me. "Georgette," she said, "I want you to be proud of being black. Why do you think I sent you to live in Jamaica? So you'd have the experience of living in an all-black country."

I turned and stared at her. She had sent us to Jamaica while she and my father were fighting. No one had said anything about Black Pride. Besides, just because I liked Shirley Temple didn't mean I wanted to be white. I liked how jolly she was and how everyone seemed to love her.

"What's the matter with you, staring at me like that?" Lately, Mother was growing more and more annoyed with my silences. I rarely spoke, even when addressed directly.

"Fine!" she snapped. "Turn it off. Go set the table for six people. Eric and I are having guests. You and your brother can eat early in the kitchen. Don't forget to set out wine glasses."

After that day, I was not allowed to watch Shirley Temple at my mother's, but on the weekends that I stayed with my father I could watch whatever I pleased. Often we watched my shows together. Laura Ingalls and her Pa had a special relationship; she was the best loved of the three children. Daddy appreciated the scenes with the daughter and father fishing or horseback riding or having heart-to-heart chats by the fireside. Pa always steered Laura in the right direction.

"Would you like us to do stuff like that?" Daddy sometimes asked. I giggled. I couldn't imagine my father up on a horse or holding a fishing pole as he stood thigh-high in a creek.

"No, Daddy, I like us just the way we are," I would reply.

"And I love you just the way you are too, sweetheart. Family is all we got," Daddy would say, and then give me a big hug. Those tender scenes lasted only a year or two. By the time I was thirteen, I hated him treating me like such a baby. It was so sickly sweet, it made me want to gag.

A few weeks after Malcolm and I ran into Amanda at the restaurant, I made a quick trip to Boston. Amanda and I had sex, of course. Afterwards, she joked as we lolled in the bedroom of her town house.

"What do you call a straight woman after two drinks?"

"A lesbian. Ha ha, very funny." I got up and started to look around for my clothes. "This doesn't mean anything." The room had been redecorated; it was pretty, almost girlish. The ivory duvet and curtains were accented with embroidered blue and green pillows. Stenciled flowers in the same colors adorned the pale cream walls. The modern glass-and-steel furniture had been replaced with a walnut wardrobe and end tables. A squashy, comfortable armchair and ottoman wore cotton slipcovers. They looked lived-in, as if someone actually sat by the fire and read. Five years ago, we never sat in the chair; whenever in her bedroom, we were screwing or sleeping. I wondered if Cheryl had softened her. In all the time Amanda and I were together, she had not changed so much as an ashtray or the placement of a throw rug in her interior design.

"Come on, Georgette, stay awhile. Cheryl's out of town. We can order in and play all day, if you like." Amanda pulled me back into the four-poster bed.

"Did you fuck other women in here while we were dating?" I asked.

"Do you really want me to answer that?" Amanda whispered, nuzzling my neck.

"Yes."

"No, I never cheated on you."

I knew she was lying, but a sudden warmth filled me at the thought that she still cared enough to lie. Nevertheless, I couldn't stop myself from bringing up her girlfriend.

"This is wrong. I'm sure that Cheryl would be devastated. I'd have been."

"Watch who you're calling an adulteress. I'm not the only one in this room who's cheating." Amanda kept her tone light, but I could tell that she was teetering at the edge of annoyance.

"It doesn't count for me. I'm not really cheating on Malcolm if I do it with a woman. Especially not you." I knew what a hypocrite I was being. I wanted to hurt her feelings. To my delight, Amanda recoiled and momentarily dropped her hand from my breast.

"You've changed," she said. "You've gotten much harder. You're being kind of a bitch."

"I know." I smiled and kissed her.

A few hours and several fucks later, she asked me why I was with a man. I shrugged and said that I didn't really know.

"C'mon, Georgette, that's no answer. I know you. You're a dyke through and through. You can't tell me that you're suddenly straight." Amanda fondled and nipped as she pressed for an answer. I never understood how her touch was able to soothe and ache at the same time—as if her hand or maybe my body could not distinguish between a caress and a jab. Finally I told her what had happened during my last trip to Jamaica a few years before. The story that I wove about the whore of Babylon might have been the correct answer. Besides, it was as good an explanation as any other answer I could give.

A few days after I slept with Amanda, I came home to find

Malcolm, a man black enough to satisfy anyone, in my apartment leaning over one of my notebooks.

"What are you doing? Get away from that." I snatched the book off the kitchen table. Malcolm had a sheepish expression.

"I'm sorry. You weren't home yet so I let myself in. It was just lying open there. I couldn't help myself."

"That's private. You're being invasive. My mother used to do that to me all the time." I was nearly crying from embarrassment and fear. Earlier in the day, I'd written up the sordid details about sleeping with Amanda.

"What are all those lists and things? Like, *Pick up clothes, water plants, check date on milk before drinking*. What is that?" Clearly, Malcolm felt more curious than guilty.

He was talking about the lists that I keep in my notebook. All the things that I have to do each day, including the very mundane, like showering, cleaning up after myself, and eating meals. The lists were left over from the period of my life when I was so depressed, even getting out of bed was a challenge. They reminded me of the trappings of normalcy required to convince others that I was like them. I was afraid that without the reminders, I might fall into living in chaos or sleeping all day, or worse.

Malcolm was waiting for an answer.

"Nothing. It's nothing. I can't explain. Just stay out of my personal writing, okay?"

"Baby, I worry about you sometimes. You're so closed. When we first met, I thought, *That girl is just shy*, but it's been three years, and if anything you're just getting more tight-lipped. Sometimes I don't even know who you are. Please, I just want us to be close." Malcolm drew me next to him. This was the moment in the movies where the woman breaks down and cries, confessing everything and leaning on her man. I heard the soundtrack swelling with heart-wrenching music, but I said nothing.

may 2001

f ingers pressed on my temples, I paused and looked up from my reading. I had pored over the box of letters for two days. Now I sat at a picnic table in the park near the library reading the last. The letters had become a presence in my life; they seemed more real than the library, Mimi, and the others. At times, in the periphery, I caught glimpses of old friends and lovers, but each time I whirled around to confront one, I realized it was only a stranger with similar features, the same stance or stride or even just a shadow. I still could not allow myself to think much about the past, but an occasional memory would flood my mind; in those moments I stood rock still, washed over by scenes of my childhood and young adult years. I felt embraced and battered at the same time, bathed by memories that seemed both stinging and sweet.

The most interesting letters were from childhood friends, the most puzzling were from my parents. My father's notes were generally cryptic and brief. He'd written things like: *Thinking of you and taking care of business. Love, Daddy.* Another, more blunt note read: *Whatever happened to that long-legged blond girl? Gentlemen (and Georgie) prefer blondes!* Mother's letters were longer and more serious, detailing her work as an attorney and cautioning me to stay focused on my studies. These letters rarely acknowledged that either of us had a personal life outside work or school. She opened and ended each with a quotation from a black woman. The most recent was from 1996.

Dearest Daughter,

I hope this letter finds you well and thriving. Oprah Winfrey once said, "I was raised to believe that excellence is the best deterrent to racism or sexism. And that's how I operate my life." I've been thinking about her words since you told me that you are committed to studying Art History. First of all, congratulations on your graduate school acceptance. I am so proud to see your talents being recognized. And a full fellowship is such an honor!

But are you sure that Art History is the most marketable choice? I understand you and Malcolm have gotten quite serious, but it's not wise to be too financially dependent on one's husband. Furthermore, Eric and I will not be around forever. And the practice is keeping me busier than ever. It's so exciting to help a group of people who really need the legal aid, but the work is exhausting and it does not leave me much time or energy to rescue an adult daughter from her own foolish choices.

It also strikes me that Art History is all well and good for rich whites, but have you thought about the needs of your own community? It's more than time to give something back, Georgie. Have you had time to read that book of inspirational quotes that I sent on your birthday? I particularly like this one by Marian Anderson. She talks about real people's lives:. *"It is easy to look back, self-indulgently, feeling pleas-antly sorry for oneself and saying I didn't have this and I didn't have that. But it is only the grown woman regretting the hardships of a little girl who never thought they were hardships at all. She had the things that really mattered."*

Much love,
Mother

After work, I wandered through the downtown pedestrian mall. For a long time, I stood under a sign for Jake's Tavern. Finally, I entered the bar, squinting my eyes against the stench of cigarette smoke and sweat. The gloomy room had a few tables of patrons watching baseball and a bartender who seemed to share his customers' fatigue as he idly drew circles and squiggles in the margin of a newspaper.

I sat at the bar anticipating the tang of a cool drink. I drummed my fingers to avoid licking my lips. In the long seconds before the bartender came over with his pad and pen, I almost wanted to scream, I was so unable to contain my excitement. Just as the bartender set a tall Long Island Iced Tea in front of me, an old white woman came inside. She sat next to me companionably, as if I knew her. She seemed to be looking at me with pity. I resisted the sudden urge to lay my head on the woman's gray silk pants and ask to be comforted. For a moment, I saw my Nina and heard her voice as the woman ordered a rum punch. I closed my eyes and imagined that I was in Nina's garden with the sun on my face and the Jamaican heat blessing me with palm trees, wild spices, and vines twisting and creeping in every direction. It had been years since I sat in Nina's garden and heard her tales. Even longer years since I had really listened. Growing up, I had spent hours in that garden, sometimes hiding in the cool shade under the verandah, sometimes sitting in a bamboo chair, shelling peas while my grandmother told fantastical stories. There was a boy who weeded and tended it, but the garden was the protected domain of women. When outdoors, my brothers and boy cousins preferred the patio and the raucous splashing of the pool.

When I opened my eyes, the woman was gone. I turned back to the bar to pick up my drink, only to discover that she had taken the glass and my wallet with her. The wallet contained my money, subway pass, bank card, and everything else. Instead of floating home that evening on a buzz of alcohol, I had to walk through the streets of downtown Boston frustrated, angry, and alone. Later that night, I sat once again with my box full of letters, looking for the key.

being jenny bennett

a t the end of my third month there, John M. ran away from CARE. No one expected it from him. He was a lanky, tired-looking man on crutches. He didn't seem to have the spirit of most runaways. Nor did he, a homeless man, have the resources of someone like Kate, who had arranged a car to pick her up in the parking lot when we went on an outdoors smoke break. Kate had nimbly jumped into a yellow Bug and sped away the week before. Everyone knew, even the counselors, that it was her boyfriend Ben who snatched her. Ben was in and out of CARE upon occasion himself and his yellow Volkswagen was seen on the patients' side of the lot nearly as often as it was parked with the visitors.

I remember Kate's escape as a big deal; all the clients (we were clients, not patients, at CARE) wondered if the staff was going to send the police after her. After all, Kate had been committed there, some said by her parents, though some thought it had actually been by Ben. Later I began to realize that many of the committed clients came from families as or more addicted than they were themselves. But at the time I was very impressed with Kate. She spent the first several days in detox screaming for her drug, which I believe was crystal meth. Having recently come out of detox myself, I was sympathetic to the all-encompassing aching need I imagined she was feeling as she cried and cursed everyone. I had not been nearly as loud or violent in detox, but I had craved alcohol more than I had ever wanted anything before. In the detox room, I spent long days looking at the pockmarked walls and ceiling, hallucinating little faces grinning toothless grins at me. They spoke—telling me that if I survived the next minute, I could survive anything. So I bit my lips until I drew blood, getting up every twenty minutes or so to throw up in the adjoining bathroom; the two detox rooms were the only ones in the complex with their own bathroom, for good reasons. Occasionally a staff member would come in and take my vital signs. Most were sympathetic. One told me that at CARE they chose not to give medication to ease withdrawal except in the worst cases of delirium tremors. They thought it better if we learned the consequences of our addiction.

Kate, however, was not willing to take her withdrawal or commitment lying down. She screamed and cursed most of the time, rejecting anyone who tried to talk to her. Even when she was not the loudest person in the room, attention seemed to naturally gravitate toward her for one reason or another. For example, during meals while everyone waited in line patiently for tuna salad or Salisbury steak, Kate would walk into the lunchroom late and blithely cut to the front. Or at night when we couldn't go outside to smoke, the men and then the women were supposed to take ten-minute turns using the little windowless smoke room. Kate would continue to smoke long after the women's turn was up. Ignoring the men pressed against the glass door, she'd blow rings at the yellow, nicotine-stained walls until she was done with however many cigarettes she had brought in with her. We all took our clues from the CARE staff, who ignored Kate as completely as she disregarded the established rules of the facility. So behavior which usually would have prompted a community meeting and a lesson for all of us in managing impulsive behavior, instead went unmentioned.

I spent a lot of time watching Kate with envy. To not care at all what others thought of you seemed a path to freedom which I couldn't find. Or perhaps she did care, but she didn't seem interested in pleasing anyone—the staff, the other clients, her family—and treated everyone with the same indifference. It was clear from the moment she arrived that Kate was Number One. I was astonished the night, one week into her stay, that she deigned to speak to me. I believed that I was one of the most unassuming of clients. As hard as Kate worked to stand out, I worked even harder to blend in. I adopted the slurred accents and jailhouse expressions that others used, though I had never seen many of the neighborhoods where they lived and the closest I had ever come to prison was an intoxicated evening spent in protective custody while vacationing on Martha's Vineyard. But if I could have had three children in foster care just to be more like everyone else, I would have gladly given birth on the spot.

That night, Kate, Maxine, Veeta, and I were in the smoke room. Still detoxing, Kate wore the obligatory hospital gown, but she managed to make it look stylish by also wearing a yellow paisley silk dressing gown and dark brown leather slippers rather than the standard disposable booties that the clinic issued. The three of them were genuinely enjoying their drags and I was pretending to puff on mine when Kate turned to me and spoke the first non-abrasive words I had heard from her.

"Do you play chess?" she asked. I ran out of the room.

Later that night, Kate found me in the TV room.

"Why'd you run out of the smoke room?" she asked.

"I had to go to the bathroom," was the first thing that I could think to say. We sat in silence for a few minutes. I pretended to watch the local news, sneaking quick peeks at Kate once in a while.

"Well, do you?" she asked impatiently.

"Excuse me?"

"Do you play chess?"

I knew how to play chess. My father had taught me when I was seven, but I didn't know if that was the answer that she wanted. I was afraid it would make me look like a snob.

"It is a hard game, I think," I said. Kate gave me a brilliant smile.

"It's not so hard," she said. "Come on to the cafeteria, I'll show you how. Then we can play together."

"That would be nice." I followed her out of the room.

The afternoon that I had first gone to the Center for Addiction, Rehabilitation, and Education, I had no intention of staying. I deliberately wrote misleading information on their paperwork—a made-up social security number, a fake address, and the name *Jenny Bennett*, after a girl whom I'd particularly hated at Ellis. I didn't want CARE to know my real identity or to offer me treatment; I only wanted to know if what I was experiencing was withdrawal. For months I had been unable to stop shaking and felt unbearable panic in the early afternoons when the drinks I'd had the night before began to wear off. My goal for each day was to get through whatever I needed to do and to a liquor store or bar before those feelings set in. A few times I'd caught sight of myself, eyes bloodshot, face ashen, and movements jerky. After that, I carefully avoided mirrors. I couldn't imagine what my professors thought of me on days that I had afternoon classes; my own voice sounded disembodied, and I often wondered if I was making sense or if everyone was just humoring me. I became used to this and accepted it as the price I had to pay for drinking so heavily, along with the constant stomach pains and diarrhea.

But in the weeks since the school year ended, I had stopped going out in the daytime. I tried hard to buy enough alcohol to last each night and through the next day, but inevitably I'd run out in the early morning. I didn't seem to be sleeping—just drinking. In the afternoons and evenings as I waited for darkness, I'd lie on the futon in my studio apartment and hear strange high-pitched voices, laughter, and often a whistling that mystified me. I didn't remember my street as being so busy or so noisy. The house was not near a playground or the center of town. So where were the voices coming from, and why did they sometimes seem to be calling my name? In those long afternoons, I'd lie there promising myself that in just a few hours I could go out and get something to drink for the night. The alcohol would give me strength and perhaps through it I could find salvation if I could just hang on for the next four, three, two hours.

Through the dormer window, I could see the branches of the oak tree that shaded the house dropping shadows on the green shag carpet. The shadows were skeleton people dancing gleeful jigs. They merrily told me that I had to stay indoors, that the outside world was for normal people and that I had to wait until night when I would be invisible. Sometimes they seemed so cruel, taunting me, that I just lay there and cried. I had begun to fear for my sanity. So I needed to know from CARE, had I finally gone off the deep end or was this just a symptom of alcoholism? *Withdrawal?* Either answer I could deal with. I just wanted to know. Once you knew something's name, you had power over it.

Getting to CARE was easy enough that afternoon. I had been wearing the same clothes continuously for longer than I could remember, so there was no need to get dressed. Though CARE was only ten blocks from my apartment (during the school year, I had walked past it every day on the way to the university), it seemed like too much of an effort to walk. I called a cab. While I waited for it to arrive, I had two drinks to calm my nerves. Brushing my teeth, I spat blood into the sink. In the front hallway, I met the two women from the apartment downstairs.

"Just going out to do some errands," I explained, then wondered if it appeared odd that I was telling them anything. Perhaps normal people, people who went out in daylight, didn't explain themselves to their neighbors. In the taxi I leaned backwards and rested my eyes, hoping the driver wouldn't talk to me. Later I realized that the sight of someone strung-out making their way to CARE was probably nothing new to cab drivers in Amherst, but at the time I thought I was maintaining my dignity.

At CARE I had an interview with a woman who was around my age, twenty-eight, but in every other way she was different. She was white, clean, and sober, and where my voice sounded flat and dead, her warm intonations filled the room. She was definitely a real person. I was perhaps an alien, or at best a ghost.

"When was your last drink, Jenny?" she asked, taking notes on a form attached to a clipboard. I was determined to make a good impression on this shiny, clean-cut woman so I clearly could not tell her that I had polished off two gin and tonics less than fifteen minutes earlier. Answering this question required some thought. What would be a reasonable answer? After a long pause, I said, "Yesterday evening around ten-fifteen p.m."

"Really? Are you sure?"

She was clever, but I was not going to allow her to trip me up. "Yes," I said in a firm voice. "I was in a bar on Lexington Street with my friends, Jane and Sarah. I had several beers—Guinness. And a cheeseburger. I mean, a vegetarian burger." Drinking with friends sounded better than drinking alone, and the veggie burger would indicate that I was health conscious.

She continued to ask questions about how frequently I drank, what kind of liquor and what other drugs I had used. It was difficult to figure out the right answers, and I had a feeling my long silences belied my carefully constructed replies. After a while she put down her clipboard and looked directly at me with stunning blue-gray eyes. I wondered if I was going to faint. She was so healthy, she practically glowed. Maybe this was a person who was trustworthy. Maybe she could help me. And even if she couldn't—well, I hadn't given her my real name anyway. I could always escape. She said, almost gently, "I'm a little confused, it sounds as if you feel like everything is under control. Perhaps you can explain why you decided to come talk to us."

"I just want to know if it's due to drinking. I mean, what's happening. What I feel and hear sometimes in the morning and the afternoon. If I drink, it all goes away and I feel better, but I'm not sure it's at all related."

"Can you describe what's happening?"

As I explained the shaking, the nausea, the strange noises and panicky feelings, my voice sounded fractured and distant. I doubted that I was making any sense. But it was a relief to finally say it all out loud. The woman, whose name I had already forgotten, looked sympathetic. I thought I might be in love. Eventually, I trailed off. Vulnerable and desperate, I waited for her response. A frown, disapproval—even one wrong word could kill me off. Instead, she surprised me by asking what my plans were for the rest of the day.

"I guess I'll go home," I said, "as soon as I get up enough energy."

"Why don't you just stay here, Jenny?"

"Stay? I just came to ask if alcohol was making me sick. I wasn't planning on staying."

"Well, do you have anything better to do today?"

Now that she mentioned it, I couldn't think of a single plan for the next few months, let alone the next day—other than to drink. My world had gotten very small. I felt so slow and thick, the thought of walking home weighed me down. Even calling a cab and walking out to the parking lot might be more than I could handle.

"You really think I should stay here? For how long?"

"You could hang out until you feel better. As long as you like. A few days or longer might be good, or even just the afternoon."

"But I don't have any clothes here or any of my stuff."

"Does it really matter?" she asked. I looked down at what I had been wearing for so long. She had a point. A few days longer didn't matter at all.

CARE was no Betty Ford clinic. You got what you paid for, the staff liked to remind us. And like me, most clients at CARE were uninsured and broke. I didn't have any resources in the Amherst area other than Malcolm. My family was back in Boston, and I was not about to contact them. Besides, Jenny Bennett had no resources at all; she was an orphan, according to the story that I had told—she had been living on her own since age fifteen.

Given its clientele, CARE was partially state-funded; thus, not a lot of money went into the décor. The residential area was dingy and grim, just a bunch of little rooms with two or three bunk beds in each, some small dressers, and industrial gray wall-to-wall carpeting. Then there were four or five larger rooms for therapy groups, the visitors' lounge, the TV room, and the kitchen and dining room. These rooms, seen by visitors, were a little nicer than the bedrooms. The two detox rooms with white tile walls each had four hospital beds. That's where I spent my first week going through withdrawal. None of the windows in the entire complex opened.

On the day that I got out of detox, I was assigned a counselor named Mary. She brought me my freshly laundered clothes—I had been wearing a hospital gown and robe for the past week. She also gave me a daily schedule. Every day the same events happened, starting with Morning Meditation at seven-thirty a.m. and ending with lights out at ten. Then, scattered throughout the day, there was always a community meeting, a women's therapy group, an exercise period, family therapy, and an Alcoholics or Narcotics Anonymous meeting. Monday mornings there was a group in which we were supposed to set goals for the next week. This was always a struggle for me because I had no goals other than to avoid thinking about how I had screwed up my life. Wednesdays there was a group about food and health for women, and on Fridays there was one about self-esteem.

After going over the daily schedule and showing me the room that I was to share with Veeta and Kim, Mary took me to her office in the front of the building. The offices and outpatient clinic were separated from the residential part by a narrow hall ending with a heavy door with a large *Staff Only* sign. The warning seemed pointless since the locked door had to be buzzed open by the nurse at the main desk anyhow. For extra security, a mounted camera recorded all traffic in the passage.

Mary's office was decorated in warm colors; its walls were lined with Matisse, Bearden, and Klee prints, and an African Kente cloth hung over the desk. On a bookshelf sat photographs of friends or family. In one picture, Mary was surrounded by three unbearably lovely children and a man who gazed proudly at the camera. Obviously, unlike me, this was a black woman with a life, so when she started to ask about mine, I felt embarrassed to admit that drinking had narrowed it down to the point where there was nothing left to say.

"Why don't you tell me what brought you here, Jenny?" she asked.

"I was really sick."

"Well, yes, but what started the binge in the first place? Why were you drinking so much?" I stared at her because the question had never occurred to me. I had spent the last week wrestling to find reasons why I *shouldn't* drink. When I drank, I didn't have to worry about the emptiness gnawing inside, and the anxiety that I felt around others was smoothed away. *Why be sober* was the real question.

"Do other people in your family drink?" she asked, trying a different tactic. I thought about my grandfather's afternoon gin and tonics and my mother's endless bottles of wine. I thought of nights out at clubs in Boston with Malcolm.

"No."

"So you're a graduate student at the University of Massachusetts?" Mary asked.

"Sort of."

"Where did you go to college?"

"Harvard," I whispered, staring at the floor.

"Pretty impressive credentials." Mary smiled. "But then, alcoholics come from all walks of life." I just shrugged; she had no idea.

"All right." Mary sighed and put down her pen. "You'll start the program tomorrow morning at Level I. Here's an AA *Big Book*, a notebook to use as a journal, and a list of the first week's assignments."

Back in my new room, I looked over the literature that she had given me. The first step read, *We admitted that we were powerless over alcohol, that our lives had become unmanageable.* I began to laugh. *Become unmanageable?* When had it ever been manageable? Well, they would get no argument out of me on the first step.

If all the steps were this easy, I would be glowingly sober and healthy in no time at all.

But the next day was hard. I felt as if I had been ripped from the protective womb of the detox ward. There, all I had to do was lie in bed, sip ginger ale, and suffer. Outside, there were thirty other clients to interact with. My shyness left me tongue-tied while I observed the activity of the unit. The strict rules and routines were punctuated by clients fighting with staff, gossip in the smoke room about who was secretly dating whom, and the therapy groups where we were supposed to regularly pour our hearts out.

Those groups, along with my twice-per-week individual sessions with Mary, were the hardest part of CARE. Most of the clients would tell horror stories about their parents beating them and locking them in closets or trying to make ends meet on a too-small welfare check and government-subsidized housing. Maxine's husband was a coke addict who was trying to get custody of their kids. Another girl weighed only ninety-five pounds—she had gotten hooked on speed from diet pills. I was not about to talk about prep schools and dissertations among all that pathos. So when the counselors turned to me and asked if I have anything to say in group, I always said no.

The first two weeks were painful, but after a while being in a residential addictions program suited me surprisingly well. Life at CARE reminded me of Brookwood Hospital. I tried to take Harmony's advice from years ago when she told me that there were worse things than being thirteen and locked up at Brookwood.

"Relax. Just hang out and people-watch. You'll probably be here awhile. I like that spot myself," Harmony had said, pointing to a chair close to the door. "From there, you can keep your eye on the ward—you know, see who's being buzzed in and out—and still look out on those pretty lawns that they won't let us use."

"If they won't let anyone out, what are all those wooden chairs and benches for?"

"Oh, they'll let patients and their visitors use the lawn. I meant they won't let any of *us* use them." She jerked her thumb toward her chest and then back to me. I never found out what she meant, but I liked the complicity of her "us."

At CARE, I missed the booze but I was delighted with how simple life became when all major decisions were taken out of my hands. The staff dictated the structure of our days—when to sleep, when to wake up, which meetings we went to, the daily forced walk to the park—everything was planned and neatly penciled into the weekly schedule that they gave me as soon as I got out of the detox room. I didn't even need my to-do lists at CARE. Their handouts covered all events, major and minor. I liked checking the schedule occasionally to make sure that I was in the right place at the right time, but in truth that was unnecessary. All I had to do was relax and follow the other female residents; there was no place else to go. Actually, with the exception of the weeks spent lying on my futon, living at CARE was the least complicated that my life had ever been. Parents, friends, lovers were cleanly excised from my world. I had told no one where I was going; consequently, no one knew where to find me. I was spared the phone calls and visits that plagued other clients at least as often as this "support" soothed them. Anyway, by the time I had gotten to CARE, my drinking had left me almost completely isolated. It was unlikely that anyone was looking for me.

The only real disappointment was that the glowing woman who had interviewed me only did intakes; she didn't work directly with clients. So until Kate came, I had nowhere to focus my affections.

Veeta told me Kate's name and that she had been to CARE a bunch of times. None of the other clients liked her, but I noticed immediately how beautiful she was—really dark hair and eyes that looked at everything with disdain. I asked one of the nurses about her, and at first he said that he couldn't talk about another client with me, but then he relented and told me that she had *borderline personality disorder*. When I asked what that meant, he said, "You'll see."

The first day that Kate joined us in therapy, the counselor, Emily, asked Maxine to explain the rules of the group.

"Please, like I haven't been here before," Kate said, rolling her eyes and slouching.

"Maxine can refresh your memory just in case," Emily replied, nodding at Maxine to continue. Maxine was a wispy woman who appeared wan and exhausted at first glance but had a surprising bossy streak and a penchant for gossip.

"Whatever," said Kate. Her voice was sullen, but a smile played at the corner of her lips. Personality and pretense were so entangled with Kate that it was impossible to tell what was real and what was an act.

"Okay. The most important rule is that whatever is said in here, stays in here." Maxine started to recite the rules that I was hearing for the fourth time in less than two weeks. "That means that you can't talk about what happened in group outside of group. No leaving the group in the middle. No touching or hugging anyone without their permission, even if they're crying. No threatening of other group members. Try not to use graphic language when describing using drugs or if someone hurt you. No violence, like you can't throw chairs or anything like that. That's about it. Okay?"

"Okay, Kate?" Emily repeated, looking hard at Kate. Kate looked at me and smiled. She stood up and in one smooth motion kicked her metal folding chair across the room.

"Fuck this shit," she said, walking out of the room. As she passed my chair, Kate's fingertips brushed my shoulder. I wondered if the others noticed that she had broken all of Emily's rules in a single gesture.

"Well, let's get started, shall we?" said Emily. "Does anyone have any feelings about what Kate just did?"

On the Fourth of July, there were no groups; instead, we had a picnic and a barbeque in the park. I was a little worried that someone who knew me from my other life would come by, but no one did. It was one of those perfect days. The sun lit the sky bright blue and the grass blades rippled gently—an invitation for picnickers to lie down and quietly doze. Steve had ordered pretty much everything that the clients asked for, and we cooked because he, like most of the staff, had the day off. The anorexic girl even ate without having to be supervised by staff.

Some of the clients played Frisbee and others just sat and talked. John M. sat and smoked endless cigarettes with Nick as they played checkers on a park bench. Veeta and Maxine seemed delighted to take charge of the food preparation. The two gave orders on everything from how to light the grill to how many napkins to pass out. No one bristled at their bossiness. There were no outbursts, no tears, no arguments. Not even any dramatics from Kate, who was the calmest I had ever seen her. Generally she was mercurial, flirtatious, and coy with all the guys one minute, stormy and angry with the staff or almost rude with the other clients the next. But the holiday away from structured treatment agreed with her. Kate and I lay on our backs in the grass and dandelions near the gazebo reading Rilke poems out loud from the book I had brought. That was the first day I believed a life without alcohol might be bearable after all. I didn't want the soft haze of a drink; I just wanted to bask sleepily in the sun, surrounded by the buzz of contented conversation and people who knew and liked Jenny Bennett.

The previous Fourth of July had also been perfect in a different way. Or at least it started out perfect, and then turned sour. Malcolm and I had spent the weekend at my uncle's house on Martha's Vineyard which had a small but vibrant black summer community including many African-American celebrities, professionals, and elite. Seeing Malcolm mingling and laughing with my uncle's guests, anyone would have thought he'd grown up in the wealthy enclave, not me. He was perfectly at ease, standing tall in a polo shirt, chinos, and docksiders, his head held high, almost regal. Tucked away in the corner of the great room, which opened onto the deck above the water, I watched Malcolm and thought again how lucky I was to have him as a buffer against my relatives and family friends. When I came alone to these functions, I was bombarded with questions about school and career. Behind the bright queries lay the disappointment that, at nearly thirty, I was unmarried and unfocused. In my mother's eyes was the fear that I was still as moody and miserable as in my adolescence, and unspoken but present was the quietly smoldering anger about the years I had spent loving women. People asked about my dissertation, but when I spoke of Gender and Representation in Twentieth-Century African-American Painting, their eyes glazed over and my words sounded esoteric and unwieldy even to me. In a family of doctors, lawyers, and businessmen, my choice to study African-American Art History was considered eccentric, if not willfully self-indulgent.

But hiding in Malcolm's shadow that day, I was able to drink glass after glass of wine unobserved. He worked the room while I sat quietly watching the golden-red sun set over the water. The few times that anyone approached me with a question or comment, the small talk, usually so painful and awkward, tumbled out of my lips like cool water on a hot day.

Later that night, upstairs in a guestroom, Malcolm accused me of being cold.

"You should have been networking, trying to hook me up with some job possibilities. You just sat there like a cold lump of dough."

"Is this cold, baby?" I asked, undoing my top three buttons so that he could see the negligee I'd brought to wear for him. He frowned.

"Malcolm, graduation is almost a year away. You worry too much. Come to bed. I can hook you up!" I gave an exaggerated wink and made my voice throaty and lewd to make him laugh. Finally he started chuckling.

"You're pretty cute," he admitted. "But I'm cuter."

I waggled my eyebrows, grinning as I pulled him down. His weight on my chest was comforting while we kissed. But he came back to the topic a few minutes later.

"Seriously, Georgie. Your mother and stepfather know practically every important African-American on the eastern seaboard. And your father has done business with lots of them. It's like your upbringing left you completely unaware of the real world. You just don't get how hard it is to succeed as a black person. I'm fighting discrimination at school, in the job market, everywhere. And the one time you could extend yourself to help a bit, you do nothing at all."

I refused to respond. Instead, I lay on the bed staring and calculating how long it would be before everyone left the party so I could make a quiet trip to the liquor cabinet.

"It's obvious that you don't care," he said, biting off words as if they tasted bitter.

"Oh no. Is the 'Man' out to get you?" I said. Alcohol made my voice hard and mean. I spoke deliberately, slowly, but Malcolm's response came bursting out so quickly, it surprised both of us.

"Bitch!" he snapped, looking angrier than I'd ever seen him.

I buttoned my shirt back together and sat at the edge of the bed with my arms folded across my chest. Malcolm leaned against the furthest wall, breathing heavily. He seemed to expect an explosive retort. I stared back silently.

"What is wrong with you?" Malcolm demanded.

"*Bitch*," I repeated finally. "That's quite original. I'm afraid you'll have to do better than that if you actually want to make an impact."

Malcolm didn't answer, or I didn't hear him. I was concentrating intently on the sound of my slippers flapping against the hardwood floor and the terse click of the door shutting behind me.

"Then Frank smacked me into the kitchen wall. He gets like that when he's drunk."

Darlene was describing the last fight she'd had with her boyfriend. Several of the other women in the group were nodding. As usual, Kate sat smiling nonchalantly with her feet stretched out into the center of the circle. She could have easily been relaxing in front of a television or sitting with a group of friends drinking a beer.

"How did you feel?" Mary asked. She was running the women's therapy group that day.

"How did I feel? Like someone just beat me upside the head," Darlene said, poker-faced, and then ruined the effect by winking at the other group members. Veeta, Maxine, and Kim grinned.

"But what was going on in your head, knowing that the man you care about was treating you that way?" Mary was a careful prospector who would briefly smile at the wisecracks then continue to mine us for details, feelings, and fallout. I had vowed on the first day that I would not give her anything of myself.

"When I get beat, I get paralyzed," one of the other women volunteered.

"Yeah, it's like you can't move except to try to protect your head," another agreed. "It is the most helpless feeling in the world."

Generally these conversations quickly fell into a comparison of bruises and broken bones, but today was different. The room felt very close. My eyes hurt as they tried to adjust to the light, which seemed to keep shifting from too dark to too bright. Darlene was crying softly.

"Just feel so trapped," she kept repeating. "There's no place to go. The thing is, I love him so much I can't breathe. You know what I'm saying? I'm afraid if I can't get clean, I'll lose him, and then it feels like I'm going to die."

I felt myself float up to the ceiling of the room. I could see everyone sitting in a circle looking at Darlene. I saw myself staring at my feet. I didn't understand what everyone was getting so upset about. People come and people go.

"Jenny, do you have anything to share?" Mary's voice was sudden and loud. At first I couldn't speak, but then I managed to whisper, "No," from my perch on the ceiling.

"You're crying and you look like you have something to say. Perhaps you have some feedback for Darlene?" Mary prodded.

"I'm sorry, but I can't relate," I said. "No one has ever hit me before." I hadn't noticed my tears.

"That's okay if you've never shared Darlene's experience, but maybe you can just relate to the emotion."

"No."

Kate suddenly got up. "Can't you just leave her alone?" she said to Mary. She walked over and put her arms around my shoulders, completely ignoring the rule about no physical contact. I was as surprised as anyone.

Kate was a white woman with wild black hair that she kept clasped behind her neck with large, jeweled barrettes—the handmade kind sold in expensive boutiques. But I knew for a fact that she had next to no money. She and Ben didn't work, making do with disability checks and the occasional drug deal. Yet her clothing looked as if it stepped off the pages of the old *Sassy Magazine*: short pleated skirts, cotton T-shirts, leggings, and those trendy, clunky platform shoes. The look that pretends to have been on a thrift store rack but was really bought at Urban Outfitters or the Gap.

I had come to CARE with only the clothes on my back, and although in my second week I got a two-hour pass to go home and pack a suitcase, I still wore baggy, worn clothing chosen to make sure that no one glanced at me twice. I couldn't figure out whether Kate liked me because I was not a threat or if my frumpiness was a challenge to her makeover skills and fashion sense. After we became friends, we would spend the hour between evening chores and bedtime trying on makeup and combing each other's hair. Those evenings, CARE was transformed from the Center for Addiction, Rehabilitation, and Education to a teenage slumber party.

John G. used to tease us when we emerged, perfumed and made up. "All dressed up and no place to go! CARE ain't no prom, ladies. This ain't no Girl Scout camp!" John G. would laugh and nudge John M. in the ribs. John M. would look up from his game of checkers or crossword and laugh so hard he'd begin to wheeze.

"Fuck you both! Fuck you all," Kate always said, but she smiled.

I remained stuck at Level I for nearly a month. People who had entered after me progressed from Level I to II to III to graduation, while I spent my time doing the same Level I homework assignments over and over again. I wrote out the ways alcohol had affected my life a dozen times and repeatedly listed my transgres-

sions against others; I filled sheets of paper with healthy alterna-
tives to drinking, and I could recite both the twelve steps and
twelve traditions letter perfect. Yet the study habits that had served
me well in college and graduate school seemed useless at CARE.
To move up a level, a client needed to gain the unanimous votes
of all her peers. Actually, you really needed the counselors' stamp
of approval, as the clients' votes were often vetoed by the counselors. Landing at CARE was proof that addicts were incapable of
making good decisions, the counselors often reminded us. CARE
was not a democracy, they liked to point out.

Kate said that the two of us made up the remedial class in
what she called, almost affectionately, the CARE Detention
Center. The difference was that Kate didn't care whether she progressed; in fact, she seemed almost proud of her inability to move
past Level I. Every sneer, every smirk, every smart remark indicated
that she found the whole program a giant waste of time.

"I'm just doing time, waiting for things to calm down.
Getting my strength back up to go back out," she explained to me,
as we played cards on the afternoon that the women's group had
voted down her promotion for the second time.

"Don't you want to graduate?" I asked.

"Jenny, this isn't like Harvard! Graduating from here doesn't
mean much other than you can play the CARE game with a little
AA religion thrown in for good measure." Kate threw down a face
card with vehement disgust. Picking up the discarded queen
would give me gin; it would allow me to beat her for the first time.
I ignored the card.

"Well, I know it isn't a Ph.D., but it is something, isn't it?" I
was anxious. Contradiction might lead to abandonment. "I mean,
it means that you're getting well. You want to be sober, right?"

"Look, wanting to be sober has nothing to do with it. Like
Veeta, she's been through CARE three times already. She graduated

and graduated and graduated some more. She'll graduate again next week. And three months from now, she'll be strung out again. But she thinks she's more committed to sobriety than me 'cause she can go from Level I to IV in a few weeks. What a hypocrite. Besides, those bitches have it out for me. And the staff too. They'll never vote me up out of spite."

I noticed that Kate had not really answered my question, but I didn't say anything. The reason why Kate wasn't moving ahead was clear, but my impasse mystified me. I dutifully completed assignments and wrote in my journal. I never harassed the staff or fought with other clients. Actually, I was the model patient. Yet time after time I was turned down with the comment that I wasn't really working.

Once or twice each week there was a graduation at CARE. Graduation meant that the client had completed all four levels of the program. Rehabilitated graduates were ready to face the outside world without the comforting protection of alcohol and illegal drugs. As for legal drugs, there were plenty of those to go around. Many of the clients were seen by the clinic psychiatrist and prescribed medication to mute mood swings, calm panic, and lift the depression that ruled our lives. My only visit to the psychiatrist took place in my second month at CARE.

Mary came and got me out of group that day to meet Dr. Harding. He was a short man with balding red hair and a brusque manner that left me feeling like a type, not a person.

"You are feeling depressed," he stated.

"No."

"It says here that you don't speak in groups and that you isolate. It says here that you are always reading." Dr. Harding stabbed my chart with stubby fingers.

"I guess."

"Why are you always reading?" He sounded suspicious, as if reading were something unsavory, akin to heroin or cocaine. I remembered sixth grade at Ellis, when I had brought a book to recess every day. My teacher eventually began to take it away, urging me to join the other girls at jump rope, jacks, and four-square. "Socialize, Georgette!" she'd command over her shoulder, striding from the courtyard into the school, carrying my book, as I stood with my back against the wall staring into space.

Now I stared silently at Dr. Harding as he asked his irrelevant questions. He really didn't seem to require answers. After a few minutes, he scribbled on my chart.

"We'll start you on Prozac. Twenty milligrams a day."

That night, Kate and I sat in her room. I was doing homework and she was flipping through a fashion magazine from the supply Ben had brought last time he visited.

"So Dr. Hard-On gave you some happy pills?" Kate asked, grimacing.

"Yeah, Prozac."

"I knew someone on Prozac once who killed someone."

"Well, that's encouraging," I said.

"Oh my God!" Kate gasped, and threw her hands to her face. "Jenny, did you just make a joke? I can't believe it. My morose little Jenny has finally cracked a smile." Kate hugged me and tried to rub my head at the same time.

"Obviously, the Prozac is working already," I replied. As I pushed her off, I laughed for what seemed like the first time since Malcolm left.

"What are you doing anyhow? More fabulous homework?"

"Yeah, Mary usually collects journals on Thursday, so I'm trying to catch up."

"Let's see." Kate grabbed my notebook off the bed before I

could stop her and read aloud. "*Tuesday afternoon, it was raining and we couldn't walk in the park. Instead, we had aerobics in the dining room with a Richard Simmons videotape.* Gee, Jenny, this is some real exciting stuff you got here. What the fuck is this shit?" Kate tossed my journal back.

"Hey, at least I write in my journal!" I couldn't believe how loose and carefree I felt. Suddenly, I was secure enough to risk a little teasing.

"Ha! That shows what you know. For your information, Miss Jenny Goody-Two-Shoes, I do write in my journal. I figure poor Emily needs a little excitement in her life. It's obvious she isn't getting any action." Kate went to her dresser and pulled a green notebook out.

"Listen up, Jen!" She stared to read: "*Ben and I dropped ecstasy that night. We had incredible sex. First I blew him. Then we got out my vibrator—*"

"Kate! You aren't going to turn that in, are you?"

"Sure, I do it all the time. You should too. Why don't you write about your boyfriend, what's-his-name, instead of Richard Fucking Simmons. Live a little."

"His name was Malcolm, and we aren't going out anymore." I thought about the last time that Malcolm and I had sex. Afterwards, he tried to hold me. I loved him for the effort, but I was tense and rigid as a board. I stared at the ceiling waiting for him to fall asleep. When his breathing slowed, I carefully got up, went downstairs, and poured a glass of red wine.

After a month stuck at the first level, I was finally promoted in late July. By that time, almost everyone who was at CARE when I first arrived had already gone. Veeta had graduated a few days before. Her entire family came: kids, boyfriend, mother, and sisters. Part of me was jealous, but having heard her complain about her sisters a thousand times, and about how abusive her mother was, I also felt superior. At least I didn't pretend to be close to my family.

The first assignment of Level II was to write out a life history. I had no idea what they wanted me to say. *I was born. I drank. I ended up at CARE. End-of-story. In the middle, I had a moment of happiness with my boyfriend, and then it was gone.*

"I'm out of here," Kate told me right before she left. "Don't tell anyone."

"What?" I was confused. I thought that she meant that she was leaving the smoke room. She pulled out another Marlboro and lit it off the butt of her last one.

"Jenny, you are such a dunce. I mean, Jenny, I'm breaking out. I've had about enough. This isn't life; it's pretty much the damned loony bin."

For a minute I stared at her, unable to believe that she was really going. Then I gave her a quick hug and whispered my real name in her ear. Kate's eyes widened. She kissed my cheek. My eyelids felt heavy and I closed them involuntarily while I savored the sensation. It was so rare to feel another person's touch at CARE. When I opened my eyes again, she was gone.

Kate's desire to leave was incomprehensible. Inside CARE it was possible to forget Malcolm for whole stretches at a time. Memorizing the AA steps, praying, reciting daily affirmations, and attending all those therapy groups and meetings neatly filled in the cracks in my mind where thoughts of him usually resided.

Kate snarled and complained and ran away. I worked hard, crying each time I did not get to progress a level, reassuring my counselor that, yes, I wanted to be there and, yes, I was committed to my sobriety. But somewhere deep down, I was just going through the motions. I had no real desire to get sober permanently.

* * *

John M. ran away from CARE in the middle of one of the daily walks. As the rest of us headed down one park path, he turned on his crutches and limped away in the opposite direction. The staff couldn't follow him for fear of losing everyone else. I watched him go, knowing that in less than two weeks it would be my turn to leave. I had finally, after three months, finished the program. I wasn't graduating because my counselor said that if I wasn't willing to open up and talk, then there was nothing more that they could do for me.

Although I was enraged and terrified, I was following the staff's recommendation that I leave. There really wasn't any other choice. Living at CARE had been standing still in time. For so long the world had been whirling around me, and fear had ruled my life. CARE was certainty—the certainty of a daily routine, the certain righteousness of AA, the fundamental sameness of all the clients' stories though the details differed. At CARE, that certainty prevailed and with it fear was kept at bay. Watching John M. go, I couldn't help but think that empty-handed, limping, and homeless, he was better equipped to face the outside world than I would ever be.

That afternoon Mary was late coming to get me for our session. When she finally rushed in she apologized.

"I'm really sorry. Our staff meeting ran over. Things are pretty crazy around here with two runaways in one week."

"It doesn't matter," I said, following her toward the front of the building.

"What do you think about Kate and John leaving?" she asked. I just shrugged.

"You don't have any thoughts or feelings at all? I thought you and Kate were good friends. Are you worried about her going back out and using? And you're leaving in a few days, aren't you worried that you might go out and use again?"

"I guess. I don't know. Kate can take care of herself." I thought about telling Mary about watching John M. leave and my realization in the park, but I couldn't find the words. I even thought of telling her the name that I had whispered in Kate's ear, but it was too hard to give away what little power I had.

"Well, she must have thought you were pretty good friends. We found a note in her bureau. She wanted you to have her things." Mary pulled a cardboard box from underneath her desk. On the top, I could see Kate's paisley dressing-gown. Suddenly, I felt a small fragment of resistance break off. I almost felt like crying.

"What are you feeling right now?" Mary asked.

"I don't know. I don't have the words."

"Do you think you could draw a picture?"

"Maybe."

After the session, I carried Kate's box back to my room and went through it. There wasn't much left of the woman I'd probably never see again. Under the clothing I found some fashion magazines, and under them there was a green notebook. Feeling vaguely guilty, I opened it up to the first page and read about how pissed off she was at her parents. And how everyone was a shit. But a few pages in, I saw the name, *Jen Bennett*.

She's a girl who I like a lot. She's cool but really sad. I don't know what her deal is. She never says anything about herself, but she listens all the time. I like her though because I can tell she's a fabulous person. I wish I knew her story.

I put down the notebook and tried to identify the feeling in my throat and stomach. It was deeper than any recent sensation, and I had a hard time naming it. But somehow the feeling seemed faintly familiar, like something from a long time ago. The resistance was shifting, and with the thaw came emotions like fear and maybe some hope as well. I changed from my jeans and T-shirt into some of Kate's clothing. Looking in the mirror, I could hardly recognize myself in the maroon turtleneck and short black pleated skirt. My legs wore gray tights painted with purple and maroon flowers, and on my feet were a pair of knee-high brown leather boots.

I took the stack of magazines with me out to the nurses' station, where I checked out a pair of scissors and some glue. Sitting down at a table in the dining room, I began to make a collage. When I glanced up, Mary was looking at me, but I wasn't sure if she really saw me.

"Maybe we can work something out so that you can stay, Jenny." Mary smiled as she extended the offer.

"That's not my name," I murmured. She didn't seem to hear.

why i drank
(or, the answers)

i 'd been in rehab for more than three months when the counselors realized I had been lying about my identity since day one. A social work professor who had begun some research project at the clinic ratted me out. I didn't know the professor, but she must have recognized me from the university, and my story quickly unraveled from there. The counselors went into a long staff meeting to decide whether to throw me out or not. After about two hours, Mary emerged and gave me a thumbs-up and a small smile. She solemnly presented me with a list of questions that had to be answered "with complete openness and integrity" in order for me to remain at CARE and progress to the next level of the program. She pointed out that I was lucky to be given a second and even a third chance in the program since I had been so resistant all along.

I didn't feel lucky. After months of numbness, my emotions had come flooding back as anger. I felt angry with the staff and their questions. Angry at their assumption that only a person with some dark mystery would drink herself to death. There was no mystery, no hidden trauma in my life, only a love of the numbness that alcohol could bring. Furthermore, I was appalled at the endless parade of clients arriving, leaving, and returning to the rehab, sometimes within days of their supposed recoveries. These men and women shared their most intimate secrets as if the group's insights could somehow alleviate their suffering. Dragging out their horrors for the group's scrutiny, they became exposed in the world. Then they went home to their same lives, still themselves; only now a layer of protection had been stripped off. Was it any wonder that so many relapsed? Yet CARE was now handing me a list of intrusive questions and demanding answers that I was not willing to share even if I had known the truth.

When was the first time that you used alcohol or drugs?
When did you start abusing alcohol and drugs?
Describe your childhood.
What was the most frightening thing that ever happened to you?
Did you get along with your parents while growing up?
What have been the significant relationships in your life?

Finally, I wrote Mary a letter starting with the last question. Elaine was my first girlfriend, if you didn't count the previous Thanksgiving night when I furtively made out with one of my brothers' girlfriends in the hallway outside my room. That far more experienced girl had left me with a hickey I had to hide from my boyfriend and an unexpected embarrassing longing to sleep with some of my classmates. I didn't actually like most of the girls at Ellis but suddenly found myself fascinated by their lips and necks when they spoke in class. I daydreamed about Sarah especially. We were both in the school play each year, and I pictured us dressed in the Shakespearean costumes as she cornered me in one of the dark recesses backstage and slipped her hand into the bodice of my dress.

I began to frequent the women's bookstore in Cambridge, carefully comparing myself to the real and fictional people described in the lesbian literature that I bought and hid behind the novels lining the shelves of my room. Starting to date Elaine seemed to settle the nagging fear that had begun to haunt me. Deciding that I was gay was a relief, and telling my parents was almost a delight.

I came out one Sunday night in the fall of my senior year of high school. I'd gotten caught in a lie that I told frequently.

"Where have you been?" my mother had accosted me as soon as I stepped in the door.

"Dad's." I kept my tone of voice casual. After hanging up my coat, I tried to get to the stairway, but my mother blocked access by standing in the middle of the narrow front hall of our duplex. I was startled that she was pushing me on the topic; it was seven years before Clinton's election, but my family had already been practicing our own version of the military's *Don't Ask, Don't Tell* policy for a long time.

"Don't you dare lie to me, Georgette Collins. Michael called yesterday and he says he hasn't seen you in weeks. Don't you have any idea how worried I get when you pull this shit?" My mother shook as she yelled. I stared, open-mouthed. I had been thirteen the first time I stayed out without permission. After nearly four years, it seemed odd that she still cared.

"Mother, you are ranting like some crazy woman. You're totally out of control. I was at a friend's house, okay?"

"No, not okay. Number one, the agreement was that you spend weekends with Michael. Number two, at this point, I can't trust a word that you say. If this behavior doesn't stop, I'll send you to the island. You can see how you like being stuck in the middle of nowhere with my mother to answer to."

"Number one, I don't like staying at Daddy's. Number two, I'd be thrilled to go live with Nina. Anything to get me out of this hellhole." I mimicked her tone—a trick that my older brothers had always used to infuriate me.

"What's wrong with staying at your father's? You'd be lucky to end up with a man as decent as your father instead of one of the little dropouts you date."

"Number one, if Daddy's so great, what are you doing with Eric? Number two, I'm not interested in any man like my father. And number three, I'm not interested in any man at all." I stopped trying to get around her. Now that we were finally at a moment of truth, I wanted to play out the scene. I was relishing her reaction.

"What is that supposed to mean?"

"It means I'm a lesbian." My announcement was triumphant. I felt like I had won a victory. It felt even better when she slapped me. Next she started to cry and call for Eric. I went upstairs to my room.

And that brought me right to *Did you get along with your parents while growing up?* The answer was obvious. By the time I moved in with Elaine, I had run away enough times that my parents were exhausted. They didn't put up a fight to stop me from living with my lover, though I was still a minor and my school had three months left before graduation. We were all worn out and slightly dazed from other clashes: college (I hadn't applied), my increasingly sporadic visits to my father (though I was supposed to go every weekend), and my refusal to actually speak to the therapist my school had mandated I see weekly.

"I'm going," I threatened. "You can't stop me."

"How do you propose to pay rent or for your food or transportation, or anything else for that matter?" My mother sat poised over a legal brief, highlighter in hand and glass of wine nearby, barely looking at me.

"I've gotten a job. It's only twelve hours a week, but that'll be enough as long as Dad still pays my tuition. My girlfriend says I don't have to pay rent." I waited for my mother to ask me about the job. I wasn't sure whether I was going to tell her the truth— that it was dancing in a dyke bar. Part of me was worried that she would get upset enough to put a stop to it. I was still underage and would be working under the table. But another part of me wanted her anger. I wanted her to swoop in and rescue me from the reck- lessness that I had cultivated for the past several years. Mother didn't ask.

"We'll miss you around here. We'd like you to stay." Eric was always trying to smooth things over. "Right, Verna?" Standing behind her, he put his hands on her shoulders and gave her a lit- tle shake.

My mother was silent, then she put down her pen and looked directly at me. "Georgette, you're not a child. I can't force you to do anything. But before you leave, I think you should consider whether you're burning bridges because you actually want them gone or because you've fallen in love with the sight of the fire."

Mother's attention only lasted a few seconds. She picked her highlighter back up and returned to her work. I shrugged. Her question was not worth considering.

Home from Howard for spring break, Chris helped me move a few boxes of books and two suitcases to Elaine's apartment in Central Square. Actually, Elaine lived less than a mile from my mother's house and merely a subway and bus ride from my father's, but I felt a sense of independence that made the move take on the weight of a momentous occasion.

* * *

So why was it that so many gays and lesbians were alcoholics and addicts? I was quite pleased with myself for coming out, and people who love themselves don't go around killing their brain cells, right? Life was grand when I went to live with my vegetarian lover and her organic-yoga-leftist friends. Elaine and her four roommates lived in one of those boxcar apartments on the top floor of a three-family house. Each room was directly behind the others and opened into the next through a set of French doors. The apartment ended with a large eat-in kitchen and a bathroom, cleaned according to the rotating schedule posted on the refrigerator. A smiling '50s housewife scrubbing shiny faucets decorated the paper along with the caption, *Thou Shall Not Piss Off Your Housemates*.

The others were all out of school already and working a series of slacker jobs. They thought my homework assignments were hilarious. Our favorite game was to get really stoned and repeatedly roll across the floor to play "telephone" by whispering messages through the cracks in the doors between the rooms. By the time sentences like, "Georgie needs to know about the battles of the Civil War," traveled from Elaine's room to the front bedroom and back, answers were garbled into, "Generally, Abe blinked then uselessly granted the medieval gore." My final semester at school was not a great success.

We dropped acid sometimes to hear ourselves think better. My trips resulted in the wild, colorful paintings that adorned Elaine's walls, or page after page of nonsensical journal entries that I would reread later to glean some psychedelic wisdom. In my ordinary life, I wanted the clarity that I got during those eight-hour journeys then immediately forgot as I awoke, bleary-eyed and cotton-tongued, the next day. Other times, Elaine and I spent the day alone together in bed; often we didn't even have sex. We just liked being together. Lying there on the mattress on the floor, she would kiss the scars on my arms and cry. I loved her, or at least I thought I did. I loved that she cried.

But that wasn't the very first time I used.

At the beginning of ninth grade, I was thirteen and still trying to belong. Not too long after one particular party, I stopped caring. Why should a square peg keep on trying to fit into a round hole?

As soon as I walked into that suburban mansion, an unfamiliar boy offered me a "rum and bug juice." Maybe those were the days before children were drilled about drug and alcohol abuse in schools. Or maybe I just hadn't absorbed those lessons. In any case, although I'd never tasted liquor before, it didn't occur to me to refuse.

Like all the other partygoers, this boy was disheveled in that clean-cut preppy sort of way. He had translucent skin and dark untidy hair. The punch had stained his lips red. I don't remember anything about that night except for the boy. He shot out questions even faster than he poured drinks.

"You go to Ellis, right?" he asked. "I've heard about you." That question made me self-conscious and thus required another drink to answer. He also asked if I was a virgin. Did I know Mark James, the black kid who went to his school? Did I tan in the summertime and had I ever seen Arthur Ashe play tennis? Did I listen to reggae or rap? Did I smoke weed? How did it feel to be black? And then, when I couldn't stop laughing, he asked whether this was my first time—drunk, that is. No, I lied (somehow it seemed important to hide my naïveté), I get bombed and smoke pot all the time. Much later, upstairs in a dark bedroom, the boy asked, "Is your pubic hair kinky too?" I let him unzip my jeans to find out. I remember being so pleased with those jeans. They were Calvin Klein, a forgive-me present from my father instead of the no-name brands that my mother usually bought. The night of my first drink was the night of my first blackout. I was so upset the next day when I woke up with a pain drilling beneath my eyebrows and wearing someone else's pants and underwear. I knew that it would take a long time to guilt-trip my father into buying another pair.

The following summer, on the island, I didn't like anyone. For the first week of August, I barely came out of the room that I shared with my cousin Nancy. I ignored her when she tried to talk to me. I spent my days listening to my Walkman and reading books. I screamed at Alex and Chris when they knocked on the door. Even my littlest cousins tried to get me out of my shell by offering me their crayons and construction paper. I was nasty to them all. Finally, my stepfather marched into the room and without a word lifted me up and carried me back out through the louvered doors onto the patio. He dropped me into the deep end of the pool. I came up sputtering to see my family standing around laughing. I thought about it a second and had to laugh too.

For the rest of the summer, Alex, Nancy, my cousin Jason, and I drove around the island every day. We stopped every few miles to buy food by the side of the road. We stuffed ourselves with fruit, coconut meat, grapenut ice cream, and spicy jerk pork. Sometimes we bought Ting and sometimes we got Red Stripe beer. At night we hung out at one of the nearby resort's club and casino. We danced and gambled and got drunk, ignoring our parents completely. Once we drove all the way to Montego Bay for an all-night reggae concert. Lying on a blanket under the stars, I felt the rhythm and got stoned for the first time. At first Alex tried to stop me, then he shrugged and said I might as well try it sooner or later. The rest of the month passed in a warm buzz. By the end of August, the best feeling in my life was blacking out and feeling nothing at all.

* * *

I knew that the folks at CARE would assume that blacking out the first time was one of the most frightening things that had ever happened to me. But actually, it didn't even make the top-ten list. The scariest was my father's heart attack. My parents had always predicted each other's deaths.

"You're going to give your mother a stroke," Daddy said the day he came home to discover my brothers and me balanced on the side roof. We had dressed my Barbies in evening gowns and seated them in dump trucks for the ride over the shingles, through the air, and into the yard below.

"Let's not tell your father. This will kill him," my mother said dry-eyed, standing over me in the hospital the day after I opened my artery for the first time. Ten minutes later, she began crying and handed the telephone to me. "You'll have to call him. I can't bear to give him the news."

In a way, it wasn't a surprise to get the news from Mother about a month after I came out of the closet. In a way, I had been waiting for it. One day after school, I was lying on my bed reading lesbian erotica. My mother entered my room without knocking. She was home early from work. I shoved the book under my pillow.

"Mother—" I began to snarl.

"Michael's in Mass General. He collapsed at work."

"What's wrong with Daddy?" My mother looked blurry, and my mouth tasted of metal.

"He's finally had a heart attack. This afternoon while you were at school. I didn't want to interrupt your calculus exam, but I called Alex and Chris. They're both flying into Logan tonight. Eric will be home any minute, he'll drive you to the hospital."

Many hours later, my brothers and I were allowed to see him one by one. During my turn, I couldn't stop crying. My powerful father looked frail among all the technology; there were monitors blinking, motors humming, and plastic tubes everywhere. His usually chestnut skin was the color of meat left too long in the freezer.

"What's wrong, little girl?" Dad whispered.

"I'm so sorry, Daddy. I'm sorry."

"Georgie, this isn't your fault," he claimed, but I didn't believe him. He must have said something to my mother though. That weekend, she and Eric knocked on my bedroom door. As usual, I was lying in bed, but this time I just stared at the ceiling.

"Honey," Mom sat beside to me, "your dad's heart attack had nothing to do with you. He just needs to take better care of himself, and take medication." She pulled my head into her lap. Resting my cheek on her thigh, I curled into a loose fetal position. I felt very young.

"Mama, are you sure it wasn't because I told him I was a lesbian?"

"Georgette, that's silly. You know better than to think that." Mother tugged at me so that I was half sitting up and half leaning against her. She kept her arms around me until I felt loved and cared for. Eric was silent, but he held my hand too.

And that was what growing up was like, feeling young and loved sometimes, guilty and angry other times, and once in a while terrified out of my mind. I imagine everyone's childhood was like that.

When I finished writing out my answers with "complete honesty and integrity," I flipped through to the very last page of my journal. In tiny, almost indecipherable letters, I put my addendum on the inside back cover: *There you have it. Answers to all your questions. My life in a nutshell. When I drank, how drunk I got, and why I was drinking. Have you found the key to my sobriety? Do you think that you actually know me? Think again. What if I told you that I made it all up? Am I in recovery now?*

brotherly love

i had been in other hospitals over the years. There was the series of short stays on adolescent wards as a teenager when my parents were desperate to find some answers. The hospitalizations mostly coincided with my school vacations. Being crazy in my family was bad enough but missing school was considered unacceptable. Then there was the time when I was twenty-one that Amanda tried to have me committed. I spent a week in Brookwood biding my time, planning our breakup. But this was my first time at a state psychiatric hospital, and it was a whole different world than the airy white buildings and green lawns of my earlier trips to the loony bin.

Farrell State was a dumping ground for uninsured or underinsured adults. I arrived there when the staff at CARE decided that my safety was "compromised." I had lived in the center's halfway house for several months after my graduation from their residential detox. I thought things were going well. I wrote in my journal, attended five AA meetings per week, went to the gym daily, and secretly cut up my arms in the bathroom each night. I didn't realize that I wasn't being as discreet as I thought until I woke up one morning to find a police officer in my room, ready to escort me to Farrell.

The Farrell grounds looked like a cross between my older brother's boarding school and an abandoned army base. A quadrangle of ugly brick buildings made up the wards. Several were empty, remnants of the days before de-institutionalization. I was alarmed by the staff that doled out privileges, restrictions, and medications seemingly at random. Several doctors and nurses seemed angrier than the patients. At the same time, somehow, I was privately satisfied to be there. Farrell was the bottom, no doubt, and after years of seeking it, I had finally arrived.

While the other hospitals and CARE had insisted that I go to treatment and therapy, the Farrell staff didn't seem to care what I did as long as I remained vertical. A patient could sit in the green plastic chairs lining the corridor, staring into space for hours, or she could spend all day muttering to herself if she chose. But within ten minutes of lying down on one of the uncomfortable sofas or trying to sneak back into bed for a nap, a nurse's assistant would start screaming in my ear that sleeping during the day was not allowed. Consequently, my two favorite forms of escape, alcohol and slumber, were denied to me. Perhaps I would never have bothered trying to "get well" if they had just allowed me to curl up occasionally. So maybe they actually knew what they were doing, but I thought it was plain malice. Anyway, as it was, I knew after a few days of being constantly shaken awake that I had to get out of Farrell as soon as possible.

Anna Walker was my social worker. Her biggest concern was that I had no place to go. CARE had informed the hospital that I was not welcome back in the halfway house, and I had lost my apartment months earlier. My lack of plans for the future worried her, Anna Walker said. I offered completing my degree as a full-time activity, but research and writing weren't considered enough to fill the gaps between AA and therapy. I pointed out that plenty of people just worked on their dissertations all day, and Anna Walker pointed out that my last dissertation attempt had resulted in drinking all day.

"Besides," she said on my seventh day there, "how are you going to support yourself?" We were at a standstill. I needed a plan. Anna Walker was one of those do-good liberal women, mostly harmless, except this one held the key to my discharge. My strategy was to make her feel guilty enough to release me.

"What about going to live with your family?" She brought up this idea several times.

"Not an option."

"Can you explain why?"

"No. It's a black thing, you wouldn't understand." I figured she'd fall for this clichéd reply.

"Please, Georgette, will you try to work with me? I really want to help. I care about you. Won't you let me in just a little?" I began to whistle the song "Getting to Know You" from the musical *The King and I*. She sighed and told me that I could go. I wasn't sure if she had gotten the reference. One of my problems was that I always whistled off-key. Sometimes even I didn't recognize my songs.

We had done *The King and I* at Ellis when I was in Class One. I had loved Lisa Andrews, the junior who played Anna. My part was an anonymous member of the royal family. But in my fantasies, I had the role of Princess Ying, the mischievous favorite, and Lisa petted, hugged, and gently scolded me. I even imagined her inviting me home to live with her family. Watching them congratulate her on opening night, I wasn't disappointed; they were wonderfully, perfectly ordinary. The mother, father, and two younger Andrews moved around the assembly hall with ease. Each time they paused to chat with another family, I was reminded of models posing in the L.L.Bean catalogue. That night, my mother wore the protective shell that she donned when nervous; it included a brash persona, talking too loudly, and a forced smile. I could never understand how she could be so cool and poised in the courtroom, yet guarded and miserable when socializing with a room full of white people. She stuck out even more than I did, and my father just sat moodily flipping through his appointment book. That too was a façade, but he wore it to hide his feelings for me.

Anna Walker had short dark hair instead of a shoulder-length red ponytail. Her long patterned skirts and muted shirts were completely unlike Lisa's preppy clothes, but some of my feelings were similar. I was torn between my desire to have her rescue me and my impulse to torture her.

Months earlier, I had listed my brother Chris as the emergency contact on the CARE intake forms. I never thought that the number would actually be used. But ten days into my stay at Farrell, a nurse came and got me out of the solarium where I had parked in a corner, leaning against the lemon-yellow walls, escaping into a world empty of feeling and ties. The brightness of the paint mystified me as did the name, *solarium*. Just because we were mental patients didn't mean we didn't notice that the plants were plastic, the ceiling was peeling, and the single mesh-covered window faced a brick wall.

"You have visitors in the Day Room," the nurse said. I gaped and followed her down the hall. Chris was waiting on a plastic-covered loveseat. His complexion nearly matched the tawny furniture. He was the lightest of us three, a fact I had envied when very young, then pretended to scorn as a teenager. Across from him, Alex perched on the edge of a stained, tattered armchair, his leather briefcase balanced on his knees. I could almost see his skin shrinking away from contact with the hospital; his discomfort and need to be elsewhere were palpable.

"What are you doing here?" I felt rather stupid for asking, but they were so foreign to the Farrell universe, it seemed impossible, incongruous, that they were in front of me. For years, I had been an alien faking an existence in the normal world. In here, my brothers were the bizarre ones. Even if I didn't quite fit in at Farrell, I belonged.

"I think we're supposed to be asking you that." Chris grinned, then looked serious as he got up and gave me a hug.

"What the hell do you think you're playing at, Georgie? Mum is frantic." Alex stood up as well, still clutching his briefcase. "She hasn't heard from you in weeks. She says you haven't answered your voice mail. A letter for you came to their house, saying that your student loans are due because you're no longer registered. When she called Malcolm, he said that he hadn't seen you in months. Then Chris gets a call from some therapist woman who says you're at this place. What's going on? How long have you been here?"

"Not that long. Not even two weeks. Alex, you really can put that down. It's not going to be contaminated by touching the floor." Confused by an odd mixture of guilt, shame, and resentment, I couldn't quite decide whether or not to go on the offensive. So even as I struck out, I didn't mention that I had spent the past six months living at a program for alcoholics and addicts. Nor did it seem the right time to complain about Mother reading my mail.

"Okay, George, I'm trying to be patient. Why are you in a state mental hospital?" Alex sat back down and put his briefcase on the floor. He had the calm tone you use to soothe an overtired child. At the same time he managed to sound martyred.

"I am here because I don't have any insurance," I said in an equally stoical, forbearing voice.

"Oh, for God's sake, Georgette. Stop acting obtuse. You know exactly what I mean." Alex turned to Chris and rolled his eyes. "She's doing this on purpose."

I didn't know what compelled me to be uncooperative. Something about Alex and his six-figure salary, mahogany office, nice wife, and perfect life struck me as unbearably smug. Alex had been my favorite brother growing up. As children, we often ganged up on Chris. We teased him and voted as a bloc to veto his choices of games and TV stations. Both of us had been rebellious as teenagers while Chris was much more eager to please. Then one day, I had woken to find my closest sibling a conservative attorney while I was still caught in the throes of a hard adolescence. Now Chris sported dreadlocks and an earring while Alex wore three-piece suits. The metamorphoses had happened years before, but I still hadn't forgiven my brothers for switching places without my permission or knowledge.

"Georgie, please tell us what's wrong. Let us help," Chris intervened.

"I'm just feeling a little lost since Malcolm broke up with me." I chose an excuse that I thought they'd understand. Admitting to the razor blades and unrelenting anxieties seemed shameful, though perhaps they could guess that part; they had witnessed my teens.

"I never liked him anyhow. He always acted like his shit didn't smell," Chris responded promptly. Alex remained silent. Malcolm and he had gotten along well. After family dinners, they sat in my mother's living room having conversations so dull I could never remember their topics. They played early-morning games of racquetball and evening basketball whenever Malcolm was in

Boston or on the few occasions that Alex came to visit me in Amherst.

"He said I wasn't black enough," I confessed, near tears.

"That's crap and you know it." Chris didn't sound surprised, but at least he defended me. "Are you going to let what that jerk says put you in a hospital, Georgie? You're stronger than that. You don't have to get so upset about these things. Instead of getting depressed, why don't you get mad?"

"I'm not really depressed. I'm not really anything." Most of the time, this statement was true. I hated how their presence had already begun to penetrate my bubble.

"Something must be wrong. People don't just end up in a psychiatric hospital."

"I seem to." I started feeling a little sorry for myself.

"Georgie, we want you home with us. If you need treatment, you can get it in Boston. I'm sure Mom and Eric will pay for it. Or you can always ask Dad. Right, Alex?"

"Georgette, you don't belong here," Alex said. It was impossible to tell if he was agreeing with Chris or just irritated at the idea that someone in his family was in a loony bin.

"You don't understand." I couldn't explain how Malcolm's rejection had pushed a giant *off* switch in me. Since the breakup, I had been off-kilter, out of focus, and as numb as an android. I had never talked to my brothers about the ricocheting of my childhood. Always moving between white schools, my mother's Jamaican roots, and my father's African-American neighborhood had left me precisely nowhere. Being with Malcolm had meant belonging somewhere, until that fragile place dissolved.

"Why are you so positive we don't understand? Georgie, what do you think my dreads are about? Why do you think I went to Howard?" Chris asked. "My identity is just as important to me. I just stopped letting other people define it a long time ago."

Embarrassed that his words came as such a surprise, I told them I needed to go to the bathroom. Talking to them had begun to break through the anesthesia that made the world flat and dull. Inside, emotions were stirring, and I needed to regain my composure. It was important not to care.

In the bathroom, a nurse with crossed arms stood over a young woman who had been put on the floor. Karen mopped the faded linoleum with a dirty white towel. She was one of the disabled patients; her empty wheelchair stood waiting for her to complete the job. I stepped over a pool of urine to get to a toilet. Afraid the stall door would swing open, I pushed it shut with one hand while I peed. The only locks at Farrell were those that kept us in.

"Next time you'll think twice before wetting yourself on purpose," I heard the satisfied nurse say. Different parts of me struggled between an abhorrence of such casual cruelty, desperation to get out of Farrell, and an inexplicable relief that there was no place further to fall. Desperation won. I decided to ask my brothers for help.

When I got back to the Day Room, Anna Walker was talking to Chris and Alex. "Georgette can leave as soon as she's ready. All we want is to be sure that she has a place to go and some sort of support system."

"We want her to come back to Boston with us. She can stay with me. Or our mom would be glad to have her. She's not that tight with Dad." Chris spoke before he noticed me in the doorway. When he saw me standing there, he asked, "How does that sound, George?"

"I'm not coming to the city with you. I'm staying out in Amherst. I want to go back to grad school. I'm going to register for the spring semester."

"Why don't we go in my office and discuss this in private? I'd like to help facilitate this discharge in whatever way I can," Anna Walker offered.

Chris and Alex allowed her to usher us out of the room, but they exchanged glances with me. I could tell they too had pegged her as the pleading, wishy-washy sort of white woman who was easily manipulated by those racism-awareness workshops. The type who believed in "white privilege" and the rights of angry blacks. There was a brief moment of connection between us. The first in years. After arriving in Anna Walker's office, the moment dissipated as quickly as it had come.

Both Alex and Chris insisted that I return to Boston with them. But the two disagreed about the spring semester. Alex thought I should register and put my recent insanity behind me. Chris kept on saying that a person couldn't just get well in a few weeks. He demanded that I stay with him at least until summer. I drifted away from the room. The practiced listlessness of recent months was useful.

"You can't expect her to just go back to normal like nothing's happened. Look at her, she obviously needs help. The Ph.D. can wait."

"Why is she studying that African-American Art nonsense anyhow?" Alex demanded. "There's no future it. She needs to do something practical like law school. Why not focus on a profession like Library Science or Dental Hygiene?"

"There's no reason to rush things. Georgie can move home for a while and think things over. Isn't that so, Ms. Walker?" Chris asked.

"Perhaps it would be best if Georgette took some time off to focus on her recovery." Anna Walker oscillated back and forth, first agreeing with one then the other. She seemed impressed by both men.

"She has nothing to recover from," Alex burst out. "Black

people don't go crazy. That's for rich, bored white folks with too much time on their hands. She needs to pull herself together."

I snapped back into the room. Suddenly, I was on my feet shouting.

"Fuck you, Alex! I don't need to do anything. You need to get out of my face."

"Georgette, calm down," Anna Walker said.

"You calm the fuck down. Get rid of him. Both of them. I want them out of here." I started pacing back and forth in the tiny office, kicking the back of Anna Walker's metal desk on each leg of the trip.

"Georgie, stop it. This is self-pity and self-aggrandizing. Nothing more." Alex seemed unfazed.

"I said, get rid of them!" I warned.

"Maybe you'd better go." Anna Walker turned to the two men.

"I'm not going anywhere without my sister," Alex said in a voice like bedrock.

"Get out!" I knocked over the floor lamp then swept the clock, Kleenex, and papers off the end table.

"Georgette! Sit down, now! Sit on your hands," barked Anna Walker in a voice as hard as Alex's. Startled, I abruptly dropped back into my seat. She was not quite the pushover that I had believed. Anna Walker came around her desk and knelt near my chair.

"Can you explain what made you so upset?" the social worker asked. I shoved her.

I was in four-point restraints in a room barely large enough for a single bed and chair. Chris sat beside me. For a long time I stared at the ceiling tiles, not saying anything. I was ashamed that my brother was seeing me immobilized, tied down like some kind of animal. And a wave of exhaustion had swept over me.

"Where's Alex?" I asked eventually

"He's waiting outside."

"Does he have to be such a jerk?"

Chris didn't answer for a little while. Finally, out of the blue, he asked, "Do you remember Alex when he was away at boarding school?"

"Not really. Sort of. I remember he had that homeboy shuffle that Mom hated. And he was into rap right away when the rest of us thought it was just noise. I thought he was the baddest big brother a girl could have."

"Did you ever wonder why he got sent to Sherman-Moss?"

"No, it was after Mom married Eric and we left the suburbs. They didn't want us in the city public schools."

"But think for a second. Why did Alex end up going to a boarding school when you and I went to private day schools?" Chris looked at me as if he expected me to remember something forgotten. I didn't know the answer to his question. I had never thought about it.

Anna Walker came into the room with an orderly just then.

"Georgette, do you want to get up?" she asked. When I nodded, she told the orderly to unlock the cuffs. A few seconds later, I was sitting up, rubbing my wrists.

"Look out the window," said Chris. I stared down at the grounds. It was a gray winter day. The trees had lost their color long ago, and the sky looked as if it had forgotten the sun's existence. Alex sat in his brown overcoat on one of the benches near the circular drive. Though I could see the wind whipping black tree branches around, Alex's back was stiff and straight; he was as rigid and immobile as I had been minutes earlier. I turned to Anna Walker.

"I'm ready to go home with my brothers today," I said. I was surprised that my voice, usually so flat and toneless, sounded hopeful, even expectant.

"I'm glad. I'll go talk to Dr. Johnson about your discharge."
Anna Walker left the room as quickly as she had come. In some
ways, I thought, she is like me. Mild and serene one moment,
gravelly and rough the next. But she feels, she cares, she's alive. I
wondered if I could be those things too.

Chris came and stood beside me. He hugged me hard.

"Hey, girl. When I said get mad, I didn't mean quite that
mad." He whispered as if our parents could hear him. I couldn't
quite manage a laugh, but I smiled because I felt less alone.

nina

(part ii)

may 2001

t he box had become an addiction in itself. Each day at lunch, I sat in the park reading letters and journal entries, piecing together fragments that never seemed to quite fit. The day after my wallet was stolen, I found a letter from Malcolm.

Hello Georgie,

I wish you would write or call, even if it's just to let me know that you're okay. I tried calling both your brothers to find out where you are. Neither of them would tell me. Chris was pretty nice; I got to admit, he's a good man for a Rasta-wanna-be. But Alex, he nearly bit my head off. You were totally right when you said Alex is wound real tight. Look, Georgie, it's your prerogative if you want to pull a disappearing act. But I miss you, and I thought we had something real happening between us. Just call, okay?

M.

After finishing the letter I sat still, people-watching for a while. Across the green, I could see the chess player, the one with the green-rimmed glasses. I remembered his shocked face when I threw him out of the apartment. I slowly lifted my hand and stroked my collarbone, remembering his smooth touch. How desperate I was for touch in my sterile life, yet how frightened.

"Why do you do it with those guys if you don't like it?" I remembered Keisha asking.

"I hated Malcolm," I whispered to myself, as if that statement somehow answered the long ago question. The words startled me since my boyfriend had been gentle in bed. Sex had been softer than velvet; his open arms had sheltered and steadied me when I had been spinning out of control, and he had swathed the gaping rawness of my twenties with purpose.

"I really hated him," I said louder this time.

"Hated who, Georgie?" Lydia suddenly appeared beside me. Her yellow miniskirt was dirty and needed pressing. The scarlet V neck dipped dangerously low into a just budding cleavage. She wore far too much makeup for a young teen.

"No one," I responded. "Nothing."

"You know, you real closed-mouthed, Georgie. Don't you ever tell nobody nothing?"

The little snort of laughter that burst out at Lydia's question surprised me. I felt silly, almost giddy. I shocked myself by trying to tease the girl. "No, I don't tell nobody nothing, Lydia. Do you tell anyone anything, Miss Mysterious Young Lady? Or do you just appear and disappear around here like a poltergeist?"

"I tell you lots of things," Lydia said plaintively. "I tell you everything, you just don't listen."

"Okay, sorry. I'm listening now." I braced myself for a lurid tale of adolescent sex or drugs or worse yet some story of parental neglect. For a moment, Lydia looked at a loss for words.

"School really sucks. I got remedial 'cause I failed two classes last year," she finally said. "It's not fair."

"Why?"

"Everybody's telling me what to do all the time. Teachers, principal, my Pops. Everybody."

"What have you got to do right now?" I tried to focus the expected monologue in hopes of hearing a tangible problem.

"Math. I can't do decimals. And I'm supposed to bring in a portrait of someone I know with a paragraph about them for Language Arts. I can't draw worth shit."

"Well, *that* I can help you with." I smiled. "Get out some paper and we'll draw someone in the park."

"No. I want to draw you. I draw you and you draw me, okay?" Lydia sat down and took some colored paper out of her bag.

"Okay," I agreed, picking up a pen. And an event that should have been so momentous passed without notice as I began to draw for the first time in years. Later that night, in bed, I shook, fearing I might have broken the latch to a gate which had been deliberately shut. But at that moment with Lydia in the park, I didn't think of consequences, I just helped the young girl with her homework.

The next day, I returned from my lunch break to be greeted by Mimi's excited face. The other librarian was flushed and held her hand to her chest as if trying to still a beating heart.

"You'll never guess what!" Mimi announced in a voice of affected drama and mystery. I felt some curiosity but I refused to take the bait. I had been wary of Mimi since her remark about lesbianism. And the woman seemed too interested in my clothing and social life. I was never sure if my colleague's questions were friendly concern or fuel for gossip with Janet, Marie, and the other librarians. I preferred silence and loneliness; they were safer.

"I'm sure that I don't know," I said as I tried to step around Mimi, who blocked access to the reference desk.

"A man was just here to see you—a handsome man. He said that he'd be back in an hour. You never told us that you had a boyfriend!" Mimi pursed her lips and arched her eyebrows with exaggerated coquetry. "What other secrets have you been hiding from us?"

Instead of answering, I pushed past the other librarian and returned to work. Part of me worried that it was one of the men that I had recently slept with. All my worlds were sliding together, colliding perhaps, as past and present merged, the dream world and waking world overlapped, and my strange, floating after-hours life and sterile library life started to interact. The thought terrified me.

An hour later, I looked up from helping a college student search a computer database to discover Alex standing near my desk, watching me. When he saw that he had my attention, he gave a stiff wave. As I approached him, he seemed to both hold out his arms and flinch backwards at the same time. Our hug was sideways and awkward, half back pat, half shoulder collision.

Alex explained that he had come into town on business and wanted to take me out to dinner. Earlier that afternoon, he had seen Grandma Annie, Aunt Fran, and various cousins. "They never hear from you," he accused, "You're a bus ride away, yet I see them more than you do." I found myself promising to visit my father's family next week and my mother's soon afterwards. I even mumbled something about making it down to Florida sometime soon. I wasn't sure if the promises were ruses to make my brother shut up or if they reflected an actual desire to reconnect with my family. Either way, Alex seemed satisfied, and we agreed to meet at a restaurant later that night.

* * *

"How's the painting going, Georgie?" Alex asked over dinner. He had waved the waiter down with an expansive gesture and ordered two steaks very rare, without consulting me. He didn't seem to notice that I barely picked at my meal, nor did he comment when I shook my head no at the proffered carafe of wine. I responded that I had pretty much given up my artwork.

"Why? You're really talented. I thought your collages meant the world to you."

"How can you even ask me that, Alex? You're the one who thinks that art is impractical—you think everyone needs to have a profession like you." I was genuinely surprised by my brother's reaction.

"Well, yeah. Everyone needs to be able to make a living, but does it have to be all or nothing? What's wrong with having a good job *and* being an artist? I mean, if you really love it."

"I can't make collages or montages anymore. The work, I used to think of it as a mosaic of memories. Now my memories are mostly gone. I don't think about the past anymore. I don't dream; I don't create. I just exist."

"Are you happy at least?" Alex asked. "Are things easier now?"

I had no idea how to answer that question. The random men, Lydia's insistence, Mimi's prying—all those things were certainly difficult, but perhaps existence was easier. Existing did not consume me. However, Alex's question reminded me of the conversation I'd had with Chris the day they had come to Farrell.

"Alex, were you happy at Sherman-Moss? Were you homesick?" As I spoke, I realized that I knew little of my eldest brother's inner life. He was the stodgy voice on my answering machine chastising me for not visiting our parents, or he was the conservative opinion at Thanksgiving dinners—but what were his joys and desires, and who were his heroes? I didn't know.

"Happy? I'm not sure. I know the school changed my life.

Without Sherman-Moss, I wouldn't be who I am now. Instead of a lawyer, I'd be hanging on a street corner smoking ganja, or instead of being satisfied with Sylvia, I'd be Daddy. It's like I tried on a few identities and settled on this one. It's okay. I'm pretty content."

"Is being content enough? Do you ever want more?"

"George, to tell you the truth, I've always been a little envious of you. Not the craziness or the drama-queen antics, but your passion. Sometimes when we were growing up, you seemed ablaze with it. Sometimes, I don't even know if I feel that way about Sylvia. I love her. I'm content, but I'm not passionate. Every once in a while, I think I'd be willing to give up a little safety for a fire or two."

"Mother used to say that I burn all my bridges," I smiled.

"Yeah, but those were some glorious fires." Alex took off his glasses to polish them. He pressed his forefinger and right thumb to his eyes for a quick minute. Then he replaced the glasses and gave me a big smile.

"So, did you ever find your true-true name?" he asked.

"What?"

"Yuh true-true name, gal. De name yuh keep to yuhself an stay silence bout. Sometime animal-name. Sometime made-up name. Dinya remember, nuh? De name yuh tell nobody so yuh can cheat de obeah." Alex screwed his face into an outraged old Jamaican lady. Then he gave a very un-Alex-like giggle.

"Ah, no man! Obeah not real. Me name is Georgie Collins and me gwine shout it out loud!" I laughed too.

february 20, 1998

Yesterday I got the call.

"My mother is dead," my mother said.

I am going to edit my life. There are too many memories that I don't need.

empty house

t he day of Nina's funeral. We all flew back to Jamaica to attend. Even my father came, though he and my mother had been divorced for twenty years. After the burial, we sat around the living room. It was like being transported back in time; Nina's house was filled with aunts, uncles, and cousins. The cook kept coming out of the kitchen with dish after dish. We stuffed ourselves on salt fish fritters, gingered chicken, callaloo, and fried plantains. Then, just when we thought that eating more was impossible, generous dessert platters appeared with carefully arranged fruit, rum cake, and bread pudding. I kept forgetting why we were there and expecting Nina to come in the room any moment with a sarcastic comment about our greedy bellies. Every few minutes, someone would smack his lips and mention how good it was to be home.

It was not until the food was gone and the younger children were in bed that the family grew solemn again. Uncle Denton sat with his head in his hands. Mercy leaned against him and Aunt Ella against her. My mother looked terrible. Her eyes were haggard and her mouth sagged, the lips too exhausted to hold their usual pursed line. Every few minutes, Alex and Sylvia hovered near her, asking if they could get her a drink. I think she finally agreed to a glass of rum punch just to get them to leave her alone.

Dad looked more uncomfortable than sad. At one point, he shook his head. "I just remember the last time I was here; your grandmother was reading me the riot act for not being a good enough husband to her daughter." Everyone nodded. We all had memories of being dressed down by Nina.

"Mama, she nyingi-nyingi all time. Me never have a moment of peace in this house!" Mercy declared. But she smiled even as she kissed her teeth, pretending to be Nina. "I can hear her now. Cha, Mercy, yuh doan care. Mercy, yuh lickle an facey; Mercy, wha mek yuh pickney so haad-headed?"

"Yeah, Nina was always on my case about something. I was a wild teenager, but she straightened me out," Alex explained to Sylvia.

Chris and I looked at each other. Nina loved the wild Alex; it was the older, conservative one who frustrated her. She was angriest with him the summer when Keisha came with us to the island. I had begged Mother's permission many times to bring my lover and been refused. Perhaps as a peace offering, she had volunteered instead to pay Keisha's way. The first week, Alex had flirted outrageously with her. I knew Keisha had had a crush on him in high school, but I was surprised at Alex's behavior. They practically made out on the sofa one night as Keisha snuggled up to him and Alex caressed her arms. Later in the pool, they horsed around; Alex threatened to pull off her bikini top and Keisha ran away squealing, but slow enough to let him catch her and throw her in. I was irritated with Keisha that day, but even more disgusted with Alex the next week when his law school girlfriend showed up and he gave Keisha the cold shoulder.

A few days later, we all got ready to go dancing. My cousins, brothers, Keisha, and I were sitting in the living room discussing our plans when Sylvia twirled into the room in a little black dress with a pleated skirt. Keisha stood up, spilled her drink, then tripped. Finally, she mumbled something about being too tired to go out and left the room. My cousin Nancy got up and followed her out, giving Alex a sour look over her shoulder. Later, when the three of us were alone in the kitchen, Chris and I confronted him.

"Alex, last week you had your hands all over her, and now you act like she doesn't exist. What's wrong with you? Can't you at least be civil?" Chris said.

"Keisha and I were just having fun a few days ago. She knew I wasn't serious." Alex shrugged. He opened a bottle of Ting and started to make a bun and cheese sandwich. Our disapproval didn't seem to concern him.

"So you're serious about Miss stick-up-her-ass Sylvia, is that it?" I asked as I took the bottle opener from him to pop the cap off a beer.

"Yes, that's it," he replied.

"Keisha's much better for you." I wasn't sure whether this was actually true, but I felt obliged to defend my friend.

"I'm not going to take love advice from some plastered dyke dropout, Georgie. So, you can keep your opinions to yourself. Keisha's not our type of people."

"What's that supposed to mean?"

"She's too . . ." He trailed off for a few seconds and then finally answered, "She's rough."

"You mean she's too poor," Chris said. I wasn't sure what Chris's smirk meant. Was he as offended as I was? I also wanted to know why Alex had called me plastered, and I wasn't a dropout; I'd merely decided not to go to college right away.

"No, that's not what I mean," Alex scowled. "It's not a money thing. Just look at her family. She has six brothers and sisters."

"So what?" I said. "Mom has five. For that matter, Daddy has four siblings."

"That's different, and you know it. Nina and Grandma Annie were married to their children's fathers. Besides, they lived in a different era. People had large families back then. For God's sake, Georgette, Keisha's fifteen-year-old sister is pregnant. Her little brother has been arrested. You know what I'm talking about."

"Yeah, I know you're a snob. I know I'm ashamed to be related to you. Keisha goes to M.I.T., by the way. Remember, I'm the one who's a dropout!" I looked to Chris for support.

"How can you treat Keisha that way? We've known her since we were like ten," he chimed in. "Why are you so disrespectful to a sister?"

"Keisha won't make it through M.I.T. Believe me, I've seen it dozens of times: at prep school, in college, and now in law school. It's not that she's poor. She's rough," Alex said in his stubborn voice. I recognized that voice—he wouldn't be changing his mind. At that moment, I glanced around. Nina was in the doorway, stiff and furious. I had no idea how long she had been there. Had she heard Alex call me a dyke?

"Wha mek yuh want act like Big Man now yuh in law school? Yuh boasie like backra-massa in Great House an all else is licky-licky? Yuh tink das right to check Keisha den treat she like she wutless? Georgie, Chris, oono galang now to sleep. Me gwine to talk to Alex an jook him til he member who for he is."

Chris and I obediently fled. Nina grabbed the beer out of my hand as I passed her in the doorway. She gave me a stern look. I was indignant. After all, I was practically an adult.

Now, ten years later and nine months sober, I was a graduate-school dropout, Chris's dreadlocks tumbled down his back, and

Alex didn't remember that Nina had liked Sylvia even less than I did. In his mind, he had "straightened up" into the perfect grandson. As he sat with his arm around Sylvia, he was probably estimating his share of the inheritance and wondering what the taxes would be on the villa.

By midnight everyone was asleep except me. The older folks and children had gone to bed early. Alex and Sylvia soon followed. Chris and several of my cousins lasted longer, playing music and rounds of cards, but eventually the rum punch and ganja knocked them out. After the last had disappeared, I went to Nina's room. Her bedroom had always fascinated me—it was kept spotless by the housemaid, but every surface was cluttered with Nina's possessions. Bottles of perfume, hair care products, and makeup covered the cherry vanity and bureau. A matching credenza sat in the corner; lace topped the polished wood. Books, religious pamphlets, a music box, and other trinkets lined the shelves. As a child, I had longed to explore the tantalizing drawers, peek in the little flower-papered boxes, but I had only been allowed in the room on special occasions or to serve her coffee on the mornings that Nina declared her old bones deserved to rest in bed. The entire room had seemed rich to the senses, and along with touching everything, I had wanted to taste, smell, and drink in the room. Now, I buried my nose in the bedspread and sniffed deeply, rewarded by Nina's scent, minty and green.

Surreptitiously, as if someone might catch me, I opened the center drawer of her bureau to discover a packet of letters. I tossed those on the bed—I would read them when I was done snooping. Also in the dresser, I found a bundle of silk scarves; my favorite one, emerald with yellow embroidery, joined the letters. A handful of silver bangles followed. I realized that if I claimed my memories of her now, I wouldn't have to compete with my cousins for mementos as we packed up the house. Suddenly I couldn't stop; I gathered beads, earrings, hair bands, a velvet sack of dried pot-pourri, matches, and more. Crying, I looked in her desk where I harvested a box of thin brown cigars, toffees, unrecognizable foreign currency, an abeng, and a pocket watch. In the desk's cubbyhole, I found a delicate egg decorated in fiery colors. Did Nina smoke? I didn't think so. Where had she traveled? I had no idea. Had she been abroad? The papier-mâché egg looked more European than Jamaican. Who was *SLM with love*, the engraving on the watch? It didn't matter. Faster and faster, I flew around the room; at this point, I was barely examining the items anymore. I just threw anything that caught my eye onto the bed until it was piled high with Nina's essence, and I threw myself there as well. I turned off the night-table lamp and released the mosquito mesh so that bed was draped and I was protected and enveloped in darkness. I cried, and then coughed so hard that I thought I would vomit.

I remembered lying under that bed during one of my mother's visits to the island. Chris, Alex, and I had been living with Nina for a few months at that point, and I knew better than to go into her room without permission. But I needed a place to hide out from the mother I both missed terribly and hated because she had abandoned me. When I heard footsteps outside Nina's door, I scooted under the bed as quickly as possible. From the floor, I could see Nina's house slippers and my mother's high heels.

"Verna, when are you going to be taking these children home?" Nina asked.

"I don't know. After things are more settled with Michael, I suppose. It's not good for the kids to be around the two of us fighting. When the divorce is final and Michael starts behaving like a grown-up—then they can come home."

"As I hear it from Mercy, your husband isn't the only one acting the fool. You're dropping your pants for one man while you're still married to another."

"Mama, I need you to do this for me right now: not judge me. Besides, I thought that you liked having them." My mother's voice sounded impatient like when I was whining.

"They need their mother. Especially Georgie."

The last thing I remembered hearing was my mother saying, "Georgie's fine. She'll be fine." Hours later, I woke up when Nina pulled me out from under the bed. She hugged me tight. The way I remember it, my mother was gone by then, but that can't be right. I have it mixed up. She wouldn't have left without saying goodbye.

For weeks afterwards, I would cry every night at bedtime. Nina would come into my room and sit on the bed, rubbing my back. She promised me that everything was all right even though it seemed the world was ending.

"Hush now, sweetness," she'd say. "You mustn't carry on so. Everything cook and curry." I hugged her and felt warm, but I still missed my mom and dad.

The night of Nina's funeral, I lay in her bed shaking until the tears finally stopped. I reached up and switched the light back on. For a moment, it seemed that I was lying amidst a pile of junk. Objects that had seemed so precious minutes ago were now just lifeless, brittle reminders of Nina's death. *What is all this disorder and bangarang?* I could imagine Nina demanding. Then I noticed that my hand sat on a thick pad of off-white drawing paper, and I remembered a desk drawer that had revealed a Starling Candy tin filled with colored markers. Although I had never seen Nina draw or paint, I was scarcely surprised. After all, she always had exactly what I needed when I needed it. The discovery of the pens and paper must be significant, I thought. It must mean that I should make a farewell picture of Nina.

A quick trip to the kitchen for glue and scissors, and I was ready to begin. While there, I grabbed provisions—a loaf of hard-dough bread and a jar of guava jelly. After a few seconds of hesitation, I took a six-pack of Red Stripe beer from the refrigerator. I had not drunk anything since CARE, but now was as good a time as any to let go of the sobriety that I had never really wanted. On my way back to Nina's room, I unbolted the doors to the verandah and stepped out into the garden, where I collected a crocus sack of soil, a handful of begonias, and a few sprigs of sage.

Sitting on Nina's bed that night, the collage grew almost by magic. I began by pasting on the paper snippets of silk and burlap from the crocus sack to form a textured foundation. Next the beads, leaves, potpourri, and flower petals were pieced together to make Nina's garden and verandah. I tried to use the soil for the picture's earth, but it wouldn't stick so I smashed it hard to stain the paper. The walls of the house were made from the label of the jelly jar and the paper wrapping from the toffees. The roof was thatched with matchsticks. I paved the long drive with rings and bottle-caps. I saved Nina's body for last and used parts of everything to build it: mosquito netting, money, cigars, and sage. I broke a bottle of perfume against the headboard and used the glass splinters for her hair. Ignoring my bleeding right hand, I painted the final touches with mascara, markers, and lipstick. I was staring at the collage wondering what to do next when I heard my father's voice.

"Georgie, baby girl, what are you doing? Have you been up all night?" Dad was standing in the threshold of her room. I wanted him to go away. He didn't belong there. But he entered anyway. I shrugged.

"Did you do this to your grandmother's room?" he asked.

"What?"

"Honey, Verna and your aunts are going to have a fit."

"Daddy, come here," I said. Michael pushed the mosquito

netting aside and sat carefully on the edge of the bed. I started to cry again as I leaned against my father and he put his arms around me. It was nice to be held. I closed my burning eyes and drifted. Daddy smoothed my hair and patted my back.

"Come on, little girl, give me a little smile," he coaxed when I couldn't stop weeping. "Laughter is the best medicine of all." As he gently massaged the knots in my shoulders, I suddenly grew angry. I had been the one who comforted my father while he mourned the divorce and was devastated by my mother's marriage to Eric. He had been the one who needed looking after and cheering up when he had a heart attack, and in the months in 1989 when he was laid off. Then there were the years when he called incessantly to complain about this woman who had done him wrong, that colleague who was a brownnoser at work, and the way my ungrateful brothers and I didn't come home nearly often enough. For my entire life, I had refused him nothing and been the perfect little girl for him without a thought for my own needs and desires. How dare he come in now and swoop down with hugs and kisses and stupid little truisms as if he were a savior? It was too late for that. How dare he even come to Nina's funeral?

I felt like I was about to explode. I was glad moments later when Verna, Aunt Mercy, and Aunt Ella came in with their shocked screams. I watched while Verna pointed out the dirt, glue, and trash littering the room and staining the bedspread. I saw Daddy's lips move in my defense, but I really couldn't hear what he was saying. The women began to clean furiously, and the maid was called. In the ensuing bustle, I slipped out to the patio where the garden boy was burning garbage. I dropped the collage onto the heap and watched the flames shoot toward the sky. As soon as I got back to Boston, I would apply to school in Library Science. Alex was right. It was about time that I got practical.

michael

june 2001

t he final letter in the box was from Keisha.

Hey Georgie,

It seems like forever since I last heard from you. Jason is walking now and getting into all sorts of trouble! I am as big as a house and tired all the time. Dr. Stevens says that it is going to be a girl this time. I say who cares? I just can't wait to get this child out of me.

I've been thinking about you a lot lately, when we were kids and the crazy shit that we did. Teasing your brothers and all that. How is Chris anyhow? Still trying to be a Rastafarian? What about Alex? Has he still got that Buppie thing going on?

I'm pretty happy with Sammy. We're both working hard and he's going to school part-time. Believe me, shit isn't easy and sometimes I regret not having finished M.I.T. But we all make choices that we got to live with.

So how are you holding up? Last I'd heard from my

grandma, you had graduated from Harvard with honors and everything. And you were all ready to head to graduate school. You go on girl! Are you still dating Mr. Malcolm Man? He still talking trash to you? If he is, let me know. I'll come up there and kick his butt back and forth between Boston and D.C. And while I'm at it, I'll kick your old girl-friend Amanda's butt for good measure.

How are you going to let your so-called lovers tell you that you aren't black enough, thin enough, sexy enough, strong enough, successful enough, whatever? You've got to stop hanging on to other people's words. You've got to let it go. Just let it go. You're you, Georgie Collins, my best friend. And believe me, I know what I'm talking about. Aiight?

Love,
Keisha

I sat in the park idly sketching the group that circled the chess players. Yesterday, I had bought a set of markers in exotic colors, and all day at the library I imagined myself sweeping pen over paper, capturing the summer afternoon and thus somehow recapturing a part of myself or my youth that had disappeared. In an odd, fanciful mood, I drew the men in purple ink and the women in turquoise and green. Though I was lost in deep concentration, I was not startled by Lydia's voice or the girl's shadow, which appeared suddenly over the half-finished sketch.

"Hey, George," the girl said. "I got an A on my portrait!" Her clothes and face were cleaner than the day before, but the cleanliness just made her appear younger and more fragile.

"That's wonderful, Lydia!" I exclaimed. I was not entirely sure if I wanted the teenager to stay and talk or if I preferred to remain alone and in silence.

"Now I've got to write a poem for class. A dumb poem! Can you believe it?"

"What kind of poem?"

"My choice. Sonnet, Pantoum, Villanelle, or Ghazal." Each word was pronounced carefully, each syllable distinct.

"Learned some new words, have we?" I smiled.

"Huh?"

"Nothing. I'll help you, if you like. Have you chosen a subject?" I pointed to the bench beside her. In one smooth gesture, Lydia collapsed in the seat and drew a ball of paper out of her bag.

"Here." Lydia's voice returned to the sullen tone of our first meetings. She threw the crumpled paper at me, slumped over the picnic table, and rested her head on crossed arms in front of her.

I smoothed the crumpled paper open. I glanced at Lydia, trying to make sure that I had the girl's permission to read the draft. Lydia refused to meet my eye, and after a minute I went ahead and read the paper. I couldn't make sense of the poem, which seemed incoherent and did not adhere to any of the forms that the child had listed.

A leather chair is not a luxury
    A leather chair is a leash.
A cigar is not for smoking
    Cigar smoke is for hiding.
An apple is not a fruit
    Apples are full of poison.
A home is not a home
    A home is a heartache.
A mirror can still reflect though I'm all she sees.
A garden is only safe until it is invaded.
A memory is not a memory
    If the memory is a grave.

This is not a poem
   This is a portrait of me.

"I'm sorry, Lydia, I don't really see what the poem is about," I said, handing the paper back. I wanted to tell the child that I had just barely gotten *my* art back, I had just barely recovered a small sense of self. I didn't want to have to try to interpret poetry or jeopardize my fragile peace with the frightening images that threatened to encompass me while reading the poem.

"You wouldn't! You don't get anything. You don't listen," Lydia said as she stuffed the paper back in the bag. I felt attacked by the sourness in Lydia's voice and her almost violent motions as she crammed the paper as deep as possible into the recesses. With equal savagery, I shoved my rising emotions down. I would not feel. No sullen, raggedy teenager could make me, even if that teenager had vulnerable eyes and spoke words that begged to be heard.

"I'm sorry that I'm so stupid. Maybe you better go and find someone else to help you with your homework."

"The poem," Lydia said with wounded dignity and a stiff little voice, "is about my father."

"Well, why . . ." I began to ask, but I forgot the question before the first words came out of my mouth. "Why . . ." I began again, and then trailed off.

"Why indeed," Lydia said, and without waiting for my response, she picked up her bag and left. I remained sitting on the park bench. I was puzzled by the girl's final words. I couldn't decide if Lydia's voice had been bitter or merely curious. For a few minutes, I tried to go back to my markers and drawing, but I was unable to reimmerse in the beautiful colors and the exotic lines. Eventually I found myself growing angry. I decided that I should confront her. No matter how difficult the girl's life might be, I deserved courtesy and respect. Instead I got adolescent histrionics each time I tried to help.

It had been years since I visited my father's family regularly, but that evening I found my way back to my Aunt Fran's brownstone. Stuck between the most well-kept streets of Mattapan on one side and a block of public housing on the other, Fran's neighborhood had always seemed embattled to me. The window boxes and tiny front yards were scrupulously tidy. Children raced up and down the street on bicycles and scooters while teenagers and women kept an eye out from front stoops. Some of the buildings were made of crumbling brick and the occasional barred window belied the general feeling of friendly safety on the block.

I stood in front of Fran's door for several minutes trying to recall the weekends and holidays that I had spent there and at Grandma Annie's as a child and teenager. But any fond memories that I had of my aunts, grandmother, and cousins were overshadowed by how much I had hated feeling like the outsider and tourist on the block. And the barbecues, ball games, and block parties were weighed down by the heaviness of my father's unhappiness with his marriage and his smothering affection.

After the divorce, we occasionally had Thanksgiving dinner with my mother's family, but more often my brothers and I ate with my father. Usually Grandma Annie would say grace and Daddy or one of the uncles would close the meal by having us lift our glasses. I must have been twelve or thirteen during the last holiday meal that I clearly remembered. Later ones were too alcohol-blurry for me to really recall. During that last one, I looked up just as everyone else solemnly bowed heads. To my surprise, Grandma's head was erect. She saw me looking and winked. In a somber voice, Grandma Annie intoned:

Some people got treats
But they ain't got teeth
Some people got teeth
But they ain't got treats
We've got our teeth and our treats
So praise the Lord, say hallelujah
And let's eat.

After a few seconds of stunned silence, the family erupted into laughter, except the littlest cousins who could not figure out the joke. Later that evening, my father loosened his belt and then lifted his glass to declare, "Home is being surrounded by family and loved ones!"

"Here, here!" We all clinked glasses while stamping our feet, a Collins family tradition. It was one of our first holidays after the divorce, and I couldn't help missing my mother. Later, Daddy pulled me onto his lap and drew Alex and Chris close.

"Are we okay? We're okay," Daddy half-asked, half-stated. "I know your mother isn't here, but we're still okay, right?"

"Sure thing, Daddy," Chris and I chorused almost in unison. Daddy buried his face in my hair gratefully. I worried that he might be crying or drunk.

"Yeah, Daddy, we're all right," Alex said, but he scowled.

Thanksgiving with Daddy's side of the family really had been okay, even fun sometimes, but my best memories of Aunt Fran's neighborhood were when Keisha and I had escaped to wander the city by ourselves.

I don't know how long I stood on Aunt Fran's stoop lost in thought, but eventually I knocked firmly, then rang the doorbell. Lydia answered.

"Hey, Georgie," she said, sounding unsurprised. Whatever

had made her angry earlier in the day was clearly forgotten. "Most everyone is in the back room. The rest of us are on the Nintendo in the basement. I'm beating all those boys' asses at *Tomb Raider*."

Faced with the girl's indifference, my frustration faded and I let her wander off. Heart pounding, I headed down the narrow hallway, through walls lined with brown-green wallpaper and framed photos of family members whom I barely recognized. In the back room, my Aunts Fran, Audrey, and Constance and Grandma Annie sat along with several grown cousins, uncles, and strangers. As always, the women formed the nexus in the room. Even if the men were not actually sitting at the periphery, they were somehow on the margins. My cousins had grown heavier, especially Peggy and Charla, who looked as if they had kept the weight of their last pregnancies, while the older men and women were thinner and more worn than I remembered. Squeezed on the floor, leaning on laps and tottering around the room, were several very small children.

My father was missing, as was my cousin Tameka, and my brothers no longer lived nearby. While I could smell the faint scent of tobacco, the room lacked the stinging smoke of years ago. I remembered Alex saying something about everyone becoming so much more health conscious in recent years. Other than those differences, the scene was an exact replica of my childhood memories. The plastic-covered couch and wing chairs were empty since no one found them comfortable. People of all shades were crowded on the rest of the furniture: two La-Z-Boys, the beige settee that Grandma Annie's great-aunt had brought up from South Carolina (no one knew how long ago), an armchair upholstered with worn knobby fabric, and several straight-back chairs pulled in from the kitchen.

I stood and soaked in the room for a few seconds before Peggy glanced up and noticed me. In those seconds, I experienced a strange feeling of ghostliness, as if unseen I were not really there.

"Georgie!" Peggy's voice was loud enough to command everyone's attention. "Hey, Georgie. Ma, Georgie is here."

"Oh, hi honey." Fran smiled. Somehow I had assumed that she would be shocked to see me. Yet she almost sounded as if I stopped by frequently. Her grin was perhaps a little wider than usual, and the way that the pale laugh lines under her eyes crinkled up seemed to demonstrate her pleasure. But I sensed no astonishment or anger that I had stayed away for so long, just delight at my presence. The next moment, I was enveloped in the family tradition of being hugged, kissed, and fussed over by every adult in the room as if I were still small. Then each child was urged to give Cousin Georgie a kiss. Each dutifully pursed her lips or presented his cheek for mine. I watched their faces carefully trying to ascertain if they really wanted to be kissed or were merely submitting to this ritual because they had no choice. But they did not seem to mind or even really notice since their attention was on each other. I was one more grownup, part of the background, barely acknowledged though I was a stranger in their lives.

"Well, someone get Georgie a chair. Georgie, do you want something to drink? Are any of you young people going to get your long-lost cousin something wet? Or does an old lady have to do all the work around here?" Grandma Annie started to raise herself laboriously from the armchair with plenty of groans and sighs, knowing full well that every person under thirty in the room would immediately leap to their feet. I did want something wet. While my Jamaican family was a mix of teetotalers and beer drinkers who occasionally celebrated with rum punch, my father's family enjoyed alcohol in as many different forms as possible; I knew the bar in Fran's house would contain most hard liquors and liqueurs, as well as multiple cocktail mixes.

"I would love a gin and tonic," I said gratefully, watching one of the men head for Fran's bar. When he returned, I gulped it as if I were dying. With the liquor buzzing through my system, I felt more real and the ghost Georgie seemed to fade.

"Where's Daddy?" I asked. "Is he coming around today?"

My aunts and grandmother glanced at each other while most of the men looked at their feet.

"I'm not sure, baby," Aunt Audrey said. "Since that mess with Tameka, he doesn't stop by so often. But who knows?"

"Who knows?" Grandma Annie piped up. "He might be by later. Michael is a good boy." At her words, Uncle Edward, Fran's husband, grimaced and strode out of the room. His back was rigid and his movements were jerky though quick. A couple of other men I didn't know followed him. I wasn't sure what had sparked that little drama, given the aunts were always in a huff about something or another and the entire family adored a good bicker every once in a while. Meanwhile I sucked on my ice cubes and listened to the women gossip.

As the evening passed, I found it easy to curse, laugh, and shout my joy. I felt embraced by my past.

When Peggy asked me what ever happened to Malcolm, I managed to make the story of our breakup so funny that Uncle Henry roared and mopped his face. Aunt Constance had tears in her eyes and fanned her chest with outspread fingers. My cousins whistled and laughed when I imitated Malcolm's angry young black man routine. Any remaining librarian primness was cast off in favor of a joking, earthy Georgie. Aunt Fran was the only one who did not seem amused.

"But are you okay, honey?" Fran kept asking.

"Fuck him," I replied. "I'm absolutely fine. Everything is all right." Afterwards, it was easy to decide to stop by a liquor store on the way home.

getting practical

i had started working at the Boston Public Library on Valentine's Day 2000, barely two months after graduating from an online degree program in Library Science. I knew I was lucky to get a reference job with virtually no experience. However, just in case I was unappreciative of my luck, Alex called me the morning of my first day, reminding me that he had called in a favor from a college friend to get the preliminary interview at the library, and warning me not to mess up. I didn't need the warning. I was already terrified that first morning when I walked up the long flight of steps and presented myself to the head librarian. While I had done well in my studies, the online classes made it easy to rarely leave my apartment and I wasn't entirely sure whether I'd be able to actually stand interacting with the patrons.

But my supervisor, Esther, was reassuring and kind. She smiled warmly and said that all new employees found their first day nerve-wracking. She introduced me to Mimi, who immediately took me under her wing, and though I was initially wary of her friendliness, I ended up liking her quite a bit. Often, she had

all of us giggling hysterically with her imitations of upper man-
agement and bawdy jokes that she told during lunch breaks. At
least once each month, a group of us went to the North End to
have dinner at her uncle's restaurant. She boasted that her uncle
served the best Italian food in the city, maybe even the state. The
cuisine was very different from the Jamaican and African-
American foods served by my families, but the company was fun
and I enjoyed these outings thoroughly.

My life as a librarian felt different, quieter, maybe more peaceful than any other life I had lived before. For the first time in
memory I had a regular source of income that did not rely on
other people's good will. I was not dancing on a box for tips from
an admiring audience; I was not dependent on my family or my
lovers or a university financial aid office to survive. And for the
first time, I was not painting at all.

I never had visitors, and everyone in the apartment building pretty
much kept to themselves. So the knock on my door startled me, but
when I discovered my father and my cousin Tameka standing in the
hall, somehow I was unsurprised. Tameka was Aunt Fran's youngest
daughter. I barely knew her since she had been in kindergarten or
first grade when I finished high school. She must have been at least
seventeen or eighteen by now, but she looked diminutive next to my
father who, as always, loomed larger than life. Even though the girl
was small, even dainty, and she kept her eyes on the floor, she
seemed to radiate energy and happiness. My father had his hand on
the small of her back as he guided her into the apartment. I brought
them into the living room, where they sat side by side on my sofa.
I sat on the floor cross-legged, unsmiling. I waited.

"Georgie," my father began, and then stopped and then began
again. "Georgie, Tameka came to me yesterday with some good
news."

Tameka started talking in a rush, words tumbling over each other: "Ma and Daddy are really angry. And Daddy will barely talk to me except to say that I need to get the situation taken care of soon. So I went to Uncle Michael for help because they won't listen. I got a full-tuition scholarship to the University of Chicago, and Daddy still wants me to go. But I want to have this baby. She's mine. I don't care about Chicago. I never did. I think Ma agrees with me, but she won't really cross Daddy so she's upset and crying all the time now."

As I watched Tameka talking, I found it difficult to concentrate on the unspoken question behind her words. I wondered whether Tameka really knew the baby was a girl or if she was just hoping. She seemed both excited and nervous and impossibly young. It was hard for me to remember being that age or being that naïve.

I looked at my father and waited. Eventually, Tameka's monologue trailed off when she realized that neither my father nor I were really listening. At first, I tried to wait my father out—to force him to ask outright for whatever favor he wanted. But he was a patient man, and eventually I couldn't stand the silence. I had to ask.

"What can I do to help?" I offered. My father's lips spread into the heart-melting smile that I knew so well—half-smile, half-smirk, and completely boyish. He was a rogue, and the entire family knew it, but we loved him for his boyish charm. He took out a cigarette, raising his eyebrows in the pretense of asking permission. I nodded and handed him an ashtray while Tameka explained further.

"Uncle Michael. He suggested . . . I mean, he thought that maybe since I can't stay at home anymore, I could stay with you, just until the baby is born or until I get on my feet. You know, get a job or whatever. I can't stay with my boyfriend either. He still lives with his mom and brothers. They don't have any space anyhow. Besides, he's mad at me too. No matter how much I explain, he won't listen. All he keeps on saying is that he's not ready to be a father, and he keeps yelling that I've got no proof that the baby's his besides."

"These young men today," my father frowned. "They don't take any responsibility for anything. It makes me really angry to see the boys around here behave so badly. You know what I mean, Georgie? So you can see what a bind Tameka is in. And I know you've got that extra little room. You could set it up real cozy. I'd take Tameka in myself, but I'm sure that she'd be happier with you. A woman's touch in her time of need and all that. Besides, it wouldn't look right."

After my father spoke, there was another long silence. Tameka kept her eyes down, but she seemed genuinely happy. My father stared into space. No one looked directly at anyone else. I glanced around the rather bare living room—my old furniture was long gone, abandoned in Western Massachusetts along with Malcolm, my Ph.D., and the perfect future that had never really existed. I had been back in Boston for over two years, but this librarian life was just beginning to feel real to me. This apartment was just beginning to feel like a home. In the past few months, I had begun to decorate, to make the rooms really mine. I had started with the study, which I had painted bright yellow in a fit of whimsy. I brought out my books from storage and lovingly organized them on the study's bookshelves along with a jumble of thrift store knickknacks. Next, I brought my favorite rug from my mother's old condo in Cambridge, and the room magically transformed into a haven where I could drink tea, relax, and read. As soon as I had enough money saved, I planned to buy new furniture for the living room first and finally the bedroom. I was excited to build a space that was truly mine, not decorated to suit Amanda's taste or made over to reflect Malcolm's interests. Maybe one day I would even have friends from the library over to visit, even throw a dinner party. Isn't that what real people with real lives did?

I had no intention of painting or making collages, not ever again, but I thought that I could build a future here, maybe a bit muted or pale compared to the Georgie of the past, maybe solitary and quiet, but real nonetheless. I didn't really want the emotional chaos that was sure to come with a pregnant teenager. I was so lost in thought that I didn't realize that Tameka was talking again.

"—I wouldn't be any trouble. And Uncle Michael says that Ma and Dad will eventually come around if we give them time."

"Can Tameka count on you to help? What have I always taught you about family?" Daddy asked.

"Friends are friends but your family will always be there," I repeated one of his favorite sayings back to him, thinking about how my brothers had loved to mimic Daddy's sayings after he left our mother. "You can do anything that you set your mind to!" Alex would sneer. "Blood is thicker than water!" Chris would throw back, or, "He who hesitates is lost!" "Walk softly and carry a big stick." Alex would always puff his chest out and give a jaunty Daddy swagger when he said that one. By the time my brothers got to, "Honor thy father," they would be laughing so hard they gasped for air.

"That's right, little girl," Daddy said and smiled. Suddenly, I felt exhausted. I agreed to let Tameka stay with me. Not that my answer had ever been really in doubt, but I hustled Daddy and Tameka to the door as quickly as possible. I longed to be alone. Standing in the hallway once more, Tameka gave me a shy hug and headed toward the elevator. Daddy lingered to clasp my arm. "Now you'll take care of little Tameka, won't you?" he asked.

I nodded.

"Don't let the family down, now," he warned

"I don't want to have to clean up someone else's mess, Daddy. I have enough messes of my own that I'm trying to get out of." That was the closest that I had ever come to denying my father anything.

"You are a good strong girl, Georgette. I know that you always do the right thing." Daddy leaned over and kissed my cheek. I bit my tongue to keep from flinching. Warm blood filled my mouth, and I vowed to never speak to my father or his crazy family again.

I went back into my apartment to prepare for her arrival, and by the time Daddy brought her back with her suitcases two days later, I had a heart-to-heart talk completely prepared. Daddy just stayed long enough to reassure Tameka that she'd be fine and to remind me of the obligations created by family ties.

"Call me if you need anything," he said over his shoulder as he headed for the stairs. "And you girls have fun!"

As soon as he was gone, I sat Tameka down. Over a cup of tea, I carefully explained to her the difference between a baby and a mistake. I told her how much I regretted not going to college immediately after high school, how it had messed up my own life and my relationship with my parents and brothers. I reminded her that my friend Keisha had never even finished college because she had gone and had a baby instead.

"But Georgie, she's glad that she had the baby. I know she is. Keisha and her kids are always coming to visit her grandma, and they're doing really well. She's real happy. I can tell. Besides, I heard Mrs. Irving tell Ma that Keisha is the only one of her grandchildren who made good." Clearly, Tameka was neither as meek nor naïve as I had originally believed. She still would not look me straight in the eye but her voice was determined, and she twisted a tissue in a hard angry knot that made clear she was no pushover.

"Is Keisha your best friend or mine?" I demanded, though I

had not seen Keisha in five or six years, and I could not remember the last time that we'd written or spoken.

"Yours," Tameka grimaced, still unconvinced.

"Well, let me tell you something about Keisha Irving, and I've known her since before you were even born. She's always wearing a mask. She'll never tell you how she really feels. She might say that she's happy. But believe me, she's dying inside. If you have this baby, you'll end up just like her. No prospects and no real life."

I wasn't sure whether Tameka believed my description about Keisha, so I looked her in the eye and explained what she needed to know, what I had to make her believe for her own good. "Tameka, I know that you think you can count on friends and family for support. But the only person that you can really count on is yourself. Don't count on your parents. Don't count on my father or Grandma Annie or any of the other aunts and uncles. And especially don't count on me."

A few minutes into my speech, tears began rolling down Tameka's cheeks. She wept silently in the hopeless kind of way that I recognized and rather admired. But her crying just stiffened my resolve.

"You need to get practical," I said. "It is a cold, hard world out there. It is a cold, white world and you don't have any business bringing a baby into it just so you won't feel so lonely. Do you think that white people are going to look at you with your belly pushed out to here and see how smart and wonderful you are or give you a job so that you can pay the rent? No, they are just going to see another knocked-up irresponsible black girl. Someone who doesn't even know enough to use a condom."

"Uncle Michael says—" Tameka began.

"My father says a lot of things," I said coldly.

"But he promised you'd help." Tameka was almost as stubborn as I had been as a teenager, and no wiser.

"Believe me, I am helping! Helping you avoid making a decision that will ruin the rest of your life."

Tameka stuck to her convictions for a few days, but I worked on her, ruthlessly pointing out all the difficulties she would face as a pregnant teenager and all the fun that she would miss if she gave up her childhood to become a parent too soon. By the third day, we were both worn out from the discussion. The radiant skin that I'd noticed earlier in the week now looked sallow, my throat was scratchy and my voice hoarse. Her eyes seemed bruised and weary.

I knew that I was a disappointment to my cousin. She did not confront me directly, but I overheard her on the phone with one of her friends. She said that I had betrayed her. She never said anything about me to Daddy during his visits, at least not in my presence, but I wondered if she complained to him when they were alone together. I considered suggesting to her that if anyone had betrayed her, it was my father by telling her that I'd take care of her, but I didn't say a word. Daddy mostly visited while I was at work and I found myself feeling oddly jealous that I rarely got to see him. With his jokes and smiles, Daddy had a way of lighting up any room. Some evenings, I'd get home from work and Tameka would announce that I had just missed him. Then she'd go into the study that I had turned into a guest room and shut the door, leaving me feeling unexpectedly lonely despite having lived alone most of my adult life.

Sometimes Tameka stayed in the little study for hours on end. I had a feeling that she was avoiding me just as I was avoiding the messages piling up on my voice mail from Tameka's parents. Even my brothers got into the act and left me messages—probably at my father's urging. They all had opinions about what to say to Tameka and how to handle her situation. But I didn't bother to listen beyond their first few words of greeting. I already knew how to handle it, but it was slow work destroying someone else's dreams. Eventually Tameka gave in, and less than two weeks later it was all over. I delivered her by taxi to her parents' doorstep and went home exhausted.

Mother called that evening and I tried to tell her about Tameka, but she seemed more interested in hearing about Daddy.

"I don't even want to hear about Fran or her kids. Your father has no right asking you to help his dysfunctional family. Divorcing him was the best thing I ever did. Michael never grew up because they never made him grow up—" My mother was working herself up to a full-fledged rant when I interrupted her.

"Mother, I need to hear that I did the right thing by Tameka. I tried to help, but what if I was just thinking about myself and not about her when I said she should go back to her parents?"

"Well, get real. You need to help yourself before you think about anyone else, Georgette Collins. Oprah Winfrey said if you want to succeed, you need to surround yourself with only people who are going to lift you higher. Do you think Tameka is going to be lifting you anywhere?"

"Mother, please. I'm sure that Oprah is not out there telling black women to dump their pregnant cousins. Aren't you the one who is always talking about unity and giving something back to help others?"

"Georgette, are you listening? Have you heard a word that I said? I wasn't talking about Tameka just now; I was talking about your father. Don't surround yourself with folks like your dad because he'll just bring you down. You've just gotten your life back on track, and Michael comes bursting in as usual sowing chaos and getting everyone in a tizzy. Stay out of it." Mother continued to talk about Daddy, making me wonder if he was right when he said that she was still obsessed with him after all these years. After a few more minutes of listening, I realized that I was not going to get any reassurance from her, so I told her I was too busy to talk but would call her back later. After the phone call, I erased all traces of Tameka's visit from my apartment. When my father called to ask how we were doing, I hung up on him.

georgette (2001)

i sat in my study with all of the letters fanned around me. Now that I had read them, I was unsure what to do. Keep them and remember or discard them and forget? Was this the choice the box offered? My excitement mounted when I considered getting rid of the letters that had haunted me all spring. I imagined tossing the box, closing the door to the study, and walking away. At the last moment, I couldn't make myself throw them out.

Instead, I picked up the small notebook full of my teenage anger. Was there some answer in there that could explain how I had arrived at this place? Ruffling through, I noticed the end was full of blank pages. I picked up a pen. *I remember,* I wrote and then stopped, closing the notebook. I carefully put it back in the box and returned the letters there as well. I sat holding my words in my lap. After a few minutes, I got up and searched the bookcases. I found a red-and-gold dyed egg swaddled in a piece of emerald silk. I wrapped the box in the cloth and tied it with a mint-green ribbon. Clearing a spot on one of the shelves, I laid the box of letters to rest. The egg rocked gently alongside.

Later that evening, I walked through the downtown pedestrian mall. Although it was nearly eight, the sky was still light. I was glancing at jewelry and clothing in shop windows when I nearly tripped over a pair of feet sticking out on the cobblestones. Sitting in the doorway of a closed shop was Lydia. Since the girl didn't look up, I knew I could escape unnoticed. I even took a few steps past until my steel shell molted, leaving me exposed. Just a moment before, the evening sun had illuminated Lydia and the shops. Now twilight enveloped the scene like a fog. I did not know which way to turn.

Finally, unable to move forward, I turned back and squatted by Lydia. I could barely make out the girl's pinched face in the sudden darkness.

"What's wrong, Lydia?"

"I'm cold, George. Don't you feel how cold it is?"

"No. Do you want my jacket?" I tried to wrap it around Lydia's shoulders.

"No!" The girl pushed me away with surprising strength for her scrawny frame. "I'm asking, don't you feel it? Don't you feel anything at all?"

"I feel fine." My voice cracked as I replied. "You don't look so good though." I helped Lydia stand up and offered my shoulder. Lydia limped along beside me, down Tremont Street to the bus stop. I ignored the stares from other passengers as I carefully braced Lydia against me, taking the girl's weight as we descended off the bus and made our way to my apartment. At home, I fed Lydia bun and cheese and mint tea, comfort food from my Jamaican summers.

"Hey, this is pretty good stuff," Lydia said as she ate her third piece of bun. "I didn't figure you for the cooking type."

I rolled my eyes and explained that I'd bought the bun from the West Indian grocery a few blocks away. "My grandmother and her cook tried to teach me how to make bun, but in the middle of each lesson they'd get all distracted, and it always came out completely burnt or half-baked. If I ever dared complain, Sonia would talk nonstop under her breath about people who eat a lot but are too lazy to cook for themselves."

"I despise cooking," Lydia said. "I've got better things to do."

"How yuh nyam so much and loaf so much?" I asked in a crabby voice, pretending to wave a big spoon in the air. I was not sure if Lydia understood the patois but she giggled at the mock scolding tone. Then we finished off the bun as we talked about grumpy grandparents and favorite foods and nothing much at all.

When we were done eating, Lydia asked if she could look around the apartment. I trailed her from room to room while she wandered.

"This place looks like a hotel suite," she said finally. "All empty and sad."

"Who are you, Martha Stewart? You didn't even see the study. It's the best room." I felt defensive and surprised at how much her criticism stung. I ushered her into the little room as if it were some inner sanctum, but she just wrinkled her nose. Again, I felt oddly disappointed. Lydia seemed tired and a bit bored, until she spotted the nude photograph hanging on the wall.

"Hey, Georgie. Is that you looking so hot? Will you take my picture? I need a picture of me all sexy and cute for my boyfriend!" Lydia pulled at her blouse until it was hanging half off her right shoulder, then she arched her back and pouted a little, imitating a supermodel pose. I pulled her shirt straight and shook my head laughing.

"You shouldn't be worried about boyfriends or looking sexy at your age. How old are you? Twelve? Thirteen? You should be reading books, playing softball, and the like. Stuffed animals and Barbies—that sort of thing."

"Were you playing with dolls when you were my age?" Lydia snorted.

"No," I admitted. *But I should have been,* I added silently.

While Lydia browsed through my bookshelves, I tried to organize my thoughts into wise advice. I wanted to come up with a proverb or truism about valuing youth. Finally, I mumbled something about the golden days of childhood, but Lydia was already flopped on the floor next to a pile of books, the photograph completely forgotten. I sat cross-legged on a pile of pillows. Together we looked through the books she had pulled off the shelves.

"What's this one?" Lydia asked, pointing to a picture book filled with vibrant graffiti-like images. The spine and dust jacket were pristine as if they had never been handled, but I recognized the crowned monster on the front cover. The creature's baleful, toothy grin appeared both seductive and devouring.

"That's a picture by Jean-Michel Basquiat, an African-American artist. Actually, Haitian and Puerto Rican. He was pretty famous, but a lot of people thought he was overrated. Kind of a pet project for some white critics." As I told her about Basquiat, I heard my mother's scorn in my voice.

Lydia flipped through the book and began reading aloud from a poem by Maya Angelou. Toward the end, a sealed envelope fell out from between two pages. Lydia handed it to me and then half-closed the book, using her thumb to mark the page.

"Aren't you going to open it?" she asked.

"I'm not sure whether I'm up for any more old letters."

Lydia looked disgusted. She took the envelope out of my hands and tore it open.

"Hey, careful!" I warned as Lydia began reading.

December 1997

Dearest Georgie,
    I spoke to Verna yesterday, and she tells me that you've

gone missing. I hope you're off having grand adventures. Of all my grandchildren, you seem to lead the most exciting life. When I look at your cousins and brothers, I'm always amazed that almost all of my descendents turned into such a staid and dull lot. But grand adventures or no, I hope to be hearing from you soon. I know you'll be fine, but still I worry.

In the meanwhile, I'm mailing your package to your mother in case she finds a way to pass it along to you by your birthday. I saw the enclosed book the last time I was in the States, and I thought that you might like it. Now, generally, I don't think much of most Haitians, but when I saw the picture of the dragon on the front, it got me pondering the night you were born. Did anyone ever tell you that story? I was right there in the hospital room with your mother. Most babies give a cry or two at first or maybe a wail, but you came out of Verna's belly with a mighty roar. And your eyes were wide open looking straight at me while you stuck your arms straight up in the air like the victory sign. If I remember rightly, it had been a hard labor, but the doctors and nurses, Verna, me—every single person in that room—just started laughing and crying when you appeared. Even then, we could all tell that you were going to be the strongest, stubbornest, feistiest one in the family. A fighter and a survivor.

I told your parents to give you a big tough name. So they named you after Saint George, the dragon-slayer. He saved children, rescued princesses, slew some dragons, and tamed others. They adored him, eating from his hand and walking at the end of a leash like meek little puppy dogs.

So I thought you'd like the artwork. And I know that I like the poem. I've walked the ocean floor quite a few times myself. The charm is in not being afraid.

Georgie, I've got so many stories to tell you and not much time left here for doing it. You need to come home soon. Please keep this letter and book safe, and they will keep you safe from harm.

Your loving Nina,
Doris Louise Babson Groves

Before Lydia had even finished the letter, I began to cry, partly because I missed my grandmother, but even more because I couldn't remember all her stories. And the few scattered tales that I did remember were jumbled in my mind. As I sank deeper into misery, I felt a hand shaking my shoulder. I looked up at Lydia's frightened face and remembered how scary it was as a child to see adults fighting or crying. I rubbed my face and smiled.

"Are you all right?" I asked.

"Yeah, I just want to know who's Nina?"

"My grandmother," I explained. "From my mother's side of the family."

"Oh." Lydia looked startled. She put down the letter and we finished reading through the book.

"Do you think your grandmother could really walk on the ocean floor without breathing?" Lydia asked when we came to the last page.

"No, I think she probably couldn't."

"Were you really named after that guy? A saint?"

"Probably not. She just liked to tell stories," I said, shrugging and yawning. Lydia seemed satisfied with that answer so we kept looking through my books; taking turns reading aloud the lines we liked the best.

At almost midnight, Lydia admitted to being pretty tired and asked if she might lie down. I said sure and gave her a duvet and pillows. I made us both a hot toddy of lemon tea mixed with brandy. Lydia sat on the living room sofa, eyes drooping heavily. One knee was curled underneath her while the other propped up her chin.

"I really wish . . ." she began, and then fell silent.

"What do you really wish?" I asked.

"Sometimes, I just wish that I could leave this place. You know, start all over again someplace where no one knows me and no one expects anything of me. Go missing." Lydia's voice was very soft. It was clear that she was half-asleep already.

"When I was small," I said to her, "Nina would tell me these amazing stories, colored every which way. And I'd close my eyes and lean back, just drinking in her voice. She provided the words, and I painted pictures in my head. They weren't fairy tales—not like the kind that you read in a book—but they weren't quite real either. By the time I was your age, all I wanted to do was paint the pictures I saw in my head when I was at Nina's house."

Before I even finished my thoughts, Lydia was asleep. While she slept, I wrote my letter of resignation to the library. I went back into my study and grabbed the milk crate of porn magazines, which I dumped into the garbage along with the rubbers and all but one carton of cigarettes. I found Nina's letter on the Oriental rug where Lydia had dropped it. I picked it up, but I didn't reread it. Instead, I put it inside the box of other letters sitting on the shelf, then turned off the lights and went to bed. A few minutes later, I was asleep as well.

In the morning, without even opening my eyes, I knew Lydia was gone. I couldn't quite remember the events of the night before. But I knew that I was unemployed and had virtually no money in the bank. Although I was lonely, I also knew that I felt better this morning than any morning in perhaps forever. I lit a cigarette and for several minutes I lay in bed blowing smoke rings at the ceiling.

Turning onto my side, I saw a single sheet of paper covered with an adolescent looping script, shaky letters garnished with embellishments and flourishes. Girly writing. I picked up the paper and read the note that Lydia had left for me.

Hi G,

I had the wildest dream last night. You were there and me. Also, a dragon and some serious wild animals, all monsters like from a nightmare. But I wasn't scared because there were a lot of strange and wonderful people too, all shapes, sizes, and colors. The craziest mixed-up shit. It was horrible and great at the same time.

All the people and animals partied all night long and lots of other stuff. I can't remember it all right now, and I got to go anyway, but I just wanted to tell you that your grandma was right! By the end of the dream, everyone was tired and drooping. And guess who were the only ones left standing.

Lydia

As I read Lydia's words, I found myself yawning again. I sat up slowly, stretching and feeling the ache in my muscles. After a few seconds of staring at nothing, I found a marker in my nightstand drawer. On the blank side of Lydia's letter, I began to sketch the girl's portrait from memory. A few thick black strokes formed the strong lines of her face. Smaller, delicate lines hinted at shadows under her eyes and a certain sulky stubbornness, but I drew lips that smiled slightly. Though Lydia's behavior had often been frenzied, I sketched her sitting relaxed on a park bench. Then I added a few long loosely drawn lines in the background so that trees and overgrown plants surrounded the girl.

When I was done drawing, I looked at the picture and sighed, liking it though not entirely satisfied. I needed to add more details to the background and wanted to work on the girl's features some more, but it would do for now. I folded up the paper and slipped it into my nightstand drawer.

Also from **AKASHIC BOOKS**

WITH OR WITHOUT YOU BY LAUREN SANDERS
317 PAGES, A TRADE PAPERBACK ORIGINAL, $14.95

"A wickedly crafted whydunit . . . Sanders shows a surprising ability to simultaneously make you feel infuriated with and sorry for her borderline-schizo heroine."
—*Entertainment Weekly*

"Sanders' vibrant, vigorous second novel is a sendup of America's obsession with pop culture, B-list celebrities, and prison life . . . In lyrical, potent prose, Sanders navigates the terrain of loneliness, obsession and desperation with the same skillful precision as her vulnerable, calculating protagonist."
—*Publishers Weekly* (starred review)

KAMIKAZE LUST BY LAUREN SANDERS
*WINNER OF A LAMBDA LITERARY AWARD
287 PAGES, A TRADE PAPERBACK ORIGINAL, $14.95

"Great courage must account for such complete disregard of political correctness, and great sensitivity for such sadness."
—Amanda Filipacchi, author of *Vapor* and *Nude Men*

"Lauren Sanders's novel *Kamikaze Lust* makes a connection between unrealized lives, sexual repression, and the fear of death. In her hands, what is usually clichéd or gratuitous is hot."
—Amy Ray of the Indigo Girls

SOUTHLAND BY NINA REVOYR
*WINNER OF A LAMBDA LITERARY AWARD AND A FERRO-GRUMLEY AWARD;
A *LOS ANGELES TIMES* BEST-SELLER
348 PAGES, A TRADE PAPERBACK ORIGINAL, $15.95

"What makes a book like *Southland* resonate is that it merges elements of literature and social history with the propulsive drive of a mystery, while evoking Southern California as a character, a key player in the tale. Such aesthetics have motivated other Southland writers, most notably Walter Mosley."
—*Los Angeles Times*

"If Oprah still had her book club, this novel likely would be at the top of her list . . . With prose that is beautiful, precise, but never pretentious . . ."
—*Booklist* (starred review)

JOHN CROW'S DEVIL BY MARLON JAMES
226 PAGES, HARDCOVER, $19.95

"Set in James's native Jamaica, this dynamic, vernacular debut
sings of the fierce battle between two flawed preachers . . . an
exciting read."
—*Publishers Weekly*

"*John Crow's Devil* is the finest and most important first
novel I've read in years. Marlon James's writing brings to
mind early Toni Morrison, Jessica Hagedorn, and Gabriel
García Márquez."
—Kaylie Jones, author of *A Soldier's Daughter Never Cries*

SOME OF THE PARTS BY T COOPER
*A BARNES & NOBLE DISCOVER GREAT NEW WRITERS PROGRAM SELECTION
264 PAGES, A TRADE PAPERBACK ORIGINAL, $14.95

The novel that's changing the way we define "family." The
Osbournes, Sopranos, and Eminem are only "some of the parts"
that make up the whole story of the new American family.

"A wholly original novel that's both discomforting and com-
pelling to read."
—*San Francisco Chronicle*

THE FALL OF HEARTLESS HORSE
BY MARTHA KINNEY
*A SELECTION OF DENNIS COOPER'S LITTLE HOUSE ON THE BOWERY SERIES
100 PAGES, A TRADE PAPERBACK ORIGINAL; $11.95

"I love this book. How Martha Kinney created this utterly
unique and powerful piece of writing . . . is beyond me. As a
grateful and admiring reader I can only thank her for this
work and eagerly await more."
—Amy Gerstler, author of *Ghost Girl*